MW BANKS

BORN OF GODS

THE BOYHOOD OF ALEXANDER THE GREAT

A VIRTUAL FILM

novum ✦ pro

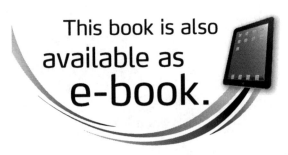

www.novum-publishing.co.uk

© 2019 novum publishing

ISBN 978-3-99064-704-2
Editing: Hugo Chandler, BA
Illustration and cover design created
by Andrew Cachia, Malta
Cover design, layout & typesetting:
novum publishing

www.novum-publishing.co.uk

Contents

PROLOGUE

ALEXANDER of MACEDON lived in the third century before the birth of Christ. All subsequent generations have recognised his having been worthy of the title 'GREAT' by virtue of his character, his conduct and his exploits. He achieved the longest and most comprehensive campaign of military success and exploration in all recorded history. His minting and putting into circulation the horded gold of Persia's Emperors was the foundation for widespread economic progress in the world as he knew it. His belief in the essential brotherhood of human beings – that we are divided only by our culture – was so way before its time that, try as we might, we cannot live that belief, even today, some twenty-three centuries later. His strong, polytheistic, spiritual faith enabled him to unite with races he had defeated on the battlefield, in marked contrast to the monotheistic faiths of the twenty first century, which have evolved, and remain, viciously divided through cultural difference, self-centred prejudice, savage bloodshed and misery.

To ALEXANDER the concept of 'holy war' would have been incomprehensible. Unlike so many of the individuals who have wielded absolute power over the centuries, ALEXANDER – in his brief life – did more good than harm. He, nonetheless, has had his detractors, but as he himself said *"It is kingly to be criticised for doing good."*

The Syrian, Roman Citizen, and fellow General, ARIAN, writing some four hundred years after the death of ALEXANDER, from malaria whilst in Babylon, summed up the man who became a king at just twenty-one as having:

"Great personal beauty, invincible powers of endurance and a keen intellect ... as being brave and adventurous ... strict in the observance

of religious duties and hungry for fame. *Most temperate in the pleasures of the body, with a passion for Glory only, and in that insatiable. With an uncanny instinct for the right course in a difficult and complex situation, and most happy in his deductions from observed facts. In arming and equipping troops, and in military dispositions, always masterly. Noble was his power of inspiring men; of filling them with confidence, and − in moments of danger − of sweeping away fear by the spectacle of his own fearlessness. When risks had to be taken, he took them with the utmost boldness. His ability to seize the moment for a swift blow, before the enemy had any suspicion of what was coming, was beyond praise. No cheat or liar ever caught him off guard, and both his word and his bond were inviolable. Spending but little on his own pleasures, he poured out his money without stint for the benefit of his friends."*

ALEXANDER stands at the head of all the Great Captains of History, by virtue of his being the only military leader to have been tested, and never defeated, in every form of warfare. No less brilliant was his administrative and logistic ability, which enabled him to take the Macedonian Army across terrain and through extreme conditions, which, over the centuries, worsted many others. We know that as a teenager he had ARISTOTLE for a tutor, and that in his late teens King Philip − his father − entrusted him with the Regency of Macedon. But what can the early years have been like for the man whose twelve years of adulthood were to be ones of constant warfare, in which he crafted an unbroken string of victories, and against whom no opponent was ever successful? On learning of his death, the Queen Mother of the Persian dynasty he overthrew, said farewell to her friends; retired to bed, and turning her face to the wall, ended her own life. After his death, two hundred soldiers were sent, by a would-be successor, to assassinate his mother QUEEN OLYMPIAS. She looked down on them with unflinching contempt, and they slunk away, unable to kill the mother of the Great King. For ARIAN, the existence of such a man indicated the creating hand of a Deity. But does it? Surely, having once created such a being, no Deity could be content with contriving anything less. To date, the memory of one of the greatest human beings who have ever lived, has been better served by the written word than by film. The beliefs and achievements of Alexander the Great are more relevant and important to our overcrowded world today, than at any time since he died some two thousand four hundred years ago. In the final twelve years of his thirty-two year lifespan, he shifted the set of the ancient world to such effect, that the whole subsequent course of history – the political, economic and cultural life of after times – cannot be fully understood without reference to his career.

Spiritually and emotionally too, we are closer to Alexander than to the Middle Ages of the Christian Era. It is at least arguable, that in certain ways, we are closer to him than even we are to the Victorians. Alexander's approach to conquest was fundamentally different to every other conqueror that came after him. They, without exception, set out to dominate, whereas he was intent on integrating the peoples and religions of the lands he conquered. The Great Campaign, by which he overthrew the pre-eminent superpower of his day, changed the way in which nations came to be governed, and led directly to the preservation of Hellenistic culture, and thence to Western Civilisation as we know it.

Alexander rejected the conventional belief of his own day, that all non-Greek peoples were barbarians. He believed that humanity is not divided either by race or colour; but by culture alone. In this he was fortunate in being a polytheist, which enabled him to unite with the spirituality of other cultures. Monotheism is an ideal concept for uniting an enslaved race; but is an unmitigated disaster for uniting a world, as the previous ten centuries – up to and including our own – demonstrates all too clearly. Alexander's idea of the brotherhood of man laid the basis for Stoic thought, and predated Christianity by some three hundred years.

At the age of twenty-four, Alexander founded the important and vibrant city which bears his name, and which has always been multi-cultural, and multi-ethnic. He had Alexandria laid out on a grid system typical of many modern cities in the United States.

It is a fitting monument to the founder, whose remains, possibly, lie lost beneath its streets and houses, and has been made even more so by the building of a new, international, library in the late twentieth century.

Alexander's achievements resulted in his becoming enshrined in the literature of no less than eighty nations, and to his having a walk-on part in three of the world's major religions. In the many legends that sprung up after his death, he is depicted as king, hero, god, conqueror, philosopher, scientist, prophet, statesman and visionary. It is said that in the remote valleys of the Karakoram there are those alive today who date their ancestry from the passing of his army. During his lifetime, the Egyptian's made him a pharaoh; after his death, the Roman Senate proclaimed him a god. Until the advent of modern communications, Alexander was probably the world's most widely known individual.

In the Twentieth Century alone, Alexander has been portrayed in at least fifty written works. This output is more than the simple compulsion of a subsequent age to relate to its present an outstanding figure from the past. It is more too than the acknowledgement of a legacy, the great majority of which was good. It also reflects the appeal of an attractive and compelling human being.

That Alexander had to be the most charismatic of leaders goes without saying. He led both his fellow countrymen, and those of other lands, by the power of sheer genius and compelling personality. Not for him the grisly trappings of a secret police, or rule by decimation. Alexander left no memoirs. For us today, he is essentially what he did and how others recorded what he did. A member of the most remarkable race ever to people the earth, he stands out even amongst them. As the books and legends show, the fascination he inspires is universal. Almost every moment of his life was seemingly one of tension and activity. It was wonderfully visual; the man of action as genius.

He was born, it is said, on the night when the temple of Artemis, at Ephesus, was burnt down; on the day when his father's horse won at the Olympic Games, and his general, Parmenion, won an important victory – not to mention arriving in the world with a great shout(!) The whole circumstance of Alexander's upbringing, in the shadow of two extraordinary parents, meant that his childhood clearly signposts, even if it cannot quite explain, the monumental achievements of the man. His iron-willed, bi-sexual, philandering father, King Philip, the greatest statesman-general of his age, who, if he had not sired a genius, would probably be remembered today in the same breath as Julius Caesar. His mother, Queen Olympias, beautiful, and equally iron-willed, a mystic who outlived her adored son, and jealously traced her ancestry through the royal house of Epirus back to another son of human-immortal parentage, the warrior-hero Achilles. As a child too, Alexander began a lifelong relationship with Hephaestion, whose death in Ecbatana, just a few months before his own, so nearly unhinged even that massive intellect.

BORN of GODS

FROM out of a BLACK SCREEN
Written first in Greek then merging into English
we read:

**Αυτή η ταινία είναι εμπνευσμένη από την παιδική ηλικία
μιας ιδιοφυίας που διαμόρφωσαν τον κόσμο πάνω από
2.300 χρόνια πριν. Και πέθανε σε ηλικία 32. Είχε έζησε δεν
μας κόσμο σήμερα θα ήταν διαφορετική.**

This film is inspired by the childhood of a genius who shaped
the world over 2,300 years ago. He died aged 32. Had he not
lived our world today would be different.

Dissolve to:

1. INT/Nursery, Royal Palace, Pella, Macedon/October 351 BC/ Midnight

The face of **Alexander** fills the screen. He will be six in ten
days' time, and lies on his back, asleep in his cot. The complexion is pale honey, flawless. The chin is already slightly cleft and
the eyes deep-set. They open, staring unblinkingly into the camera; and are grey, but different. One is darker than the other. He
looks beneath the wool, fur-trimmed coverlet; lets it drop, and
lies back with a broad smile.

Alexander
Glaukos!

The room is lit by a single resin torch in a wall cresset. Its flaring light mingles with shafts of blue moonlight. Beyond **Alexander**, his nurse, **Lanike**, lies snoring lightly in a carved wooden bed. The flickering tongue and the head of a silver-grey snake, the size of a small child's hand, slides into view on the naked chest. **Alexander** tickles the top of its head, which swings beneath his chin, and rests above his left nipple. We hear the slap of a sentry's sandals outside the nursery. Still further away, shouts, laughter, and the clang of a bronze cup, dropped on a stone floor, come from a drunken supper somewhere in the depths of the Palace.

Alexander

Glancing towards the door.

> She will miss you,
> Glaukos.

Alexander throws back the coverlet, filling the shot. From it, the brightly painted walls of the nursery are revealed. Flowers, birds, animals, and a couple in an act of adoration to a bust of Herakles. There is a heavy wooden door, beyond **Lanike's** bed, and the tiny crib of baby sister **Kassandros**. Standing up, and stepping across to a three-legged stool, **Alexander** is naked, apart from the snake entwined around his waist, its tail nearly touching the floor. Holding the animal with one hand, he takes a blue, gold-fringed shoulder cloak from the stool, and puts it around his shoulders with his free hand.

Alexander
I will get you back to
the Queen

The slap of sandals fades. He runs silently to the door. Drawing it back without a sound, he peers out.

Title Card:

BORN of GODS
Intro Credits

2. INT/The Corridors of the Palace

Alexander's bare feet make no sound on the coloured, pebble mosaic floors of the palace. The only sounds are the drunken supper party in the background, and the occasional spit and flare of a resin torch from an iron sconce, wrought into a wolf head, a fish, and a cluster of flowers. Paintings of battle and hunting scenes by Zeuxis decorate the walls. He sprints round corners guarded by life-size bronze statues of Apollo, Hermes, and Demeter. We see his upper body moving along a balconied corridor, set high above the dining hall, where **Philip** and his cronies lounge on the couches. They sing, shout stories or conversations, and are attended by Blue Thracian slaves. **Alexander** runs by unnoticed. On along a corridor with, at the end, a half life-size statue of Herakles wearing a lion-mask robe and holding his club. He stops, briefly, to rub a toe for luck. On again; he stops at the end of this corridor, and takes a deep breath, before peering around the corner.

From **Alexander's POV** (point of view), we see five, low steps leading up to the corridor of the Queen's apartments. At the far end it opens out into a veranda overlooking the palace gardens. Two stone lions face each other beside the balcony. White robed women in woodland settings decorate the walls. The sconces are metal tangles of writhing snakes.

Halfway along the corridor is a deeply carved door, with a golden latch. Opposite stands the young soldier sentry **Aegis**. A bearded son of the Macedonian nobility, he is wearing a red cloth kilt, leather corselet buckled over each shoulder, ornate open-toed kothornos, and a Thracian-style helmet with a horsehair crest.

The great round shield on his left forearm is emblazoned with the gold eight-pointed starburst emblem of the Macedonian Argead dynasty. With his right hand, he rests a seven-foot fighting spear on its butt spike. His cloak hangs on a nearby cresset. At the top of the five low steps is a life-size bronze of a youthful, rounded, almost effeminate, **Dionysios**. He is smiling, and his vine clad hair cascades to his shoulders. From the garden comes the violent barking of a guard dog. **Aegis** looks in that direction, and **Alexander** glides up the steps and hides behind the statue.

Cut to:

Close Up – **Alexander** and the statue.

> **Alexander**
> Herakles come. Quickly!
> Send Aegis away.

The snake's head squirms free of the cloak and, hissing, goes around **Alexander's** neck. Blowing gently, he strokes its head.

> **Alexander**
> Wait, Glaukos, wait.
> Our chance will come.

Alexander lifts each foot in turn off the cold mosaic and warms it against the opposite calf.

> **Alexander**
> Herakles, help me.
> And Agathodaimon … and …

The whisper gives away to a smile, and the humming of a quiet paean of victory.
We see **Aegis** walking briskly towards the two lions. Slipping the great shield from his shoulder, he places it with his spear

against one of the lions. Straightening up, he lifts his red kilt and begins to pee. **CU – Aegis**, alone in the frame, looking into the camera.

Aegis
All of us who guard Queen Olympias
use the lions!
With Eos, goddess of the dawn, will come
a Thracian slave to mop up.

He lowers his kilt and reaches for the shield. With **Aegis**, we look back along an empty corridor.

Cut to:

3. INT/The Bedroom of Queen Olympias/Midnight

Alexander walks across the rich reds and browns of the patterned brick floor, towards the carved ivory and tortoiseshell bed, positioned almost centrally in the room. Three windows are set into one wall. Each has deep-blue curtains with blue ties. Either side of the bedhead are a pair of identical, eight-foot-tall standard lamps, in burnished silver. Each comprises three snakes, their bodies entwined, standing upright on splayed tails, and their upward gaping mouths containing oil and wick lamps. Only the centre of each lamp is lit, bathing the room in soft, subdued light and deep shadows. Opposite the bed is a big, pillared fireplace. On either side of the bed are chests, stools, and a single cornel wood dressing table, neatly covered with brightly coloured and stoppered flasks, terracotta pots and trays, and a pair of polished metal mirrors. The mural above the dressing table depicts a grieving Orpheus being torn to pieces by Thracian women, in the throes of a Bacchanalian orgy. The remaining walls show scenes from the siege of Troy; Hector and Andromache with the baby Astyanax, and Achilles with Thetis, his goddess mother.

Alexander approaches **Olympias**, asleep beneath a bedcover of marten furs, each one picked out in gold. He stands looking down at his beautiful, twenty-one-year-old mother, who lies facing him, with her right arm outside the cover, and her shining, dark red hair tumbling across her face, neck and shoulder. He shakes forward his heavy, blonde hair, and compares a lock against her gently waved tresses. Then, slipping the shoulder-cloak to the floor, he lifts the cover and slides Into bed beside her.

CU- head and shoulders of **Alexander** and **Olympias**. Her arm goes around him and she nuzzles her face into his hair.

Olympias

Purring sleepily.

Who let you in?

Alexander
I told the guard you
wanted me.

Olympias
Mmmmm. I do

Alexander pushes his head beneath her chin, until his head rests on her breasts.

Alexander
Do you love me best?

Olympias
I couldn't love you more.

Alexander

Fiercely.

No! Best! Better than Kleopatra,
better than the King.

Olympias

Smiling, she strokes him.

Perhaps.

Alexander

Will you marry me?

Olympias

Five is too young to marry.
Ask me when you are seven.

Alexander

I shall be six this Lion month.
I've got something for you …
… if you love me best.

Olympias

Oh tyrant! What can it be?

Alexander lifts the cover and to reveals the snake amongst their naked bodies.

Alexander

Proudly.

I've found Glaukos.

Olympias slides the back of her hand across his chest and under the throat of the snake. The head lifts. It hisses quickly, flicking its tongue.
Alexander tickles the top of its head, and it sinks back, with **Olympias** still smoothing its throat.

Olympias

This is not Glaukos.
The same kind, yes; but bigger.

Alexander

He came to my bed.

Olympias

Not for the first time.
See how he clings?

Alexander

Yes.

Olympias

He knows you well.
He is your daimon, Alexander.
He comes from the god Ammon.

The background noise from the supper party becomes, abruptly, more apparent. The party is breaking up, with shouted good nights, and slammed doors.

Alexander

I will call him 'Fortune'.
He can have his milk in my gold cup.
Will he talk to me?

Olympias

Who can say? He is your daimon.
Listen, I will tell you about your ...

They both look towards the door, listening as heavy, stumbling footfalls sound in the corridor.

Olympias

... Don't worry,
he won't come in here.

As **Olympias** finishes speaking, there comes the clang of a butt-spike on stone, as **Aegis** salutes. A door crashes open, footsteps approach across the antechamber, and the bedroom door is flung open.

CU – Philip, alone in the frame. He stands, swaying slightly, peering into the dim light. Dressed in a purple and gold chiton and open-toed sandals, the greatest King-General of the age in Greece, is an impressive yet repulsive sight. Thickset, with black crinkly hair and beard, his bare arms are fissured with battle scars, both old and very recent. The socket of his right eye, recently pierced by an arrow, has not completely healed, and is gummed with oozing, yellow matter. The cheek, eye lid and brow are puckered and livid. We see **Olympias** pull the coverlet up to her chin, while he walks to a cushioned chair near the bed. Without looking at the bed, **Philip** strips off his chiton.

Olympias

Quietly pleading.

> No, Philip, not tonight.
> It is not the time.

Philip

Roughly.

> You said that half a month
> ago, you Molossian bitch.
> Do you think I cannot count?

CU – Olympias raising herself on one elbow. Her eyes flash, and in her fighting voice, her reply cracks around the room.

Olympias

> Count you wineskin?
> You're in no fit state to know summer from winter!
> Go to your minion.
> All days are the same to him.

Now naked, **Philip** kicks away his right sandal, takes three strides to the bed, and wrenches back the coverlet, letting it fall to the floor. Having been coiled at the foot of the bed, **Glaukos** pours to the ground, catching **Philip's** good left eye.

Philip

Disgusted.

> How dare you! Witch!
> I forbid you to bring your vermin
> to my bed.

Philip suddenly notices **Alexander** staring up at him. Disconcerted for a moment, he turns away, looking for his chiton. Slipping it over his head, and looking back at the bed, he appears to see the second snake for the first time.

Philip

Pointing.

> Are you teaching him now?
> Take heed before you suffer. I will not
> have him made a howling fiend of Dionysios.
> The child's a Greek, not one of your barbarous cattle thieves.

Olympias

> Barbarous! ...
> Her voice rings around the room, then drops to a rasping hiss.
> My father, you peasant, sprang from Achilles
> and my mother from the Royal House of Troy.
> If my son is Greek, it is from me.
> In Epiros our blood runs true.

Philip

> If you are Greek, then show
> a Greek woman's modesty.
> I mean him to have Greek schooling,
> as I had in Thebes.

CU – **Olympias** and **Alexander.** Still looking wide-eyed at **Philip**, the child reaches back and clutches his mother.

Olympias

Sneering.

> Oh Thebes! It's Thebes again is it?
> Where you were made a Greek.
> No Athenian speaks of Thebes,
> it is a byword of boorishness.

Philip

Derisive, sneering.

> Athens! A talking shop
> whose time is passed.
> They are right to be silent.

Olympias

> It is you who should be silent.
> What were you in Thebes, nothing but …

Philip

Interjects, growling.

> A hostage for my brother's treaty.
> Just sixteen. Do you hold that against me?
> When all Macedon was at the mercy of
> the northern tribes, they made me a soldier,
> and I came to you a king.
> Your family were happy enough with that.

Olympias

> A soldier was it, they made you!
> And what else?
> You learned only what Thebes is famous for – battle and boys.
> The whoring came naturally.

CU – Philip. He bellows as if he were on the battlefield.

Philip
Be silent!
Have you no decency before the child?
I am telling you my son will be …

We hear a great ringing, contemptuous laugh from **Olympias**. She throws her upper body forward, supporting herself on straight arms.

Olympias
Yelling.
Your son?! *Your* son?!

Philip steps forward and raises his arm to strike her. **Alexander** jumps to his feet, and steps toward his mother's right arm. He thrusts out a hand towards **Philip's** raised arm. He is dry-eyed, fierce looking.

Alexander
Go away! Go away!
She hates you.
She is going to marry me.

For a fleeting moment, **Philip** hesitates, astonished at the child's reaction. Then he steps forward and grabs **Alexander** by the shoulders. He strides across to the door.

Olympias
Philip! No!

From the POV of Olympias, we see him let go of **Alexander** with one hand, wrench open the door, and leave the bedroom.

4. INT/Corridor Outside the Queen's Apartments

A startled **Aegis** watches from between the lions and the door, as **Alexander** and the snake are flung into the corridor. **Philip** is not seen. In a **high-speed cam shot)**, child and snake part company in mid-air. They hit the floor together, and go sliding towards the short flight of steps.

Aegis
My god!

He drops his spear, and runs towards the pair, shaking his shield from his left arm.

In **CU**, we see all three approach the top step. The snake starts down the steps, followed closely by **Aegis's** right foot. He turns and gathers the sliding, naked child into his arms.

Aegis walks back to his cloak, hanging on the cresset. He talks both to himself, and to **Alexander**, whose eyes are closed.

Aegis
Don't die on me child, please.
If I leave this post, the Guard Commander
will have me spitted …

He wraps **Alexander** in his cloak.

… And if you die, the King will.
No matter my father's a Companion.

Alexander's eyes flutter open, and throwing back his head, he gives one great howl, and bursts into tears. **Aegis** walks towards the lions, rocking him back and forth, and stroking his head.

Aegis
There, there, soldier. Don't cry.
We'll stand guard together, you and I;
Look after each other, eh?

With a shuddering gasp, **Alexander** stops crying and looks up
at **Aegis**.

Alexander
Where's my Fortune?

Aegis
What do you mean, your fortune?

Alexander
My Fortune; my snake.

Aegis
Oh, your lucky snake.
Don't worry, he'll be back …

We hear a crash, a scream, and a man's cry from the bedroom.
Aegis looks back from near the lions.

… Never mind what your father said.
It was only the wine in him.

Alexander
When I'm big … when I'm ten,
I'll kill him.

Aegis
Sh … sh … sh … don't say that.
It's God-cursed to kill one's own father.
It sets the Furies after a man.

Aegis transfers **Alexander** to his right arm and puts his left foot on one of the lions. He draws back his red kilt, revealing a curving, livid scar. A channel between two lumpy ridges, furrowing his thigh from knee to buttock. **Alexander** reaches out from the cloak, and admiringly traces the wound with his finger.

Aegis
It hurt; I can tell you;
but what taught me not to cry out
and disgrace myself, was my father's beatings.
The man who did that became my first man.
When I gave his head to my father, he gave me
my sword belt.

Alexander looks thoughtfully at **Aegis**, and then looks about them for the snake.

Alexander
Can you see my Fortune?

Aegis
He'll not be far.
He'll be back for his milk
You'll see …

Aegis walks back towards the steps.

… It's not every boy who can tame
a house snake. It's the blood of
Herakles in you I dare say.

Alexander
What was his snake called?

Aegis
Two snakes got into his cradle.

Alexander looks hard at **Aegis.**

Alexander

Frowning.

Two!

Aegis
They were bad snakes.
He grabbed them by their necks, and
er, and er, well and he ... er, was a god.

Alexander
Herakles worked very hard.
Why did he have to work so hard?

Footsteps can be heard approaching.

Aegis

Distracted.

Because his land was given
to a cousin.

The sound of splintering furniture comes from the bedroom. **Aegis** turns in that direction, and then back, as the **Guard Commander** rounds the corner at the foot of the steps.

Aegis
That's why Herakles did his labours.
No one's approached, Sir, only the King.

Alexander looks closely at his friend **Aegis.**

Alexander

Fiercely.

Herakles worked to show he was the best!

Guard Commander
Why are you carrying the child?
And where is your spear?

Aegis
He was running about the place,
mother-naked and blue with cold.

Guard Commander
No nurse?

Aegis
No, he was looking for his snake.

Guard Commander
At this hour!
I'll shake up a slave-girl to rouse the Lady.
Lanike. It's too late to disturb the Queen.

The **Guard Commander** turns and strides away. **Aegis** grimaces at his final unknowing remark. **Alexander** squirms round; puts his arms about his friend's neck, and kisses him on the bare cheek, between the eye and the top of his beard.

Alexander
If you see my Fortune,
tell him I've gone back to bed.

Aegis juggles for a moment with the child; but he wriggles free and drops to the ground. **Alexander** half turns towards **Aegis** before running down the steps.

Alexander
He knows my name is Alexander.

We **track alongside Aegis**. He talks to us and to the **camera**, as he walks back along the corridor and picks up and adjusts the shield on his left arm.

Aegis
He seems to belong nowhere amongst
his parents' endless quarrels;
too clever for children three or four
years older; but too small for their games.
Already he's on name terms with many
of us Royal Bodyguards.

He picks up his spear.

… We soldiers are his true friends.

Cut to:

The small, naked figure dashing through the flare-lit corridors of the palace, on his way back to the nursery.

Dissolve to:

5. INT/The King Archelaus Study, Royal Palace/July 349 BC/Early Morning

Philip stands looking out of a window of the study and picking his teeth with a long silver stilos. The slatted shutters are wide open, and the garden below is clearly visible. A barefoot **Alexander** (now aged around eight years old) throws a length of spear shaft, javelin fashion, to be chased after by a huge gangling, black Lion hound. Beyond the boundary wall of the Palace can be seen a succession of forested hills. **Alexander** waves to someone out of sight. He runs faster. We see him run up to **Kleitos** and another **Companion Cavalry Officer** who is in his late teens. The dog bounds over a low, ornamental wall, and joins them, the spear shaft protruding from its jaws. **Alexander** and **Kleitos** grab one end each. They run out of view, around a corner of the palace. **Philip** turns back into the study.

The one long, internal wall of the room is dominated by a larger than life size painting of Apollo playing his lyre and surrounded by the three ancient Muses; Melete (Meditation), Mneme (Remembrance) and Aoide (Song). The colour theme throughout is yellow ochre. **Philip** stands before a huge, cedar wood writing table. Standing on big, lions-claw feet, it is inlaid with lapis and chalcedony, and occupies fully a quarter of the floor space. It is cluttered with scrolls, tablets, a planning model of Northern Greece, the King's Thracian-style helmet, and sheathed dagger. Polished cedar wood shelves fill the spaces between the three windows. In the wall behind **Philip**, and on either side of the single window, in the short wall to his left, there is a recessed reading-cell. Against the wall to his right, where the Chief Secretary, **Eumenes,** and a scribe sit on stools, between the writing table and the recess, is a bronze of Hermes inventing the lyre.

There is a double doorway, through the long inner wall. **Philip** rests an arm on the back of his chair, a great Egyptian antique affair of wood and leather, surmounted by a gilded sphinx. The sphinx head theme is continued on five smaller chairs spread around the room. **Antipatros** sits in one, reading a scroll. **Parmenion** paces about the room, then stands, leaning over the back of a chair. Both these generals, and confidants of the King are bearded and, like him, have their arms covered in the folds of their chitons. **Antipatros** is tall and slim. **Parmenion** heavy, thick-set and with the bowlegs befitting a cavalry general. **Philip** jerks his great chair clear of the table and slams himself down in the seat.

Philip
The boy may not be big for his eight years;
but he's forward in everything else.
It's time to make a Greek of him.

To ween him from that …
From the women.

Parmenion
Chuckling.

His friends in Agathon's Phalanx
tell me that he can lift the butt-end
of a sarrissa to his shoulder.

Philip
Scowling.

He has too many friends in every phalanx.

Parmenion
They'll make a soldier of him.

Philip
All they'll teach him, Parmenion, is their
peasant dialect, and what else you and I
can only guess at.
What he learns from his mother
is best not thought of. We are
raising a fighting King of Macedon,
not a peasant or a priest!

Antipatros
Will you appoint a tutor or a pedagogue?

Philip
Tutor.

Parmenion
Anyone in mind?

Philip gets up, walks to the end of the writing table, and
looks down on the planning model. He speaks with pauses,

slowly, thinking, and at the end, briskly. **Parmenion** moves towards him.

Philip
You know I would rather outflank a pass
than force a fight ... But the boy ... like
this crisis at Olynthos ... cannot wait ...
I'll sleep on it! Now! Our plans!

Antipatros stands up and joins the other two.

We'll march at the end of the week,
Parmenion.
You, Antipatros, will remain at Pella
as our Regent.

Cut to:

6. EXT/By the Pella Lagoon/Morning

The rugged, tree covered hills and gorges descend to a long, narrow strip of open meadow, beside the reed and sedge-clad curve of the Pella Lagoon. No paths or buildings are visible. Amongst the pines, the rowan, the oak and the beech, the last wisps of mist are burning off in the morning sun. A succession of ducks, geese, and waders, and an occasional heron, either rise into the air, flapping and honking, or swim strenuously out into the lagoon.

Alexander appears from the reeds, followed by his dog. They run onto the firm ground nearer the treeline. Both are wet and muddy. **Alexander** stops and scrapes the mud from one arm with his hand. The dog barges up to him and licks his face without having to stretch up. Alexander hooks an arm around the animal and buries his face in the thick fur of the neck. Looking along the length of the dog's back, he speaks quietly to himself.

Alexander

So who approaches? On the big chestnut.
Brother Ptolemy? On a new horse?

The dog barks and swings round, almost sweeping the boy off
his feet. It dashes out of shot, leaving **Alexander** smiling and
holding up a hand in greeting. **Ptolemy** trots into shot. Still
barking, the dog races in behind the horse, swings away towards the trees, and falls silent, stopping abruptly to investigate a smell. **Alexander** steps up to the horse's shoulder, and
Ptolemy reaches down, and hoists him up in front of him on
the saddle cloth.

Ptolemy

Hup!

The dog races in towards them, before veering off and running
on ahead.

Ptolemy

Is that dog of your still growing?

Alexander

Yes, he's still not big enough for his paws.

Ptolemy

He's getting his mane. You were right
about him being a true Lion hound.

Alexander

It was about here they were going to drown
him. The man said he was rubbish. I untied
the stone round his neck. Come on,
Let's canter.

Ptolemy
If they don't know the sire, some won't
pay the cost of the rearing.

Alexander looks back sharply at **Ptolemy**, who urges the horse
forward. We see them front on, the horse cantering. The dog
runs into shot, overtakes the horse, and runs past the camera and
out of shot. The horse and its two riders, are now seen close up.
The horse stumbles and limps.

Alexander
There's a stone in his near fore frog.

Ptolemy
Know all...
He reins in the horse and dismounts

... Does your father know you spend so
much time with grooms and soldiers?

Alexander
Yes. He says I can ride with Silanos and
Kleitos; or hunt with Oileus and Aegis; and
Menestas ...
... Ptolemy?

Ptolemy
Mmmm.

Ptolemy leans against the horse's shoulder, picks up the hoof,
and clears the frog with his horn handled dagger.

Alexander
In the guardroom they say
we are brothers.

Ptolemy starts in surprise. He drops the hoof and the horse skitters away. In **CU, Alexander's** muddy, childish fingers expertly gather in the reins and halt horse. Wiping the dagger, **Ptolemy** strides the two or three paces to the horse's side, and, holding the ornate, red leather cheek strap, looks up at **Alexander.**

Ptolemy
They may; but not me. I would kill
the man who said that.

Alexander
Why?

Ptolemy
Because my mother is married to my father.
It would mean I'm a bastard.
You know what that is?

Alexander
Yes.

Ptolemy holds the bridle close by the bit and pulls the horse forward into a trot. There is no limp. He stops the horse, turns and looks up at **Alexander** intently and in silence for a moment.

Ptolemy
Can you keep a secret?

Alexander
May Herakles turn from me.
May the gods strike me, and I become
an outcast both cursed ...

Ptolemy

Hastily.

Whoa! Whoa! Stop, stop ... Too strong.

I absolve you. Listen.
The truth is your father did get me on mother.
When he was fifteen …

Flash shot (opening bedroom scene):

Olympias voice

Her sneering yell.

Your son! *Your* son!

Cut back (to the present):

Ptolemy

… Before he went to Thebes.

Flash shot (opening bedroom scene):

Olympias room

Contemptuous

Oh, Thebes!

Cut back (to the present):

Alexander

Imitating Olympias.

Oh Thebes!

Ptolemy

My mother was already married to father.
It dishonours them to speak of it,
and is something a man must take blood for.
Women should only do it with their husbands,
or the child cannot be recognised.
That's why they wanted to drown your dog.
For fear his strain was spoiled.

Ptolemy looks unhappy and uncomfortable; **Alexander** only serious.

Alexander

Quietly.

I'll not talk.

Ptolemy

Looking away.

Of course, if we were sworn
blood-brothers we could tell anyone.

Alexander

Fiercely excited.

Yes!

Ptolemy

Do you know what we have to do?

Alexander

Of course. Do it here. Now.

He clenches his left fist, and thrusts it down towards **Ptolemy,** who takes out his dagger.

Ptolemy

It's a solemn thing we do, Alexander …

In **CU** we see their two wrists, and the dagger point drawn across each in turn, leaving a blood trail nearly one inch long.

Ptolemy

… Your enemies will be mine,
and mine yours. Until we die.
We will never take up arms
against each other …

The both extend their fingers and they press the cuts together.

Ptolemy

… If either of us dies in a strange land,
the other will give him rites.

Alexander

Eager.

I promise!

Ptolemy

I promise.

Alexander

Pleased and excited.

Come on Brother, mount up.
He's got his wind.
Now we can really go!

A smiling **Ptolemy** prepares to mount.

Cut to:

7. EXT/The Roadway from Pella to the Royal Stables/ Later the same morning

The broad, dirt roadway shimmers in the heat. Beyond lies the now familiar succession of forested mountains. Pella is hidden from view; but its presence is suggested by the smoke from several cooking fires, spiralling up from beyond a middle-distance crest line. A few men and women stand amongst the widely spaced trees that line the roadway. All are looking away from the camera. We slowly zoom in on the roadway disappearing over the middle-distance crest line. Dust rises beyond it. Then the bobbing topknots of two horses appear and then the hatted heads of four men riding abreast. The innermost pair are Persian Envoys, and they wear round black hats. The two outside them are Macedonian chamberlains; welcoming escorts, who wear the local causia, a brown felt, pudding basin hat, with a brim upturned at the front and back. The **zoom stops,** with all four horses and riders in view, and filling the frame. We have a **Steadicam** in front of a succession of files riding over the crest line. The files pass in succession out of the bottom of the frame. There are eight files in all, with the final six files being Persian bowman, with high crowned helmets, quivers, and tight-fitting uniforms.

We track alongside, amongst the dust and the flies of the leading files, for a short distance, before picking up **Alexander** and **Ptolemy** riding up to join the onlookers beside the roadway. Then, we see the Persian files from their **POV.** The palace and the royal stables can be seen in the middle distance, with Pella Lagoon beyond.

Ptolemy
Barbarians. Persian Barbarians.

Alexander
Why Barbarians?

Ptolemy
They are not Greek, and they are
wearing trousers. Barbarians are
notorious for their trousers.

Both laugh.

Alexander
The escort are all bowmen.

Ptolemy

Persian bowmen are famous fighters.
They will have used their bows
to hunt game on the long journey
from Susa or Persepolis.

Alexander

They are envoys of King Ochos?

Ptolemy

From the Great King of all Persia
himself. I hear they've come for
Artabazos and Menapis.

Still sitting on the now sweated chestnut horse, **Ptolemy** puts
his arms around the younger boy's waist, and he rests his chin
on his left shoulder. **Alexander** twists his head around to look
at **Ptolemy.**

Alexander

Indignant.

The King will never give them up
to be killed.

Ptolemy

No. No They are being forgiven
their rebellion. The Envoys will show
pardons to King Philip.

Alexander

They'll have a long wait. He's out in the field
with the Foot Companions.
Shall I go and fetch our two guest-friends?

Ptolemy

No. There has to be an audience first.

Alexander slides off the horse. He runs towards the last file, and keeps pace with it, looking up intently at the Persian archer.

Cut to:

8. EXT/The Persians at the Royal Stables/Moments later

CU of the head of a horse sucking up water. The circular bit piece depicts a winged bull. Two hands enter the shot, and rest on the curved stonework beneath the horse's head. **Alexander** looks closely at the ornate, metal harness-work and head-plume on the horse, while its rider checks a rear hoof. Persian horses, drinking thirstily, ring the circular fountain, in the stable court-yard. In the centre of the fountain is a statue of Poseidon, god of the horse as well as the sea. The stables are built around four sides of a square, which is colonnaded along its entire length, and can accommodate some five hundred horses. The fourth side is open and faces the roadway to Pella.

The dust being stirred up by the process of unloading, watering, feeding, and grooming the horses, is considerable. **Alexander** walks through the throng to a water conduit on an outside wall of the stables. He wipes the mud from his legs and feet; looks down at his mud-stained chiton, and runs off towards the nearby Palace.

Cut to:

9. INT/The Perseus Room of the Palace/Afternoon

We enter the Perseus Room through the central span of the tri-ple-arched entrance, flanked by two blue-tattooed Thracian slaves, carrying trays of cakes and sweetmeats. In the main body of the room, six courtiers stand around in pairs, gawping. Three broad steps, curving across the width of the room, make its far end a dais. Above the dais, a mural gives the room both its name, and its most striking feature. The wall is taken up completely by a mural of Perseus, naked, but for his winged sandals, holding a helmet against his chest and dangling a satchel from the other hand, while in the act of saving Andromeda from a seemingly endless sea-dragon.

On the dais, three gold chairs have been placed at an angle facing a bigger gold and red throne. The chairs and the throne have side-tables close by.

Watched by a Persian **Aide**, **Eumenes** is settling the **Persian Envoys** in two of the chairs. The Persians are completely covered, apart from their hands and their faces, in heavily embroidered and sequined trousers, shirts and tunics. The older **Envoys** have black beards, cut square in dense masses of tiny ringlets. The **Aide**, a youth of fifteen, is beardless with an ivory complexion, and long, silky black hair.

As the Thracian slaves place the trays on the side-tables and retire, the **Aide** flashes a brilliant smile to someone out of shot. **Alexander's** high, clear, child's voice rings around the Perseus Room.

Alexander

Off-shot.

> May you live. I am
> Alexander son of Philip

Alexander walks into shot, wearing a clean, cream wool chiton, edged in blue. His mass of heavy blond hair he has 'tidied' himself, and it is still wet. Surprised, **Eumenes** steps back beyond the throne. The Persian **Envoys** glance at one another, they rise as one, and bow with serious dignity.

Senior Envoy

> May the sun shine on you,
> Prince.

Alexander
Please sit down.
Have some refreshment. You
must be tired after your journey.

Suddenly realising that they are waiting for him to be seated, **Alexander** turns abruptly, and scrambles up on to the throne, levering himself up with his right knee. When he sits down, he occupies only the front third of the seat, and his hands on the arms of the throne are in line with his shoulders. **Eumenes** looks in dismay at his sandal-toes dangling above the floor, and frantically beckons a Thracian slave, to whom he whispers an instruction, and pushes him, running, on his way.

Alexander
I have come to entertain you
because my father is out drilling
the Foot Companions.

The **Envoys** exchange another surprised glance.

Senior Envoy
His Majesty drills the army himself?

Alexander
Always, when he wants to try a new tactic.
The sarrissa and the phalanx make a good
solid front, my father says.
The thing is to make it mobile. Is this
your son?

Senior Envoy
No. This is Hafiz, the son of my brother ...

He gestures the **Aide** round beside the chair, saying;

He will be privileged to enter the
Household of the Great King next year.
On his sixteenth birthday.

Hafiz bows. He and **Alexander** exchange smiles. The **Envoys** look pleased. **Hafiz** returns to his place, standing behind the **Envoys**.

Alexander
You are not eating your cakes.
I will have one.

He takes a small nibble and swallows quickly.

Our guest-friends Menapis and Artabazos
will be glad they are pardoned.
They often talk of home.
I don't think that they will rebel again.
You can tell King Ochos.

Senior Envoy
Bows in his seat, saying,

We will not fail to do so.

Members of the Court can be seen arriving to watch the spectacle of the eight-year-old conversing with the Persians. The Thracian slave hurries on to the dais carrying a footstool. He goes down on one knee to place it beneath **Alexander's** feet.

Alexander
How many men does King Ochos
have in his army?

The Thracian slave withdraws. The **Envoys** converse in hurried whispers.

Second Envoy
The truth can only do good.

Senior Envoy

Smiling.

Doubtless our Prince can be relied upon
to remember most of it! ...

He looks across at **Alexander**, speaking aloud.

Beyond number, my Prince. Like the
sands of the sea, or the stars on a moonless night.
The cavalry of the Empire is from
Armenia, Cappadocia, Bactria, and Scythia.
Household troops, are both Persian
and Median.
Scythe-wheeled chariots ...

Alexander listens intently, wide-eyed with interest and excitement.

... Infantry, Assyrian, and from the Outer
Empire, Kissian and Hyrkanian.
Hillmen from the borders.
And towering grey juggernauts
from India.

Silence. **Alexander's** eyes narrow in thought.

Alexander
How long do they take to respond to
the Great King's summons?

The **Envoys** look at each other, this time nonplussed.

Senior Envoy

Simply.

When summoned they come.

Alexander frowns, clearly unsatisfied with the answer. He opens his mouth to speak, then closes it and smiles.

Alexander
Is there a road all the way to India?

Senior Envoy

Slightly patronising.

Couriers relay the Great King's commands,
by night and day across the Empire.
Through rivers and ravines. Across deserts.
Over mountain passes.
After winding along forest trails, edicts are delivered
for proclamation in walled cities, whose watchtowers
look down on the daily life of India.

Alexander nibbles a bit more of his cake.

Alexander
If the soldiers don't speak Persian, how
does King Ochos talk with them?

The **Senior Envoy** is startled almost to the point of incomprehension.

Senior Envoy
Talk to soldiers? The King?
The satraps of their provinces appoint
officers who speak their tongues.

Alexander

Unimpressed.

> Soldiers like to be talked to before a battle.
> They like you to know their names.

Senior Envoy

Condescending.

> I am sure that they like you to know
> their names.
> The Great King only converses with
> his friends.

Alexander

Drily, still unimpressed.

> My father talks to his at supper.

Eumenes walks up to Alexander, bows, in a formal manner, and leans towards him, speaking quietly.

Eumenes

> The King desires your presence at
> the manoeuvres, my Lord.

Alexander nods seriously, then smiles at the **Envoys**, as he slides off the throne.

Alexander

> Some of the Foot Companions are
> friends of mine.

Reaching the edge of the dais, he stops, and walks back. Standing in front of the **Envoys** he looks puzzled but determined.

Alexander

A boy here told me that people have to
lie flat on the ground to greet the Great
King. I told him that he was being silly.

Senior Envoy

Our Master rules both many peoples and
many kings. Some are kings by blood, whose
forebears ruled in their own right long before
they were brought into the Empire.
The Great King must be as far above them,
as they are above their subjects.
There is no more shame in falling down
before him than before the gods.

Alexander nods his head in understanding, while thinking about
the explanation, then he replies seriously.

Alexander

Here we do not fall down before the gods,
so you need not before my father …

Alexander starts to move away.

… He won't mind. He does not expect it.

CU of the two **Envoys.** They laugh together. One holds the
other's forearm.

Second Envoy

Lie down?! Before one who's great,
great grandfather was a traitorous
satrap of Xerxes. Never!

Senior Envoy

He drills the troops, I wonder if
he cooks his own supper!

Reaching the small crowd by the entrance, **Alexander** turns, waves, and exchanges a smile with **Hafiz**.

Cut to:

10. EXT/The Palace Garden/Evening

Philip, wearing a cream, purple trimmed chiton, sits back, at ease, on a marble seat. **Alexander** is kneeling, on the ground, opposite the good, left eye, his right hand resting on the marble seat. His left hand is on the neck of his Lion hound, whose head rests across his thigh.

Alexander
I told them not to approach you on
their bellies.
I was concerned that they would be
laughed at.

Philip throws back his head and gives a great bellowing laugh.

Alexander

Indignant.

Did they?

Philip

Immediately serious.

No; but they had your leave.
Always make a virtue of necessity,
and see you are thanked for it.
What you found out about their military
strength is useful.

Alexander
He also said that their army came from
as far away as India.

Philip
And there, they mount bowmen on
towering grey beasts called elephants.

Alexander
Yes.

Philip
I've heard this before, from men I have
found honest in other ways.
Who knows, if we live, we may
one day see for ourselves.
Talk alone will not free the Greek cities
of Asia from Persia's grip.

Alexander
I'd rather fight a battle.

Philip
Laughing.

Would you now!
Well, I'll tell you something else,
this shame will not be lifted until the
Greeks are ready to follow
a single war leader.

We hear a woman's voice calling, some distance off.

Lanike
Alexander! Alexander!

Alexander

Lanike!

Alexander and the dog stand up.

Philip

Sounds like your supper's ready.
I have decided that Leonidas of
Epiros shall be your tutor.

Alexander

Mother's uncle?

Lanike

Off but closer.

Alexander! Alexander!

Philip stands up.

Philip

Yes. He will teach you the discipline
of Sparta; a different regime from
the ways of women.

Alexander

When will he be here?

Philip

Any day now; but probably after I have
left for Olynthos.
Is that great brute the best you can
do for a dog? …

Lanike

Off; but closer still.

Alexander!

Philip

... I'll have the Huntsman look
you out something with breeding.

Alexander reaches out for the dog, and he glares at **Philip**. The
dog's muzzle twitches in the beginning of a snarl. It growls quietly.

Alexander

Shouting.

No! I love him!

Philip, displeased, starts to move away.

Philip

All right, all right. You needn't shout
at me. I was offering you a gift.

Alexander takes a great shuddering breath and replies stiffly.

Alexander

Thank you, father. I think
he would kill the other one.
He is very strong.

Philip shrugs, and he strides away.

Lanike

Still off; but now very close.

Alexander! Alexander!

Alexander and the dog race off in the opposite direction.

Cut to:

11. EXT/A Secondary Guard Post in the Palace Wall/ Moments later

Watched by **Menestas,** the single sentry, **Alexander** and the dog run from behind a hedge, across the open ground by the gate, and into the guard post.

Cut to:

12. INT/Inside the Guard Post

As **Alexander** and the dog run in, **Oileus** is sitting on one of the two three-legged stools at the rough wooden table, eating a hunk of bread with his dagger. On a wood and leather bed at the far wall opposite the door, **Aegis** swings his feet to the floor and sits up. The entire guard post is what we see.

Alexander
Gyras, keep him for me.

Lanike

Off.

Alexander! Supper time.

Gyras

Grinning.

Under the bed?

Alexander

Heading for the door.

Talking to soldiers may be beneath
her; but she'll look in here.

Cut to:

13. EXT/The Palace Garden Outside the Guard Post

We see **Lanike** walking towards us, and **Alexander** comes out of the Guard post and turns towards us. A hedge separates them. We **dolly in** on **Lanike,** a bustling, indignant, slightly over heated, and out of breath figure.

Lanike
You should know,
I am no common or garden nurse;
but a lady of the Royal Kindred.
I, like the Royal House of this
Macedonian Temenid Dynasty,
you should know,
am from Peloponnesian Argos, and
can trace my heritage back to Herakles,
on my father's side.
You should know,
I would not be doing this for anyone
less than his father's son, as I remind
the boy daily.
Alexander! Supper time!

Watched only by a grinning **Menestas** – who has heard it all before – **Lanike** walks across to the guard post and goes inside. **Menestas** continues standing still, with his back to the boundary wall, looking at the guard post.

Alexander

Unseen – voice only.

Are the workmen still on the
palace roof?

Menestas
They've gone for today;
but we have orders to check them
in again tomorrow morning.

We hear a burst of male laughter from the inside the guard post, and **Lanike** bustles out. Turning right, she hurries away beside the hedge. After a moment, **Alexander** drops to the ground, having been hiding in **Menestas's** shield. With **Lanike** still in sight, he runs across to the end of the hedge, turns and grins broadly at **Menestas**, and then he runs off.

Dissolve to:

14. EXT/The Palace Roof/Sunset

Alexander crouches beside a five-foot wooden statue of Winged Victory, on a pinnacle of the palace roof. The painted statue holds at arm's length, and facing towards the setting sun, a gilded laurel wreath. The brightest of the evening stars are already visible, mirrored by the flares on the first of the night's fishing boats setting out across Pella Lagoon.

The bleat of a single goat breaks the silence. **Alexander** leans forward to look directly down. We see into the palace garden from **Alexander's POV.** Two lines of women approach the Queen's postern from opposite directions. They wear thin, coloured dresses and have fawn skins draped around their shoulders. They all carry flaring torches, and either a reed thyrsus, tipped with a pinecone and vine wreath, or a musical instrument. Two carry systra, two twin-tubed flutes, and another two finger drums. One has a pair of cymbals. The two leading women turn outwards, away from the palace, when they reach the postern. Followed by the others, in turn, the two lines cross the garden towards the wicket gate, leading to a tree-clad hill in the palace grounds.

Alexander walks along the path of the roof-line, away from the statue, then, sitting down for a moment, starts 'walking' down the slope on both hands and feet – feet first and stomach up.

Cut to:

A ground level, Steadicam shot, from between the two lines of women (Maenads), as the postern opens, and **Olympias** emerges. She wears an ankle length, saffron robe, tied with a twisted gold and red girdle, and gilt sandals. In her shining, shoulder length, henna-dressed hair, gleams a delicate wreath of gold wrought myrtle. The procession keeps moving, with individuals walking out of the frame both to left and right.

Olympias is followed by **Hyrminia** (her favourite, Epirote, lady-in-waiting); a girl dressed all in white, with a sword worn on a telamon beneath her fawn skin, and a small boy dressed all in black, and leading a white goat on a red leather collar and lead, with a green vine wreath around its neck.

Cut to:

Alexander, in the last of the setting sun, edges sideways along the ledge at the base of an ornamental frieze depicting robed women carrying pitchers. The drop behind him is some twenty feet.

Cut to:

From the lower slope of the tree-clad hill, now in the deep shadow, the flare studded procession passes through the wicket gate, and moves upwards through the trees. Beside the wicket gate is a life-size statue of Herakles, on a square stone plinth. He wears a lion skin, with the upper jaw protruding over his forehead, and the front paws folded across his chest.

Alexander stands on the edge of the palace roof, beside the top of a workman's ladder. His arms are folded across his chest, and he looks fiercely at the ground, some forty feet below. Then he relaxes, hums a paean of victory, and reaches for the ladder. The rungs are tied to the uprights with reeds and have been designed for a man. He has to stretch out, looking down between his legs for the next rung.

Cut to:

The procession arriving in a small clearing at the top of the hill. Torches are placed in metal brackets set in the ground around the edge of the clearing, and in two on the stone alter at one end. The systrum players begin a tinkling tune. The women talk and dance. One goes around pouring wine. **Olympias** stands by the alter with **Hyrminia**, and the sword-girl, beside her. The boy and the goat wait, facing her, beneath a tree at the far end of the clearing. Without any noticeable signal, the individual dancing gives way to a swaying and stamping in unison. The flutes and the muttering finger drums swell the music.

Cut to:

Alexander as he passes through the wicket gate. He rubs the right foot of the Herakles statue. We can hear the music from the top of the hill.

Alexander
Firmly, to himself.
> God and good luck

He runs up the slope and out of sight amongst the trees.

Olympias stands, with her back close against the alter, holding an empty bowl. On her right, stands **Hyrminia**, holding the snake basket in front of her. Glaukos is clearly visible. On the left is the sword-girl, holding the sinuous bladed kopis, unsheathed, against her thighs. The music is punctuated with sharp shouts.

Maenads

In unison.

Bakchos!

The boy and the goat begin walking down the clearing. The Maenads close in behind them. The throbbing music builds to a crescendo. We move towards **Olympias,** from the **POV** of the goat. We see **Alexander** walk out of the darkness of the trees, and up to the back of the alter. He picks up a flagon of wine, pours a little out on to the alter table, and runs his finger through it. The rest he drinks. Taking a second flagon, he ducks beneath the altar, to lie on his stomach watching proceedings with his chin cupped in his hands.

The sword-girl holds the kopis aloft. The music stops. We stop in front of **Olympias**, who hands over the bowl, and takes the sword. She steps forward, holding the kopis point down in front of her, with both hands. She lunges downwards with the sword passing **out of shot**.

There is a single, shriek from the goat. The music restarts. **Alexander** takes another drink, and scrambles excitedly to his feet. He runs forward, past the body of the goat, pinioned to the ground, by the kopis driven between the shoulder blades, and the sword-girl collecting the blood in the bowl.

With wind milling arms, the Maenads dance away towards the torches spaced out around the edges of the clearing. **Alexander** imitates them; whirling faster and faster, in an arc before the alter. **Olympias** walks towards him. He staggers backwards and he falls into the arms of a laughing **Olympias**. She kisses his face as his eyes close, and his head slumps forward on to her shoulder.

Olympias
Even gods must sleep when young.

She walks back to the altar, wraps him in a red cloak, and lays him down beside the alter.

Olympias
Lie there and sleep. Soon we will
all go home.

As she stands up, we see that his feet have left bloody footprints on the front of her dress.

Cut to:

15. INT/The Bathroom of the Palace Nursery/Early morning

Kleopatra, Alexander's young sister, leans against the doorway of the bathroom. She is dark and dumpy, her father's rather than her mother's daughter. In the centre of the room, **Alexander** lies in the sunken marble bath, while **Lanike**, cleans his legs with a strigil. It is a corner room with windows in two walls, the single doorway set centrally in a third wall, and with a mural of Perdix covering the fourth. The inventor of the saw, chisel, and compasses, sits at a workbench, surrounded by numerous variants of his inventions.

Kleopatra
Now you are a schoolboy you can't
come into the women's quarters.

Alexander

I shall go in whenever I like.

Kleopatra

The Queen will love me now.

Lanike

That's enough, Kleopatra.

Alexander

Who do you think will stop me?

Kleopatra

Your teacher will. Uncle Leonidas.

She starts a taunting chant and jumps up and down.

Your teacher will! Your teacher will!
Your teacher will!

Lanike

Kleopatra, I said enough! ...

She turns and wags an admonishing finger.

Now stop it!

Kleopatra

More quietly.

You can't come in and see
the Queen! You can't come ...

Lanike turns around again. As she turns away from him, **Alexander** leaps from the bath, and grabs **Kleopatra**.

Lanike
Alexander, no!

Kleopatra screams. **Alexander** flings her fully clad into the bath. **Lanike** grabs **Alexander**, puts him across her knee, and whacks him with a sandal. He makes no sound. **Kleopatra** struggles from the water and stands by his upturned bare feet. She grins.

Kleopatra
Quietly.
>You can't come in and see the Queen.
>You can't come in and see the Queen.

Lanike puts **Alexander** back in the bath, and grabs **Kleopatra**. She sits down, lays **Kleopatra** across her knees, and whacks her in turn. **Lanike** stands up, and putting the dripping, and now howling, **Kleopatra** under one arm, she strides from the bathroom.

Lanike
Slave! Slave!
Dry and change Kleopatra.

Cut to:

16. INT/The Queen's Bedroom

Olympias sits at her dressing table, sorting through a pile of gold, gold and enamel, and gold and ivory, brooches. **Alexander** walks in enveloped in a towel. He walks up to his seated mother, and, putting his arms around her neck, he buries his face in her hair. **Olympias** leans back against him and strokes his cheek with hers.

Alexander
You smell of all the flowers
of Mount Olympus

Olympias
God of my heart,
I have a present for you.

Alexander kisses her hair, and he moves round beside her, leaving his left arm draped around her neck. **Olympias** holds up a solid gold brooch.

Olympias
A shoulder clasp for
a new chiton. Come …

She stands up.

… I embroidered it myself.

They step over to the bed, where the scarlet edged chiton is laid out beside a boy's girdle. On the floor below are new, gold studded sandals. **Olympias** picks up the chiton. As **Alexander** pushes the towel from his shoulders, she drops the chiton over his head.

Alexander
Milesian wool?

Olympias
Of course. We will clothe our
culture in the finest clothes before
this barren Spartan.

Alexander
Leonidas is family. From Epiros.

Olympias
So he is; but he travelled throughout
Greece in his twenties.

He is in love with the idea of Hellas,
rather than the reality.
For all his Athenian friends, the savagery
of Sparta is his spiritual home.

Olympias goes over to the dressing table for a heavy, tortoise-shell comb. **Alexander** works each foot in turn into the sandals. She begins to comb his heavy, still damp hair. He winces at the bigger tangles.

Alexander
Has he fought in battle?

Olympias
Never. Too fastidious.
All he wants is to produce the perfect
man, from Spartan harshness;
perfect beings, and never a thought
for the perfect life.

Alexander
And perfect women?

Olympias
Laughing.

From Epiros, possibly, from
Sparta, never. Great unwashed brutes,
half faceless, Soldier-slave,
and half brood mare ... uh!

Olympias reaches out with her unoccupied hand to arrange a lock of hair. **Alexander** leans his head back and kisses her palm.

Olympias
Darling.

Alexander
I will obey him for you.
And for justice for you.

There is a gentle scratching at the door. They both look in that direction.

Olympias
What is it?

Hyrminia
Voice off set.
Leonidas of Epiros has arrived.
Lord Chamberlain Eumenes
has arranged for you to receive him
in the Perseus Room.

Olympias
More to herself, than an aside to Alexander.

While Philip is with his soldier boys.

Alexander
He rode out last night.

Hyrminia
Voice off.
Madam?

Olympias
Send Doris in with the hair curlers.

Cut to:

17. INT/The Perseus Room/A half hour later

Olympias sits on the throne, and **Leonidas** sits in a gold chair, they sit at an angle, facing each other, with **Eumenes** standing midway between the Queen and the dais steps.

Eumenes
Prince Alexander, your Majesty.

Alexander walks quickly through the room, his hands hidden in the folds of a shoulder cloak. His heavy hair has been curled by **Olympias**, and he gives his head a brisk shake to loosen the curls. He exchanges a broad smile of greeting with two Companion Cavalry officers standing amongst the few inevitable onlookers in the great Reception Room.

Alexander walks up on to the dais, and stops, standing very upright, near his mother's footstool. He and **Leonidas** look at each other intently. **Leonidas** is in his early forties, lean, with black, wavy hair, and neatly trimmed beard. He wears a girdle; but no jewellery of any sort. After a moment, he gets slowly to his feet, and steps forward, to put a hand on each of **Alexander's** shoulders, and he kisses him on each cheek. He looks across at **Olympias**.

Leonidas
I had not expected the bearing of a
soldier, Olympias. To find the Spartan
training so well begun.

Olympias
There is rather more than
a mere soldier, Uncle.

Leonidas
He will be a credit to our ancestors,
I have no doubt …

He drops his hands to his sides, and looks at **Alexander** with the not unfriendly comment:

> ... Of course, Spartan children raise
> their eyes from the ground, only
> when addressed by their elders.

Without either speaking, or showing a trace of emotion, **Alexander** continues to look **Leonidas** straight in the eyes.

Leonidas
Yes, well ...

With a slight smile, he resumes his seat.

> ... Given time and the right teacher,
> who knows?

Olympias
You will want to settle in, of course; but
how soon before you begin his studies?

Leonidas
We will begin running, swinging the hand
weights, hurling the javelin and riding,
tomorrow. At dawn.

Alexander
Riding! Good! I will tell Kleitos.

Olympias
Is he not with the army, my darling?

Alexander
Parmenion assigned him to the Pella
Garrison. He is not pleased.

Leonidas

Kleitos?

Olympias

A brother of our nurse, Lanike.

Alexander

He's a friend of mine.

Leonidas

Thoughtfully.

> I see … You have reared a fine
> child, Olympias.
> These pretty baby clothes show
> how much you care. Now,
> we must have something for a boy.

Olympias gives a slight nod and looks away.

Cut to:

18. EXT/Pella Stadium/Sunrise

Leonidas stands beside the chariot and running track oval, leaning slightly on a sheaf of lightweight, four-foot spears. He is bareheaded but sandaled, and wears his himation, brooched at the throat. The track is part of a complex of temple, theatre, gymnasium, baths, parade square, and a barracks, built between the palace, and the first houses, stalls and steadings of the farms and smallholdings which are a part of Pella. Smoke from cooking fires rises into the clear sky.

Alexander runs around a bend, and into a long straight. In each hand he swings a dumbbell weight to the rhythm of his stride.

He wears the short-sleeved tunic of the Macedonian hypaspist, in faded red homespun with a gold cord girdle.

A file of nine spearmen pass on their way to guard duty. Either singly or in pairs, citizens walk between the palace and town on their way to or from work. Dogs of various colours and sizes scavenge the remnants of a temple sacrifice. Cockerels crow.

On the far side of the track from **Leonidas**, two members of the garrison, unarmed but for their daggers, are placing straw-filled dummies, some thirty feet apart; one inside and one outside the track.

Alexander stops on reaching **Leonidas**. **Kleitos** approaches, leading his own warhorse, and **Alexander's** skewbald pony. Both have blue saddlecloths. **Kleitos** wears kothornos and chiton and is without either helmet or arms.

Leonidas
Now for the javelins.

Alexander tosses the weights clear of the track and is handed two javelins.

Leonidas
Put only the first two fingers of your
throwing hand through the thong.

Alexander
I've thrown before.

Leonidas
Show me.

Leonidas walks into the centre of the track, and **Alexander** runs on, adjusting the first javelin as he goes. At a distance of some twenty feet, he throws both javelins in quick succession, at the same dummy. Both hit the mark. He runs back to **Leonidas,** who hands him two more javelins.

Leonidas
From the centre of the track,
one at each target.

Leonidas walks back to his original position, and beckons **Kleitos. Alexander** runs on around the bend, and into the straight towards the targets. He impales the first target with a left handed throw, followed by the second with a right handed throw. Drawing an imaginary sword, he runs on. **Leonidas** claps his hands, waves **Alexander** to him, and speaks to **Kleitos** as he reaches him.

Leonidas
Walk and trot on the forest trails
behind the Royal Stables.

Kleitos
How long do we have?

Leonidas
One hour, and then breakfast.
He hands Kleitos three of the small javelins.
Have the Prince throw these at
targets pointed out by you.

Alexander joins them, and **Kleitos** throws him the reins of the pony.

Kleitos
Smiling.
We have an hour.

Alexander
Yes!

Kleitos puts the javelins into a holster attached to his saddle cloth. **Alexander** runs off. The pony breaks into a trot by his side. Some twenty yards away, he grabs the mane and vaults on to its back.

Cut to:

19. INT/A Corridor of the Palace/Early morning

Lanike walks along the corridor, followed by eight slaves, carrying **Alexander's** two chests of belongings, and his bed. **Leonidas** approaches from the opposite direction, and they meet at the entrance to the 'Prince's Quarters'. Together they climb the eight steps on **Lanike's** left.

Lanike
The Prince's Quarters have not been
used since I was a child.

Leonidas
King Philip was never the Heir Apparent.

Lanike
No. After his brother's death, they made
him Regent for his baby nephew.

Leonidas
Smiles wryly.
And it was 'The People', of course,
Who did not want to be ruled
by a child!

They stop at the top of the stairs.

Lanike
Everyone was tired of the endless
succession wars.
We wanted a strong man, who would
do what had to be done.

Leonidas
King Philip is certainly that.

Lanike
He is good for Macedon.
Through there is a dormitory
for chosen Companions.

Lanike indicates one of two doors in the wall to their left. Ahead
of them is a small curved 'buttress' of five steps, leading up to a
single more ornate, carved door. On either side of the steps are
a statue of Apollo, his right hand resting on a silver bow, and a
stone head of Asclepius, on a tall plinth, which makes them of
equal height.

Leonidas
They will need to be chosen
with care.

Lanike leads the way towards, and up the steps, to the bedroom.

Lanike
But not until Lord Alexander has
taken his man and come of age.

Leonidas
Why Asclepius? … and his father?

Lanike
Apollo, yes …

They enter the bedroom.

> When King Archelaos commissioned
> Zeuxis to decorate the Palace,
> he hoped that his eldest son, Perdikkas,
> would become a patron of the
> healing arts.

Leonidas
And did he?

Leonidas strides across to a small door set in a far corner of the bedroom. He opens the door and peers through. **Lanike** points out to the slaves where she wants the two chests and the bed.

Lanike
No, but my Prince may well.

Leonidas
He's no longer your Prince.
Where does this lead?

Lanike
A private stairway. King Archelaos required
discretion with visiting women; but with my …
with Alexander, it will not be a problem.

Leonidas looks across at her sharply, as he pulls the small door-way closed.

Leonidas
You mean boys – men?
Lanike
Scornful.

> Men! I mean neither. Alexander has a
> fierce loyalty for his friends.

He will bestow his physical love as
a beloved gift, to reward the needs
of others.

Leonidas
Clearly puzzled.
> You cannot possibly know.
> Not at this age.

Lanike
Quietly, and with great firmness.

> I am his nurse. Is that all?

Leonidas moves between the two chests.

Leonidas
Roughly.
> No.
> His clothes are in which of these?

Lanike points to one, without speaking. **Leonidas** throws back
the lid, and bending down, begins tossing out clothes.

Leonidas
> Most of this can go back
> to the Queen.

Lanike urgently beckons an **out of shot** female slave, and immediately begins picking up the discarded clothes, then handing
them to the slave to carry.

Cut to:

20. EXT/The Forecourt of the Palace Stables/Morning

Still mounted, **Alexander** and **Kleitos** give their horses a brief drink at the fountain. Laughing together, they ride on towards the colonnaded loose-boxes and harness rooms. **Leonidas** appears between the pillars in front of them.
Kleitos dismounts and, ducking beneath the neck of his horse, takes the reins of **Alexander's** pony. **Alexander** launches himself forward, and he throws his arms around **Kleitos's** neck, and gives him a kiss on the cheek as he slides to the ground. Still laughing, he turns to see **Leonidas** glaring at him, just a few yards away.

Leonidas
Wait for me in the harness room.
Go!

Alexander
Smiling.
You said breakfast …

Leonidas
Red faced and shouting.
Go! Go! Go! Now!

With a glance up at **Kleitos**, **Alexander** walks out of shot.

Leonidas
Your behaviour is not fitting a
Companion Cavalry officer …

Alexander stops a short distance away and listens.

… This boy is a future king.

Kleitos

Blushing.

> It's not what you think.

Leonidas

> Return to your hipparchia.

Alexander pushes between them. With his back to **Kleitos**, he looks up at **Leonidas**, who ignores him.

Leonidas

> You are no longer Cavalry
> Instructor to the Prince.

Alexander

Challenging.

> I kissed him first. He has never
> tried to have me.

Leonidas

> You are dismissed Kleitos ...

Then, to **Alexander.**

> ... You! Will come with me.

Kleitos leads the horses out of the frame. **Alexander** and **Leonidas** walk towards the harness room. A pillar separates them as they move into the shadow of the colonnade.

Cut to:

21. INT/A Harness Room/Seconds later

The door is banged open, and **Leonidas** strides in, shouting. **Alexander** follows.

Leonidas
Get out! Now! All of you!
Out! Out! Now!

Five grooms are in various parts of the harness room, either stitching, cleaning or polishing individual pieces of equipment. They drop their work and hurry out by an internal door. Most of the wall racks are empty; but the workbenches contain a large number of tools, leather equipment and various weapons.

Leonidas strides over to a wall, and jerks a five-foot, black leather driving whip from a largely empty rack. **Alexander** stops ten feet behind him, and stands, bare feet slightly apart, with his thumbs hooked into his girdle. He looks towards three racked javelins, next to a peg, on which are hanging three xiphos (broad-bladed, double-edged swords).

Leonidas brings the whip swishing down on to a workbench and turns to face **Alexander**. His voice is angry

Leonidas
You were not conceived against
a barrack wall.
Do not behave and speak as if you
were.
From now on you will speak Greek,
not Macedonian. At all times.

Alexander
Alexander replies calmly.

Even slaves speak to each other
in their native tongues.

Leonidas
Your native tongue is Greek,
as your father speaks it.

Alexander
Macedonian is the heritage
of heroes ...

Leonidas
Silence!

Alexander
... the Queen says.

Leonidas
You will speak Greek! Always!

Alexander
Greek is a degenerate patois,
which the Queen speaks out
of courtesy, only to inferiors.

Leonidas
That is enough! You will do as I say!

Alexander looks again at the xiphos on the wall. **Leonidas** follows his glance, and immediately strides forward, and takes him by the shoulder.

Leonidas
You will not defy me.

He pushes **Alexander** face down over a workbench and lashes him across the back with the whip. **Leonidas** stands back, waiting for a cry which does not come.

CU of the tip of the whip resting on the workbench beside **Alexander's** right hand. The whip is lifted out of shot. **Alexander's** right hand flexes, and the fingers dig at the workbench, as **Leonidas** flogs him a further eight times in rapid succession. The only sound is the thump of the leather on the boy's back.

Leonidas

An order.

Stand up.

As **Alexander** pushes himself upright darker patches of red are already beginning to appear on the back of his faded red homespun tunic. He is white-faced and dry-eyed, as he turns and looks at **Leonidas** with hatred and menace. **Leonidas** is taken aback by the look.

Leonidas
The silence of the soldier. I approve a
man, who can bear his wounds …

He moves away to the whip rack.

… No further work until this afternoon.

He replaces the whip in the rack. The room that he turns back to is empty.

Leonidas
Alexander?

He walks to the door. There is no sign of **Alexander**, either beneath the colonnade, or in the stable forecourt. **Steadicam** in front of **Leonidas**.

Leonidas
I own I was tempted to take him by the scruff
and thrash out that defiance; but we are not
breaking in a slave.

And besides, for an eight-year-old his
self-control is remarkable.
I watched my niece, his mother, growing
up in Epiros ...

He smiles at the recollection.

... Olympias would have retaliated ...

He claws the air in front of him.

... Her nurses cheeks bore scar on scar,
where childish nails had gouged deep
furrows in the flesh.
With Alexander, you cannot but feel that he
understands the politics already.
I have travelled widely, and have all
the experience and the skills the King needed.
But I got the job solely because I am
the wife's uncle! ...

He laughs out loud.

... No one in Hellas politics likes Philip.
Except, perhaps, the son?

Fade to:

22. INT/Corridor Outside the Queen's Apartments/ Morning

An enraged **Philip** walks out, slams the door behind him, and
strides off, along the corridor, and **out of shot**. A sentry remains
rigidly to attention, in the frame, looking neither to right nor
left. The slammed door swings slowly open.

We **dolly through.** Across the forecourt of the Queen's Apartments, where two messengers stand-by, waiting at a table. On, through the arched entrance of her receiving room, where three windows overlook the palace garden. The room is all gold and white, with red ornaments, and a gold throne, two couches, with occasional tables, and a spinning wheel, in a partially screened-off corner. A log fire blazes in the arched stone fireplace. Only one wall has sufficient space for a big mural. On it, Aphrodite is shown receiving the Golden Apple, 'To the Fairest', from the boy-shepherd Paris, on the slopes of Mount Ida. The attentive **Hyrminia**, watches nervously, with two other female attendants, as **Olympias**, her face tear-stained, paces angrily about the room.

Olympias
My brother shall know of this latest
insult. Hyrminia, prepare the
writing tablets.

Hyrminia
And a scribe, Highness?

Olympias
No! No! what I have to say is between
me and the king of Epiros,
but tell a messenger to prepare for the
journey. The first snow has already
fallen in the mountains.

Cut to:

23. INT/Outside the King's Study/Same morning

Two of the *'basilikoi paides'* (royal lads or squires) open the double doors to the study, as **Philip** approaches. Motioning the waiting **Antipatros** to follow, he strides inside.

Philip
Eumenes, send for Alexander.

In the reading-cell of the study, **Eumenes** pushes a scribe on his way. **Philip** stands close against his desk, his back to **Antipatros**. He raises both arms, shakes his clenched fists in the air, and bellows aloud. Then, leaning for a moment over his desk, in silence, he turns, steps over to **Antipatros**, and puts his left hand on his shoulder.

Philip
It's like living with some hideously
powerful noble.
One with spies everywhere, and who
cannot be reduced, either by war
or politics.

Antipatros
The Queen is against your Thessalian marriage?

Philip
She, and every god who is flattered by
her scheming rites. I tell you, Antipatros,
we'll marry whoever we think fit.

Antipatros
Fit, young and ripe.

Philip
Scowling.
It is a tradition that Macedon's kings
marry to protect her borders, and
their army's flanks.

Antipatros

"A wife for every war", as the saying
has it.

Philip

Then, laughing.

Exactly! And besides, youth is more
desirable than beauty!

Philip drops his hand from the shoulder of **Antiparos** and moves
to the campaign model on his writing table. A sleet squall rattles
the closed, louvered shutters. There is no fire in the fireplace. The
wind moans in the room. **Eumenes** and a second scribe blow on
their hands. The two soldiers seem impervious.

Philip

Pointing.

Last year, the snows broke over us as
soon as we crossed the Strymon.
We never had a single skirmish in the
mountains, and by the time we reached
the Hebros, the Thracian field army had
ceased to exist.

Antipatros

Many think it wrong to abandon old
conventions, and make war when
even bears hole up.

Philip

Our men are skilled and hardy. We can
win victories in any weather.

Antipatros

Outside our borders none believe in
winter warfare.

Philip

Outside Macedon all Greece is at war
with itself. City cannot keep faith with
city, nor man with man.
They have forgotten what Sparta
showed them once. How to stand and die ...

His voice rises. He becomes increasingly passionate.

... In ten years, all Greece will obey me, and
be reborn. They will win back their pride
by looking to me – to Macedon –
to lead them.
Their sons will look to my son.

Alexander

Voice off.

Pausanias! We can go riding.

Both look towards the doors, as they are opening.

Philip

Quietly.

Pausanias! A Royal Guard for no
more than a week.
Does he know all my soldiers
by name?

Flanked by the two guards in the doorway, **Alexander** looks
like some small wild animal. Both father and son glow from their
outside exertions. One, scarred and torn by war, the child by no
more than the scratches of the forest on his bare and muddy legs
and feet. His face tanned, and his hair bleached by the sun. **Philip** goes around behind his writing table, as a serious **Alexander**
walks into the room.

Philip

To Antipatros.

We'll talk at supper.

Antipatros walks passed **Alexander** and **out of shot**. **Philip** bends down to pick-up something from beside his chair, as **Alexander** walks to the edge of the writing table. He looks straight at his father. **Philip**, wanting to be friendly, smiles and indicates the scribe's stool.

Alexander, **alone in shot**, settles himself, very upright.

Philip

Voice off.

What do you make of this?

A tangled mess of soft, gold and brown leather lands in his lap. In **CU**, we see his hands immediately begin to work at untangling the strapwork. The gold decorations are all of stags in various postures, and of differing sizes. Father and son look at each other with pleasure.

Alexander

It's a sling and shot bag …

He holds up the bag, pointing with his fingers.

… The bag goes on a belt, here.
Where was it made?

Philip

In the far north. On the plains of grass
beyond the Istula. It's Scythian.
Probably influenced by Greek settlers.
We took it from a Thracian chief.
I kept it for you.

Alexander

Thank you, father. I'll try the sling
first on hares.

Philip

Don't stray too far from the Palace.
Athenian envoys are on the way.

Alexander

Eager.

About the peace?

Philip goes back to his campaign model; but **Alexander** stays
focused and eager about the Athenians.

Philip

Yes. It seems they are in a hurry.
They asked for a safe conduct without
waiting for a herald.

Alexander

The mountain roads will be icy.

Philip

Laughing.

We'll let them thaw out before
I hear them.
When I do, you shall hear some
serious business.
Perhaps now something worthwhile
may come of a year of talk.

Alexander

Won't Sparta fight?

Philip

They've had a bellyful of leading, and
Spartans won't serve under Athenians.
So, they talk, squabble and take
endless votes. Meanwhile I act!
Never discourage your
enemies from wasting time.

Alexander

Who is representing them?

Philip

Iatrokles and Aristodemos, which will
do us no harm. Philokrates …

Alexander

Your chief agent?

Philip looks sharply at **Alexander**; as if surprised by his knowledge but he lets the remark pass.

Philip

The showpiece actors are Aeschines
and Demosthenes.

Alexander in turn looks sharply at **Philip**.

Alexander

Demosthenes! Is he brave, like the
men at Marathon?

Philip is both angered and puzzled by the remark.

Philip

Sourly.

Are all my enemies' heroes to you?
See for yourself and guess …

Then laughing.

> ... But don't ask him face to face! ...

Alexander flushes and purses his lips in irritation.

> ... Don't be so touchy. I was joking.

Alexander
How many envoys do they need?

Philip
Ten it seems.

Alexander
Ten! Will they all speak?

Philip
Of course, but I won't hear them until
the next afternoon.
An evening reception should curb
some of their eloquence.

Philip crosses to the doors. Opens one and beckons. Both doors are opened. **Philip** goes back to his writing table. **Pausanias** walks in.

> ... You will wear court dress.

Alexander slides off the stool. We see him pass **Pausanias** on his way in, and we are aware of three figures, beyond the guard, in the foyer. Two stand together with their backs to the camera. The third, tall, fair and bearded, and wearing a cuirass, peers into the study as the doors close. He will be identified as **General Attalos**. He sees:

Pausanias in **CU**, settling himself on the stool just occupied by **Alexander**.

Pausanias is eighteen, with strong, coarse features, and a thin, wispy black beard. **Philip** walks into the shot, and stands very close against **Pausanias**, and begins caressing the inside of the young man's thigh with his left hand... He speaks seductively.

Philip
Who is waiting to see me?

Pausanias
Two craftsmen from Pella's Guild of
Armourers, and General Attalos.

Philip
Shall I see them now, or shall we keep
our curious general waiting?

Pausanias
He only arrived from the front half
an hour ago.
He sent the Eromenos Guard for wine.

Philip
Who is that?

Pausanias
Euphorion.

Philip
Ah! The youthful Euphorion. Even the
eager general would not complain of being
kept waiting while I enjoyed his nephew!

Pausanias scowls, and **Philip** laughs.

Philip
A joke, my young friend. By the stomach
of the god, you are as bad as Alexander …

Philip draws **Pausanias** towards him.

… Go and fetch Attalos.

Cut to:

24. INT/Foyer of the Study

The beautiful, sixteen-year-old **Euphorion** hands **Attalos** a
flagon of wine and a bronze cup. **Attalos,** who is still filthy
from his journey, slops out a cupful of wine, and drinks thirstily. In the background, **Alexander** is showing the sling and shot
bag to a taller, fair-haired boy, who we will recognise later as
Hephaestion.

Attalos
You should be in there.

Euphorion
I think the king prefers Pausanias

Attalos pours a second cup of wine.

Attalos
In the palace; in the field; day and night,
our family must surround the King.
We will decide his preferences.

Attalos drains the second cupful of wine. He hands the flagon
to **Euphorion**, and they each hold a handle as they watch the
approach of **Pausanias**.

Attalos

Quiet aside.

> Remember, the gods will contrive
> this one's downfall.

Euphorion looks up, both startled and innocently, at **Attalos,** who lets go of the flagon.

Cut to:

25. INT/A Guest-Bedroom of the Palace of the Athenian Delegation/First light

Aeschines, alone in the frame, lies flat on his back in bed, snoring vigorously. His hairy, barrel chest, and both feet, protrude from either end of the bedcovers.

We **pan across** to **Demosthenes**, with whom **Aeschines** shares the room. He lies on his side, with the bedcovers held close under his chin, watching, in wide-eyed disgust, his snoring companion. Without warning, **Demosthenes** mingles a string of sneezes with the snores, and sits upright. Dragging the covers around him, he gets up, and hobbles, barefoot, across the cold, green marble floor, to a chamber pot placed beneath one of the two windows.

Demosthenes stands, **back to camera**, looking out of the window. The snow, capping the peaks of the farthest hills, is tinged pink by the rising sun. Wisps of steam rise between **Demosthenes** and the windowsill. He sneezes, hobbles over to his clothes on a nearby chair, and, with a glance of disgust at the snoring figure, begins to dress.

Cut to:

26. EXT/The Palace Garden/Minutes later

Alexander walks through the palace garden, looking across at the windows of the guest-wing of the Palace. Despite a cold wind, he goes barefoot, and is wearing only a short sleeved, homespun tunic. The Scythian sling dangles from his left hand, and the shot bag is on a belt over his boys' girdle. He picks up a smooth, rounded pebble from the pathway. Some thirty yards away, a door opens. He moves to his right and leans against a stone urn on the corner of a low wall. Rubbing the pebble between his fingers, he watches **Demosthenes** emerge, stamping his sandaled feet, and flogging his arms around his well-cloaked chest. (He speaks with a heavy lisp).

We see him from **Alexander's POV**, as he sneezes, and blows his nose on the hem of his cloak, before walking away along the path, and declaiming the speech he is preparing for the afternoon audience.

Demosthenes
Lisping with frequent sneezes.

> He thinkths you should rethpect all who thpeak
> well of your achievements; but seek the fineth
> compliment of all in the belief that your
> character warranth thtill greater thucctheth, and
> in the dethire to go beyond laudatory remarkth
> about the prethent ...

Alexander walks into the frame from behind the camera. He reaches a point opposite the door and sits on his hands on the low wall beside the path, as **Demosthenes** turns and starts walking back along the path.

> ... make future generationth feel for what
> you have done.

An admiration unparalleled anywhere
in the patht. He maintainth that you thould
be the benefactor of all Helath …

Now nearing **Alexander, Demosthenes** sneezes several times,
without stopping.

… ath well ath King of Mathedon, and thould
gain, to the greatetht pothible extent, the
empire of the non-Greek world.

Demosthenes looks closely at the boy on the wall, as he walks
by, stifling a sneeze, and blowing his nose, once more, on the hem
of his cloak. **Alexander** pushes forward off the wall and follows.

Demosthenes
If you can accomplith thith, you will win
univerthal gratitude. If your rule continueth
kingly, and not tyrannical.

Demosthenes swings around. **Alexander** stops, and each frank-
ly considers the other.

Alexander
Please go on.

Demosthenes stifles a sneeze. He is both puzzled and irritated.

Demosthenes
Why are you here? Who are you?
What do you want?

Alexander
Can you tell me, please, if Demosthenes
has left his room?

Demosthenes

Startled.

> We envoyth are all equal. What do you
> want with him?

Alexander

> I only want to see him.

Demosthenes

> I am he.
> What have you to thay to me?

Alexander

Smiles indulgently.

> I know which he is.
> Who are you really?

In the background, **Aeschines** standing, with bare torso, at one
of the windows, begins a series of vigorous voice exercises.

Alexander

Excited.

> There he is!

We see an exasperated **Demosthenes, alone in the frame.**

Demosthenes

> That, ith Aithchineth thon of Atrometoth. Until
> rethently an actor by trade. Thothe are
> actor's extherthitheth he ith undulging in tho
> othtentatiouthly. Athk anyone from Athenth.

Alexander blushes and looks from one to the other in confusion.

Demosthenes

What do you want with Aithchineth?
Tell me. I know enough already.

Alexander

Now composed.
                I don't think you do.

Demosthenes

You have a methage for him.
No lieth now. What ith it?

Alexander

Why should I lie? I'm not afraid of you.

Demosthenes

What do you want with him then?

Alexander

Nothing, either with him or you.

Demosthenes

You are an intholent boy. I suppothe
Your mathter thpolith you for hith
enjoyment of you.

Alexander

Curtly.
                Goodbye.

Demosthenes

Slightly pleading.
            No. Wait. Don't run off. Whom
Do you therve?

94

Alexander

Slightly superior.

> Alexander …

Demosthenes

Sneering.

> Every other man in Mathedon claims
> himself to be the 'defender of men.'

Alexander

Quietly.

> … And the gods.

Alexander turns away, and **Demosthenes** lunges forward and grabs his wrist.

Demosthenes

> Come here. You have wathted
> my time. Don't dare go.

Without struggling at all, **Alexander** draws back to the full extent of his arm and he speaks very deliberately.

Alexander

> Take your hand off me, or you are
> going to die. I tell you.

Demosthenes drops his wrist as if it had suddenly become too hot to hold. From the window above, **Aeschines** almost achieves a pure falsetto. **Demosthenes** sneezes. **Alexander** gazes steadily at him for a moment, then he vaults the low wall and runs off.

Demosthenes

> Vithiouth child.

Dissolve to:

27. INT/An Internal Courtyard of the Palace/Early morning

Aeschines' falsetto **dissolves** into the twanging of a lyre. **Alexander** running through the garden **dissolves** into the furtive figure of **Philokrates** hurrying across a small internal courtyard.

Reaching a door, **Philokrates** looks over his shoulder, grasps the handle, and pulls it towards him. From the other side of the door, we see him come through, lean against the door for a moment after closing it, and then, turn right, and go through a second adjacent door. The lyre music gets louder with the opening door.

Philokrates stands back against the wall of a narrow gallery, overlooking the palace dining-hall, and from his **POV** we see the lyre player, **Euphorion** sitting on the end of a dining couch, immediately below. Thracian slaves are preparing the dining-hall for supper. A gong booms, and the slaves begin dispersing outwards, and away through doors in all four walls. Still playing, **Euphorion** walks across to a corner of the room. **Philip** enters through the press of departing slaves, and **Philokrates** hurries down the nine steps from the gallery to the dining-floor. **Philip** jerks his head at **Euphorion**, indicating that he is to leave, and strides across the floor to give **Philokrates** an enthusiastic welcome.

CU of them embracing. **Philip** turns on his considerable charm.

Philip
My dear friend. Philokrates.
Valued ally.

From outside the dining-hall comes the most tremendous crash of falling metal plates and smashing terra cotta. **Philokrates** starts violently and looks round. **Philip** laughs loudly and puts a hand on his shoulder.

Philip

Calm yourself. You are our honoured
guest-friend.
And besides, the companions are
in place to ensure that we are not joined
by your fellow Athenians.

Philokrates smiles nervously and speaks quickly.

Philokrates

Everything is arranged We have a seven
to three majority in favour of your plan.
Our order of speaking is agreed.
Demosthenes will speak last.

Philip

Drily.

For the old order, I have no doubt.

Philokrates

Hastily.

The status quo, yes. And its advantages.

Philip

For an undeserving Athens, living
on past glories …

Philip puts his left arm completely around the other's shoulder.

… So. To our first meeting, the 'Water
Drinker' – my noisiest critic – will bring
No surprises.

Philokrates

No. He is as rabid as ever.

Philip
No matter. In spite of themselves, they
all dance to my score.
This afternoon you will open for Athens.

Philokrates
Yes, I will introduce the speakers and
set the scene. My Lord, I must get
back before my absence is noticed.

Philip
Of course, …

They start towards the nine steps, and **Philip** puts his arm right
around **Philokrates's** shoulders.

… On the day we sign the peace,
the 'golden mule' will pay you
another visit.

Cut to:

28. INT/Alexander Outside the Queen's Apartment

Alexander exchanges a nod with the sentry and reaches for the
door handle. From inside comes a scream, a crash, and a shout
of rage. He closes his eyes, and holds up his right hand in brief,
silent supplication to Herakles. Entering, he walks towards the
bedroom door.

Inside, we see in **CU**, an amphora of kohl smashing on the tiled
floor.

Alexander walks in as **Olympias** sends the slave-girl who dropped
the kohl, sprawling, with a backhand blow to the head.

Olympias
Useless slut! Get out!
All of you. Half-wits!
Leave me alone with my son.

A slave-girl runs out passing **Alexander**. The girl on the floor picks herself up and follows. **Olympias** flings herself down on the bed. **Hyrminia**, who has been setting up the triple snake lamp knocked over before **Alexander** entered, runs out last. **Alexander** kneels beside **Olympias** and strokes her hair. She writhes on the bed, then grabs him by the shoulders, and drags him to her.

Olympias
Dionysus, my witness, speak for me!
May the gods of Olympus unite
to avenge me!

Olympias rocks them both from side to side. She moans. Clasped to her bosom, **Alexander** moves his head in order to breathe.

Olympias
Heaven forbid you should learn what I
suffer from this most repulsive of men.
May Hera protect your years of innocence.

Alexander
Is it a boy or a girl this time, mother?

Olympias
Shrieks.

A Thracian daughter! A filthy blue
painted Thracian!

Alexander
I'm sorry, mother. Has father
married her?

Olympias thrusts **Alexander** away to arm's length, her hands gripping his shoulders. Her eyes are dilated and staring; her lashes matted. Tears of rage, and kohl streaks her cheeks. Her thick red hair stands out around her face, and cascades in tangles, down across her chest.

Olympias

Her voice low and menacing.

> Never call that ... that man,
> your father ...

Alexander winces slightly as her fingers dig into his shoulders.

> ... Ammon hear me, you are clean of that!
> The day will come when the monster
> knows he had no part in you.

Olympias lets go of **Alexander**. She begins to laugh and falls back on her elbows. The laughter becomes hysterical. **Alexander** looks at her in wonder and in fear.

> Oh yes! He will learn that a greater
> was here before him!

Olympias lets her head loll back. Sobs mingle with the laughter, and its pitch rises higher and higher. **Alexander** pulls at her hands.

Alexander

> Mother no! Please, please,
> please stop! I am with you.
> Me, your Alexander.

Her breath comes in choking gasps. **Alexander** crawls up onto the bed and puts his arms around her neck. He kisses her face and then pleads in her ear.

Alexander

Don't go mad. Please, don't go mad.
I could not bear it. I will die, I will die.

Olympias moans, and lies back for a moment, before sitting up
and taking **Alexander** into her arms.

Olympias

My poor boy. My poor, darling boy.
It was only the laughing sickness.
He brings me to it; but only you shall know.
As only you know what I have to bear.
I am not mad. I know you. I love you.
Do not worry.

Alexander

When I am grown up, I will see you are
rightfully treated.

Olympias

Darling child, I know. *He* does not even
guess what you are. But I know. I, and
the God!

Olympias gets up from the bed and goes to her dressing table.
Alexander slides off the other side of the bed and goes around
behind his mother. He puts both arms around her neck and buries
his face in her hair. Abruptly, he runs from the room. **Olympias**
swings around on the stool, stretching out one arm.

Olympias

Alexander wait.

She turns back to her mirror. Wiping her eyes, and rimming
them swiftly with kohl, **Olympias** stands up and walks towards
the door.

29. EXT/The Palace Garden/Moments later

In the middle distance, with the palace in the background, we see **Parmenion** chatting with a very unathletic, chubby, pasty-faced man, with black thinning hair. He is in his early thirties, and we come to know him as **Lysimachos**. They are joined by two others.

As we **dolly in** towards the four, **Alexander** is seen running from the palace beyond them. **Lysimachos** watches him intently. **Alexander** leans across a low wall and throws up.

Lysimachos
I must get back to the library.

Lysimachos hurries forward **out of shot**. **Alexander** walks slowly back towards the palace, and we see him and **Lysimachos** enter by adjacent side entrances.

Cut to:

30. INT/An Internal Hallway of the Palace/Noon

An agitated **Lysimachos** paces around the area. **Alexander** and **Olympias** come around a corner. **Lysimachos** goes straight up to them, speaking without ceremony, abruptly; but with concern.

Lysimachos
Is the boy all right?

Olympias
Bantering.
> You forsake your books to enquire after
> my son's health, Lysimachos!

Lysimachos

Hesitant.

I was in the garden. I saw.

Olympias

Laughs.

All is well with us.

She strides on, accompanied by **Alexander. Lysimachos** watches them disappear out of sight, before moving slowly away in another direction.

Cut to:

31. INT/The Queen's Apartment/ Moments later

The sentry salutes the arrival of **Olympias**. She and **Alexander** go through to her bedroom. **Hyrminia** appears, and she joins them. **Olympias** opens a chest, and takes out a multi-coloured chiton, which she holds out for **Hyrminia**, without speaking, or even looking.

Alexander
I will wear my jewels after all.
You are right.
One should not dress down for Athenians,
even if they do think jewels barbarous.

Olympias holds out a blue-trimmed chlamys for **Hyrminia**. She continues to search in the chest.

Olympias
They are nothing these envoys. It is
proper that you out dress them.

Alexander

And besides, the King will wear jewels.

Olympias

Yes, well, you wear them better.

Alexander

And I think the blue chiton.

Olympias

I know just what suits you, darling.

Alexander

Yes; but it must be right.

Olympias gets up from the chest. She moves close to **Alexander** and combs her fingers through his heavy, wind-blown hair.

Olympias

Tsk, tsk. My lord shall be obeyed!

They smile together, and **Alexander** pulls her hand down and kisses her palm.

Cut to:

32. INT/The Guest Wing of the Palace

Philokrates walks from his room and follows a Thracian slave-guide along the corridor. They pass two other Thracians waiting outside doors. As they reach a third, the door is thrown open, and the bluff, expansive, mannered and self-confident figure of **Aeschines** strides out. We walk with them, as they follow the two slave-guides.

Aeschines

What does Philip really want of Athens?
Deep down. Is it simply to rule our city?
Along with the rest of Greece.
Or is it more important for him to be
welcomed at the Parthenon as a hero?
A saviour? A guest-friend even?
One who did not desecrate the altar
of our greatness by fire or sword.

Philokrates

Defensive.

Why ask me? I am not privy to the
thoughts of tyrants. You assume he
covets the city-state. He claims he
wants peace. Who knows? Perhaps
we are about to find out.

Aeschines looks hard at **Philokrates**, who smiles and looks away.

Aeschines

Reflective.

Soon, he will be the master of all northern
Greece. Including the corn-route of the Hellespont.
Then Delphi will welcome him.
The only question for Athens is whether
the door should be thrown open, or he
should have to beat it down.

They reach a broad staircase, and the slave-guides start down.
Another slave-guide, followed by an envoy, approaches from the
opposite direction.

Cut to:

33. INT/The Queen's Bedroom

Alexander, wearing a blue chiton, stands next to the dressing table, as **Olympias** sorts through her brooch collection. She holds a number against **Alexander's** shoulder as they talk.

> **Alexander**
> I have spoken to some of
> the envoys already.

> **Olympias**

Surprised.

> Have you? With whom?

> **Alexander**
> Aristodemos. He said I had grown
> so that he hardly recognised me.

> **Olympias**
> It is three years since his last visit.
> Such a charming man. We must invite
> him to come here on his own.

> **Alexander**
> He introduced me to Aschenes. He
> used to be an actor.

> **Olympias**
> Is he a gentleman?

> **Alexander**
> It doesn't matter with actors.

Olympias fastens the selected brooch, and steps back to check.

Olympias
You must be careful with these people.
I hope you said nothing indiscreet.

Alexander takes the blue-trimmed chlamys from a chair, and hands it to **Olympias**.

Alexander
Oh no. We talked about the war party
and the peace party, in Athens. I liked
him. He said Macedon is not at all like
he thought it would be.

Hyrminia enters.

Olympias
For Athenians, anywhere north of Mount
Olympus is lion country! Well?

Hyrminia
The King sends a message, saying that he has
summoned the envoys.
His Majesty wishes the Prince to
enter with him.

Olympias
He will be there.
Fetch the curlers, Hyrminia.

Hyrminia
They are ready, my Lady.

Hyrminia leaves.

Alexander
You must stop curling my hair, mother.
None of the other boys have it done.

Olympias
What is that to you?
You lead, you do not follow.
Don't you want to look beautiful for me?

Cut to:

34. INT/Antechamber of the Perseus Room/Early afternoon

Fully armed Foot Companions stand at each of the three sentry points, and at the foot of the stairway, which projects into the antechamber. The ten Athenians stand in a group near the triple-arched entrance to the Perseus Room. The Lord Chamberlain, **Eumenes,** two assistants and four guards, stand together at the centre entrance arch. Several prominent Macedonians, who have come to witness the audience, stand around in groups of two and three. There is a low hum of conversation.

In **CU Eumenes** points to two of his guards, who rap their spear butts three times on the marble floor. The hum of conversation fades.

Eumenes
Delegates of the Athenian Assembly.
You will remain standing inside the Perseus
Room, until King Philip invites you to be
seated. Pray follow me.

Eumenes goes through the centre arch, followed by his two assistants. The four Foot Companions move to flank the approach. The Athenians follow in pairs. **Aeschines** and **Demosthenes** bring up the rear.

Our first view of the Perseus Room is from the dais, looking back towards the entrance. A short distance from the dais is a row of ten gold chairs. A wider space separates them from a group of less ornate chairs for spectators. All the chairs have been positioned to the right of the room. There is no central aisle, and everyone follows **Eumenes** up the left side of the room, as we view it.

The dominating feature is two double rows of fully armed Foot Companions, in close order, lining both sides of the Perseus Room, from dais to entrance.

As **Eumenes** approaches the gold chairs, we see **Aeschines** and **Demosthenes** in **CU**.

The former looks about boldly and with interest, whilst the latter tends to his nose with the hem of his cloak.

Aeschines

Muttering aside.

> You are doomed already with that fever;
> but it looks as though the rest of us
> face a more blood-stained end!

Demosthenes

Sniffily.

> We are the elected reprethentativeth of
> Athenth, not common criminalth.

Aeschines

> Who elected to come through the ranks
> of Macedon without the protection of a herald!

In a **reverse shot** from the spectators' chairs, we see the Athenians filing along the gold chairs. On the dais, two thrones are flanked by two massive chairs, in red, picked out with gold. The door near the great mural of Perseus is thrown open, and **Philip** strides in. **Alexander** trots slightly behind him, and both are flanked by the imposing, military clad figures of **Parmenion** and **Antipatros**. There is nothing military in **Philip's** rich attire. The two generals are greaved, cuirassed, and wearing swords; but are without helmets. **Alexander's** head is a mass of heavy blond waves. He looks fixedly at his feet throughout.

Both sides look at each other with interest. The sounds of the spectators moving to their seats dies away. **Demosthenes** stifles a spluttering sneeze. His rheumy gaze meets **Philip's** one-eyed glare for the first time. The tense atmosphere eases, as **Philip** welcomes them warmly.

Philip
Welcome to our capital of Pella.
I trust that the coming of spring in
Macedonia is not proving too rigorous
an experience!

Demosthenes looks at him, sharply, and shakes off the arm of a grinning **Aeschines**.

Please be seated …

Philip waits for the Athenians and spectators to settle, and then says:

In putting the case for the greatest of Greek
cities, I would ask you to remember the
words of one of her greatest sons.
Even today, some two centuries later,
who can disagree with the incomparable
Perikles that:
"Every happiness depends on Liberty".

Philip nods to **Eumenes**, and sprawls back in his throne. The other three also sit, with **Alexander** now staring relentlessly at his knees.

Eumenes
Philokrates son of Tritogeneus
of Attica.

Philokrates rises and walks forward to the edge of the dais.

Fade out:

35. INT/The Palace Library/Mid-afternoon

Lysimachos sits at a small, kidney shaped table, strewn with scrolls, reaching from floor to ceiling. He watches **Olympias** pacing agitatedly beside the shelves.

Lysimachos
Now he has outgrown his nurse's care,
do you not think that he should have
a pedagogue?

Olympias swings around, her jewelled necklaces clattering.

Olympias
Never! I will never allow it! The King
knows that. Those low bred pendants who
would break the spirit of my son! ...

Olympias bears down on **Lysimachos**

...They allow his spirit no time to breathe
from rising to lying down.

Olympias thrusts her hands amongst the scrolls, and she leans over him, her eyes flashing.

... Would you have him marched about like
a slave? Like some captive thief? ...

If the King put you up to this, Lysimachos …
You can tell him, that before Alexander
shall suffer a pedagogue, I shall have blood.
By the Threefold Hekate, I shall have blood!

After a moment, **Olympias** pushes herself upright, and goes back
to her pacing. **Lysimachos** is composed, quiet.

Lysimachos
God forbid, Madam. I would only ask
that I should be his pedagogue.

Olympias in **CU**. She stops with her back to **Lysimachos**, half
looking back; but without turning around.

Olympias
A gentleman? For a servant's work?

Lysimachos
Quiet; then intense.

I believe that Achilles has come again in
Alexander. If so, he needs a Phoenix.
"Would that you, godlike Achilles, were the son I
chose for my own, that someday you
would keep the hard times from me".

Olympias turns around; but keeps her distance.

Olympias
What he asked Achilles did not grant.

Lysimachos
Had he done so, it would have saved him
sorrow. Could it be his soul remembers? …

Olympias steps back to the table. **Lysimachos** stands up, his speech becoming more animated.

> ... I think so. The ashes of Achilles and
> Patroklus were mingled in one urn. Not
> even the god could sift one from the other.
> Now, Achilles is back, with all his pride and
> fierceness; but with the feelings of Patroklus.
> Each of them suffered for what he was.
> This boy will suffer for both.

Olympias
> There is more to Alexander, as men will learn.

Lysimachos
> I do not doubt it; but for now, this is enough.
> Let me try. If he cannot do with me, I will
> let him be.

Olympias starts to move away, and then abruptly turns back to face **Lysimachos**.

Olympias
> Try! If you can stand between my son
> and those fools, I shall be your debtor.

Cut to:

36. INT/The Perseus Room/ Late afternoon

Demosthenes in **CU**, as he mouths his speech in preparation.

Demosthenes/Aeschines
Voices off-set.
> He maintains that you should be the
> benefactor of all Greece, as well as

King of Macedon, and should gain
to the greatest possible extent …

Suddenly he realises that he is hearing the words spoken. He looks
up sharply. **Aeschines** nears the end of his speech. He stands before the dais, his right hand just visible inside his chlamys. He
makes restrained but emphatic gestures with his left. Beyond
him, **Alexander** still looks down.

Aeschines
… the empire of the non-Greek world.
If you can accomplish this, you
will win universal gratitude.
If, your rule continues kingly,
and not tyrannical.

Aeschines inclines his head in a slight bow to the throne. We
see **Alexander** (vigorously ruffling any last curl from his hair
with his fingers) in **CU** with **Philip**.

Philip
Our thanks, Aischenes son of Atrometos.
A most significant and elegant speech.

Aeschines inclines his head again, and, with a slight smile on
his face, returns the five paces to his seat. He never looks at **Demosthenes**, although the latter's eyes never leave his face, despite at least one attempt at a sneeze.

Eumenes
The final speaker for the Assembly
of Athens. Demosthenes,
son of Demosthenes of Paiania.

Demosthenes stands up. He dabs at his nose and clears his throat
as he steps forward. Nearing the edge of the dais, he looks to-

wards the throne, as he begins to speak; but instead of catching **Philip's** eye, he sees only **Alexander**, leaning forward, his head tilted slightly to the left, and looking straight at him.

Demosthenes
I take a broad view of the whole
quethtion of a Peath...a, er, broad
view...er, yes, a broad view...

Flash shot:

Alexander
Watching **Demosthenes** in the garden:

'You are going to die, I tell you'.

Cut back to present:

Demosthenes, visibly shaken, clears his throat, and sneezes; but is unable to look away from the unblinking gaze full upon him.

Demosthenes
I... I... I... I... er, take a very broad view.

Murmuring breaks out in the Perseus Room. **Philip** looks at **Demosthenes** in some surprise; but he is sympathetic.

Philip
Take it point by point. No need to be
put off by a moment's dry up.
I assure you we can wait.

Alexander's glare never leaves **Demosthenes**. **Aeschines** steps forward and puts an arm around his shoulders. It is shaken off.

Demosthenes
The broad view ith. No. I'm thorry.

Everyone stands up, and the delegation members move in and around **Demosthenes**. All stand on the dais.

Dissolve to:

37. EXT/The Palace Garden/Moments later

Alexander and **Philip** walk towards a large shrub.

Philip
You could have gone out. I never
thought to tell you.

Alexander
I didn't need to. You told me once
not to drink before state occasions.

They reach the shrub and, side by side, lift their robes to pee.

Philip
Did I? Good, well, so what did you
make of Demosthenes?

Alexander
You were right, Father, he isn't brave.

Philip
Strange he should perform so badly ...

Half sensing that **Alexander** knows something relevant, **Philip** looks down at **Alexander,** both still intent on the task in hand.

... do *you* know why?

Alexander
Aeschines was an actor once, he stole
his lines.

Philip
However, do you know that?

Alexander
I saw him practising his speech in
the palace garden. He spoke to me.

Philip
Demosthenes?! About what?

Alexander
He thought that I was a slave sent to spy.
Then he thought I was someone's bed-boy.
I didn't tell him. I thought I'd wait.

Philip
What?!

Philip drops his robe and turns to **Alexander** who follows suit

Alexander
He didn't recognise me until I sat up and
looked at him, when he started speaking.

Philip chuckles. They walk back towards the Palace.

Philip
Why didn't you tell me?

Alexander
He would have expected that. Now he
doesn't know what to think.

Philip throws back his head and roars with laughter. Suddenly serious he looks at **Alexander.**

Philip
Did that man proposition you?

Alexander
He could not bring himself to ask
a slave.
He just wondered how much
I'd cost.

Father and son look at each other in perfect harmony. Each puts his arm around the other, and they walk, away from the camera, back into the Palace.

Dissolve to

38. EXT/Pella Harbour Market/Early morning – Late May 344 BC

Very **CU** shot of two eggs sizzling in oil, in an earthenware dish, over a wood fire, burning in a ring of stones. Two hunks of bread are held in shot, on either side of the dish. A wooden spatula, held in female fingers, bastes the eggs. One egg is scooped out on to one hunk of bread, which is lifted by a male hand, **out of shot**. The second egg is basted and scooped on to the bread. We watch it lifted up, to reveal **Harpalos**, aged about thirteen, short, thick-set, swarthy, with curly black hair, one clubfoot and a stutter. The cook, a pretty, grubby woman dressed in ragged red, takes two more eggs from her family vegetable stall, and cracks one into the oil.

Hephaestion, also aged thirteen; but tall, slender, fair, and with vivid blue eyes, looks at the woman's vegetable display, being tended by her seven-year-old boy and girl twins, and then jerks his head at **Harpalos**.

Hephaestion
C'mon.

They move away along the line of stalls, munching the bread and eggs. The limping **Harpalos** hurrying to keep up.

The market is predominantly fish, vegetables, herbs and spices, game, and an occasional hardware stall. Interspersed between the well-spaced permanent flimsy wood frames supporting cotton awnings, are individual sales pitches. These are simply cloths spread on the ground, displaying a few trinkets, a sword or helmet, a few items of clothing, or a single type of vegetable or animal.

The market is already well attended. Women with children of all ages. Scarred and limbless ex-soldiers. At one stall, sits a legless veteran on a wheeled trolley, surrounded by his all-female family, cheerfully selling their impressive display of herbs and spices. Water and wine sellers move through the market, dispensing in bronze cups, from amphora slung across the backs of donkeys. There is a steady trickle of individuals moving to and from fishing boats in the nearby harbour.

Smoke from numerous little cooking fires rises straight into the still, early morning sky. Scavenging crows and gulls hop and wheel on the fringes. Some eye two dogs scrapping with a carcass. Two kites wheel overhead. Cockerels crow.

Hephaestion and **Harpalos** run from the end of line of stalls, to a small isolated building near the quayside where there are two columned stoa on which notices are displayed. **Hephaestion** arrives first.

Harpalos
Any bbbbargains?

Hephaestion
If you fish, or wish to sail to
the Piraeus.

Harpalos
Ugh. Even I'd rather walk.

From a nearby stall comes a sequence of strong chords on a stringed instrument, followed by an isolated cadenza.

Hephaestion
The god himself?

Harpalos
It's nnnot the wrwrwrwright instrument
for the silver bbbbowman.

Hephaestion
That's not a lyre?

Harpalos
Never.

They pause, listening for a moment.

Harpalos
An obbbbol says the truth is nnnnot
a lyre.

Hephaestion
You're on for a half, Harpalos.

They bend swiftly, scoop up a pinch of sand from the ground at their feet, and banging it together between their left hands, run across to investigate.

The pair joining a group of some ten men, women and children gathered around a small stall selling a few weapons and musical instruments. **Alexander** puts down the kithara he has just played. **Lysimachos** picks up one of two others, which has a delicately wrought sound box and a rich patina to its woodwork.

Lysimachos
Even Orpheus would be tempted.

Alexander
It is certainly beautiful.

He takes it up, slipping the sling around his neck, and gently strumming the bass strings with the fingers of his left hand.

He looks up, and his eyes meet those of **Hephaestion. Alexander** is by far the sturdier of the two; but shorter by some six inches. As he starts to sing, we see **Hephaestion** and **Harpalos** in **CU**.

The latter gives **Hephaestion** a sharp nudge with his elbow and holds an upturned palm in front of him. **Hephaestion** does no more than glance down, and his eyes are back on **Alexander**. He hands over a coin without looking down. **Alexander**'s strong alto voice floods the marketplace, without a trace of the roughness of breaking.

Alexander
God has all things come to pass,
as he would have them be.
God ordains the wheeling eagle;
the dolphin in the sea.
He masters also mortal men,
though their pride be bold;

But to some he gives a glory
that never will grow old.

He stops abruptly. **Hephaestion** steps forward almost instinc‑
tively to re-introduce himself.

Hephaestion
Hephaestion

Alexander
Son of Lord Amyntor. I remember.
It was five years ago, maybe six.

Hephaestion
Your sling and shot bag. My father
had an audience with the King.

Alexander turns away to the stallholder, slipping the kithara
from around his neck.

Alexander
This one.

The three boys walk off into the market. **Lysimachos** hands
money to the stallholder, picks up the kithara, and follows. As
he joins them, walking amongst the shoppers, **Harpalos** limps
out of shot.

Lysimachos
You should find more time for
your music.

Alexander
Not a hope. Days are short
enough already.

Hephaestion
I agree. Why do we have to sleep?!

Alexander
One should be able to do without.

Lysimachos
Why must we die? We could do
without that too!

Alexander
Sleep makes me think of death.

Lysimachos
You?! At twelve. Surely you are
rich enough in time?

Alexander
Zeus alone knows that.

Hephaestion
Why not enter a music contest?

Lysimachos
Good idea. You could prepare for the
Pythian Games next year.

Hephaestion
Would the king let you?

Alexander
Not if I competed only as a musician.
Nor would I want to, Lysimachos.
Why do you want me to take part?

Lysimachos
To discipline your skill.

Alexander
I thought as much; but then I wouldn't
enjoy it …

Lysimachos sighs and looks away.

… Don't be angry. Leonidas has
been discipline enough.

Lysimachos
I know, Achilles, dear child; but you
will never be the complete musician if
you neglect the philosophy of your art.

Alexander
I can never be a musician, my Phoenix.
Even if I had the essential mathematics
of the soul. I have other things to do.

Hephaestion
Enter as an athlete, and take in the
music contest too.

They near the end of the of the line of stalls. Their ponies, and
the cart of **Lysimachos** are tethered beneath the trees. **Harpalos** can be seen beyond them, limping up to the ponies. A ragged, legless cripple, kneeling on a small wheeled sledge, paddles
between them, followed by a dog.

Alexander
No. I can beat the boys here because
we are all training to be men.

At the Games the boys are nothing
other than athletes,
either finished before they reach manhood,
or turning into men for whom the Games
will become a way of life.
Like being a woman is for a woman.
Perhaps if I were to compete only
against kings!

They all laugh.

Lysimachos
This has all come about in my lifetime.
People who have earned no pride in
themselves, are content to be proud
through others.
Our dead were proud less easily.

Alexander
With music, everyman's pride is ours.

They untie their various horses. **Lysimachos's** driver has only
one arm; but deftly manages the reins and the two horses. The
boys mount and **Lysimachos** steps onto the cart.

Lysimachos
You have never played the kithara for
your father's guests at supper.

Alexander
The lyre is what people want at supper.

Lysiamchos
It's what they get for lack of something better.

Looking at each other, **Alexander** and **Hephaestion** move off together.

Alexander
All right. Given the right occasion.

Lysimachos follows, with **Harpalos** bringing up the rear.

Cut to:

39. EXT/A Roadway Leading West out of Pella/Mid-afternoon

Steadicam amidst a manacled column of ragged, filthy men and women moving slowly forward in a swirl of its own dust. Small children and dogs move at liberty amidst the shuffling feet. There is little or no urging, from the random overseers, or talk from anyone. The only sounds are the thud of feet, the chink of chain links, the yelp of a kicked dog, the cry of a child, and a background screech from the wooden wheels and axles of a cart. We see individuals in **CU**, listless, staring, starving and silent, then a **voice-over** conversation between **Alexander** and **Hephaestion** both unseen:

Alexander
Survivors from Olynthos. Better they
had not lived.

Hephaestion
Fight or surrender, it was their choice.

Alexander
Yes.
All the gold in Macedon can't buy
everyone, the god be thanked.

Hephaestion
What will become of them?

Alexander
They will swell the fortunes of slave
dealers, and lose their freedom in the
households of fellow-Greeks – or in brothels.
Some of the men might become
spearmen in someone's army,
if they survive the march.

Hephaestion
They're not criminals! They are ordinary
Greeks being marched through Greece
In chains. I could weep.

Cut to:

40. EXT/The Palace Roof/ Mid-afternoon

CU of a gulley in the palace roof, from where the pair have been watching the passing column. **Alexander** leans back against **Hephaestion**, who, has an arm around his waist. **Alexander** speaks quietly; but with a fierce intensity.

Alexander
It cannot happen to you if
you are the best!

Hephaestion
What can we do?

Alexander
Ignore it. We will be the best.
We will win. Always!
Do you understand?

Hephaestion gives the golden head a look which is both worried and loving at the same time.

Hephaestion
Alexander, you won't ever go to war
without me?

Alexander
Without you? How could you even
think it? You're my dearest friend.

Hephaestion
Do you mean that? Do you
really mean that?

Alexander jerks upright, and **Hephaestion** hastily withdraws his arm.

Alexander
Indignant.
Do you doubt that I mean It? Do you
think I bring others up here? Or tell
them the things I tell you.

Hephaestion
Don't fight me. One always doubts
great good fortune.

Alexander's look softens, and he raises his right hand, back outwards, and with the palm and fingers pointing towards his own face.

Alexander
I swear by Herakles.

Lowering his arm, he leans forward, and gives **Hephaistion** an affectionate kiss on the cheek. **Hephaistion** closes his eyes in pleasure. By the time he opens them, and has nerved himself for a return kiss, **Alexander** has turned away. Looking across the rooftop, he points to the statue of Winged Victory.

Alexander
That Nike is the highest point on the
palace roof.
I can get up there. Come.

Cut to:

Alexander runs up the gulley, followed; but not closely, by **Hephaestion**. They run across a short section of flat roof and come to a two-foot-wide wall connecting the flat roof to a friezed arch. The drop is some forty feet on one side of the wall, and about ten feet on the other. **Alexander** immediately jumps down and starts to walk across. **Hephaestion** freezes, looking down at the drop. Realising he is not being followed, **Alexander** turns and walks back.

Alexander
Outstare the earth-daimons.
Such creatures always give in
when challenged. Defy the drop.

He scowls down the forty-foot drop, then looks at **Hephaestion** with a smile and begins to hum a paean of victory. **Hephaistion** steps down on to the top of the wall, and follows **Alexander** across; but more slowly.

Cut to:

Alexander and **Hephaistion** moving sideways to their left, along the ledge below the relief of young boys playing 'hockey' and other ball games, on the arch freize.

Alexander and **Hephaistion** moving up the sloping roof, to reach the statue of Nike, Goddess of Victory.

Alexander
Hold on to the waist of the goddess …
… Now grip my wrist.

CU of the hand of **Hephaestion** grasping **Alexander's** wrist. **Alexander** bunches his fist and makes no attempt to hold on to **Hephaestion**. Medium shot of the two boys and the statue. Leaning out over the drop to the palace garden, some sixty feet below, and with both arms at full stretch, **Alexander** can just reach the gilded wreath. He breaks off a leaf, and puts it in his mouth, and then reaches for a second. He has to twist and work it, before it too breaks free, and he puts it too in his mouth, as he hauls himself back to **Hephaestion**.

CU of **Alexander** taking the hand of his friend. His other hand **enters the shot**, and we see him place a gilded leaf in the up-turned palm.

Alexander
Voice off.

Now do you believe that we will go to war together?

Hephaestion closes his fingers over the leaf.

Hephaestion
I thought it was me who was
being tested.

Alexander

Laughing.

Wasn't it?
I saw Lambaros in
the garden.
Let's go and cheer him up.

They move down the sloping roof on hands and feet; but now
looking up.

Hephaestion

Is he the Thracian chief's son?

Alexander

No, king, the Thracian king, a prince.
A hostage for his father's good behaviour,
and treated here like some common
prisoner of war. It's shameful.

They reach the bottom of the flat roof, and, in turn, they stand
up, heading for the ledge of the arch.

Cut to:

41. INT/The Palace Library/Afternoon

Lysimachos searches amongst a shelf of scrolls. He checks one,
briefly, then a second. Picking them both up, he heads for the
door, passing two Thracian slaves doing some less than enthusiastic dusting. Going out, he closes the door on us.

Cut to:

Lysimachos entering **Philip's** study. **Philip** is writing and looks
up. **Lysimachos** walks up to the writing table.

Philip
Did you find a copy?

Lysimachos
Two. One written by Euripedes himself,
while he was staying here at the palace
in your grandfather's day.

Philip
Let me see.

Philip stands up. He starts walking around the writing table
when something outside the window catches his eye. He looks,
and holds out a hand to **Lysimachos**, who is moving to meet
him. He will give him the scroll.

Philip
He has the sons of all my nobles to
choose from; but no, he consorts with
a Thracian savage.

Looking between **Lysimachos** and **Philip**, we see **Alexander**
and **Lambaros** crouched on one knee and one foot, facing each
other, and piling their hands alternately one on top of the other. They are watched by **Hephaestion**, and a **Soldier-Guard**
some short way off.

Lysimachos
The bow unbent. I like to see him at
a childish pursuit.

Lambaros throws back his head, and howls like a dog, in a crack-
ing treble imitation of a Thracian war-yell. The **Soldier-Guard**
strolls towards them.

Philip
It seems he took our young hostage to
the gymnasium yesterday morning.
The noble fathers were not amused.

Lysimachos
He has become very friendly with
Amyntor's son, Hephaestion.

Philip
His age to a day. With his beauty,
we expected an older boy.

Lysimachos
To Alexander it's no more than friendship.

Alexander and **Lambaros** hold each other's heads between their
hands and plant a kiss on each other's foreheads.

Philip
Whatever that is, Lysimachos, it has
gone far enough. Go and fetch him.

Cut to:

42. EXT/The Palace Garden/Afternoon

We dolly in towards **Alexander, Lambaros** and **Hephaestion**,
as the **Soldier-Guard** approaches them. Reminded of his position, **Lambaros** hangs his head in misery. **Alexander** looks up.

Alexander
Go back, nothing is wrong. He is teaching
me his customs. I'll call if I need you.

The **Soldier-Guard** withdraws without speaking. We see the boys in **CU**.

Lambaros

When our father's die and we are kings, you
will bring your men to fight my enemies?

Alexander

And your soldiers will fight my enemies,
when we go to war, yes. It is being allies,
Lambaros. Do you understand?

Lambaros

When we go to war, yes.

Alexander

Yours was a fine oath. Say the end again.

Lamabaros

I will keep faith, unless the sky falls and crushes
me, or the earth opens up and swallows me, or
the sea rises and overwhelms me. My father
always kisses the chiefs when they are sworn in.

Hephaestion

The guard is coming back. Let's
get out the knucklebones.

Lambaros

His god always wins for him.

Alexander

No, I just try to feel lucky. You ask
your god for such little things. I
expect he gets offended. Gods like
to be asked for something great.
I save up prayer.

The **Soldier-Guard** reaches the boys and stands looking down at them. In spite of himself, he shifts his feet under **Alexander's** steady gaze.

Lambaros
What for?

Alexander
For when I need allies.

Soldier-Guard
The King, your father, wants you, Alexander.
This young lad is to stay with me.

Alexander
Very well ...

Alexander jumps to his feet and confronts the **Soldier-Guard.**

Don't stop him doing everything he wants.
You are a soldier not a pedagogue.
And don't call him 'this young lad'.
If I can give him his rank, then
so, can you ...

He looks down at his friend.

Tell Hephaestion how Red
Thracians form up for battle.

Alexander heads swiftly for the Palace. Laughing, **Lambaros** shouts after him.

Lambaros
Together we will win a thousand heads.
Chop, chop, chop!

Alexander turns around, laughing.

Alexander
Yes; but the slingers. Where
do your slingers stand?

He runs off towards a Palace entrance.

Cut to:

43. EXT/A Barrack Stadium East of Pella/Minutes before sunrise

In the twilight before sunrise, a small chariot, pulled by four white horses and carrying a **driver**, plus **Attalos** and **Euphorion**, drives briskly along a deserted dirt road from Pella.

Euphorion
No foreigners will be eating
with the king tonight.

Attalos
So, who will keep the tyrant
company in his cups?

Euphorion
Members of the Household, military
companions, and Alexander.

Attalos
Each day we become more like
Athens in our customs.
The boy should not be present.
He has yet to come of age.

Euphorion
He won't be the only one …

The chariot swings on to the empty stadium and stops.

… Harpalos, Hephaestion, and General
Parmenion's son, Philotas, will be there.
also – or so I hear.

The driver stays in the chariot. **Attalos** and **Euphorion** dismount, to stand close in front of the horses.

Attalos
At least we can rely on Antipatros
not to bring under-age children to the
supper table of Macedon's king.

Euphorion
Or allow the surly Kassandros
near a wine-pitcher!

They watch in silence as a file of four spearman march into view, at the far end of the barrack building. They march slowly, rhythmically, and in silence. Without shield, each man carries his spear at the trail. Other files follow, at an interval of one spear's length. The crimson sliver of the rising sun is just visible above the distant mountains, beyond the marching men.

Attalos goes to the side of the chariot and takes one of a pair of spears from a rack on the side of the vehicle. Returning to **Euphorion's** side, he places the butt of the spear on the ground and leans on the shaft. With his face close to **Euphorion's**, he speaks quietly.

Attalos

Tonight! ... I'll settle with
Pausanias tonight at supper
with our most subtle master.

The leading file wheels through forty-five degrees, and the length-
ening column approaches them obliquely.

Euphorion

What do you plan to do?

Attalos

Better you have no part in it. Stay close
to the king, and don't come near me all
night.

Euphorion nods as they watch the column transforming itself
into a pair of concentric circles. The two inner rings now hold
their spears in a throwing position. The outer rings hold theirs
across their bodies. They all turn inwards, to face a single, unarmed man, untied and unsupported, in the centre of each circle. Having completed the manoeuvre, they shout in unison.

Spearmen

Helios!

Attalos throws up the spear he has been leaning on, catches the
butt, and hurls it into the ground in front of him. It sticks there,
quivering. The sun bursts clear of the mountain tops and floods
the circles in bright light.

Spearmen

A single shout once more in unison.

Helios!

The men in the two inner rings hurl their spears. In **CU** we see spears being pulled from a ragged body, but without seeing the individuals concerned. Still in **CU**, three spears are slid under the now oozing body – at the shoulder, the small of the back behind the knees. It is lifted up, the hands and feet trailing in the dust. The column reforms in two lines, and marches away, with the twelve men carrying the corpse between the lines.

Attalos
We were within an arrow's flight of the
Thracian camp. When I went around the
picket-line before dawn, he was
asleep.

Cut to:

44. INT/The Palace Dining Hall/Evening

The wine-red theme of the walls is heightened by a pale gold ceiling, and mirrored in the polished, rustic, terra-cotta tiles of the floor. Three walls depict classical scenes and were also painted by Zeuxis when the palace was built at the turn of the century. One wall shows Herakles subduing the Cretan Bull and another has him supporting the sky, with the help of Athena, while Atlas brings him the Golden Apples. The third wall has two girls picking apples, on either side of the main entrance, above which is a large representation of a circular dish, decorated with Mediterranean fish. The fourth, which includes the King's Door, is strikingly different in both style and subject. Modern, and multi-coloured in its portrayal of a clad crowd, the mural was commissioned by **Philip** two years earlier, and shows Solon, the architect of the democracy of Classical Greece, addressing citizens in the Agora at Athens, shortly after being elected Archon, two hundred years earlier.

Slaves hurry about the great dining hall, arranging couches, and positioning adjacent tables, on which other slaves are distributing bowls of fruit, wine, cups, bread and knives. Slaves carrying wine and water-pitchers either take up positions around the room, or pour for guests who have already arrived, and are settling themselves in groups beside, or stretching out on, the couches.

Alexander enters through the King's Door. Bathed, with his hair washed, but not curled, he is dressed in a rich, cream wool chiton trimmed in gold, and wearing his jewellery. He nods to **Lysimachos,** and exchanges a smile with **Hephaestion,** standing demurely beside his father, who is talking to a friend. On the far side of the room, **Attalos** and three cronies stand at a group of couches with **Pausanias. Attalos** holds up his cup for a toast. They all drain their cups and he beckons over a wine bearer.

Ptolemy comes and settles himself on the couch next to **Lysimachos.** Wine and water bearers fill three cups on the table between them. **Alexander** joins them. He picks up a cup, takes a sip, and wrinkling his nose, puts it down, and picks up the one nearest **Lysimachos.**

Lysimachos
Now, now, boy-Achilles. That's
my cup you're drinking from.

Alexander
Well, I pledge you in it. If they rinsed
wine round mine before adding water
that was all. Try it.

Ptolemy
One in four is the proper mixture for boys.

Lysimachos

Pour some in mine, we cannot all take it
neat, like your father, and it looks bad to
call the water-pitcher.

Alexander

I'll drink some more to make room
Before I pour.

Lysimachos

No, no, stop, that's enough.
You'll be too drunk to play ...
You are going to play?

As **Alexander** sits down on the edge of **Lysimachos's** couch, we begin a **slow zoom** on the **Attalos** group. All five are now stretched out on couches. Six new arrivals come in through a nearby door. **Attalos** beckons to them.

Attalos

Dikon! Philadelphos! Over here!

As the six move towards him, he beckons to the wine bearers, before turning to **Pausanias**, with a smile containing a hint of contempt.

Attalos

You know the king's favourite.

Three of the newcomers crowd up to **Pausanias**, while the other three replace **Attalos's** original cronies on the couches. The room falls suddenly quiet.

From the POV of **Attalos**, on the far side of the room, we see **Philip** stride through the King's Door. **Slow zoom** in towards **Philip**.

Philip

Flagons of full-bodied Akanthian are what
we need, my friends. And no water!

The hubbub becomes loud and general, with cries of Akanthian, more wine and no water.

Close shot of **Philip** with **Parmenion**, who reclines on the couch
next to that of the king. **Philip** is flushed, not yet with wine, but
with anger. His good eye fixes **Parmenion** with a grim smile.
He holds up his wine cup before draining it.

Philip

A sovereign cure for snakebite!

He puts the cup on his table and sits down on the edge of his
couch. As he does so, he looks up, and catches **Alexander's** unblinking stare. It is **Philip** who looks away. He lowers his voice
and leans towards **Parmenion**.

Philip

May the gods hear me, I'll do it yet,
Parmenion. The Epirote bitch!
For all her powerful kin, poised like
a sarrissa at our backs, she would
be well advised not to get too cocksure.
But for them, she would be long gone.

Parmenion

Keep me for soldiering, my King.
I have no head for intrigues.

Philip

You will smell the smoke of campfires
on a campaign road soon enough ...

Philip throws back his head and gives his bellow of laughter.

> Especially now, Athens thinks that she has
> agreed peace.
> But what we need here is music ...

Philip jumps to his feet, shouting above the hubbub.

> Music! To liven our souls and
> widen our friendships.
> Who will give us a song?

A song, A song, is shouted around the room, together with names of popular singers such as 'Kallimachos', and 'Heracleitos'. **Lysimachos** stands up and addresses **Philip**.

Lysimachos
My King. Your son has a song
especially for us tonight.

Drunken Voice
Off-set.
> Let's have one we all know.
> From Kleombrotos

Alexander and **Lysimachos** in **CU**.

Lysimachos
What will you sing for us, dearest Achilles?

Alexander
A chorus from The Bacchae.

Lysimachos
Concerned.

Peleus, the mortal father of Achilles
will approve the choice of Euripedes;
but The Bacchae? ...
Will he not suspect your mother's hand
in a Bacchic triumph?

Alexander

Man's misfortune is to live in opposition
to nature. The poet tells of nature's
triumph, not the gods'.

Lysimachos

I fear the greater significance will be
obscured by a lesser enmity.

Alexander

The fear is yours.

Cut to:

Brief CU shot of the hand of **Attalos** guiding the base of **Pausanias's** cup, as, already quite drunk, he drinks and spills in equal measure.

Attalos

Off.

Drink it down, my dear Pausanias.
Time for another toast.

Pausanias

Time for (gasp) another toast.
(splutters and throws up)

Cut to:

Lysimachos, is now standing nearer **Philip's** couch, and addressing the reclining king and the whole room.

Lysimachos
My Lords. Euripedes, the Sage of Salamis,
completed The Bacchae within the walls of
this very palace, shortly before he died in Athens.
So impressed were they by this last great work,
that they awarded the play an Oscaros.
Being Athenians, they had of course made
sure, that the poet was dead, so as to be
certain the gesture would not cost them.
Friends!
Lord Alexander with a chorus from
The Bacchae.

Cries of Alexander, and the chorus, the chorus, are shouted from around the room, amid the laughter at his crack at Athenians.

Philip
Come here then, boy. Bring
your lyre and sit by me.

Cheers and clapping break out around the room. A slave brings a three-legged stool, and places it beside **Philip's** couch. Another slave intercepts **Alexander**, as he leaves **Lysimachos's** couch, and hands him the kithara, which he straps on as he approaches his father.

Alexander and **Philip** in CU.

Philip
Scowling.
You can't play that thing, can you?

Alexander

Smiling.

You must judge for yourself, Father.
Tell me when I've finished.

Alexander ripples a lengthy sequence of strong opening chords.
Philip turns angrily to **Parmenion**.

Philip

A kithara no less!

Parmenion

For paid performers only.

Alexander's Chorus

O' happy to whom the blessedness is given
To be taught in the Mysteries sent from heaven,
Who is pure in his life, through whose soul
the unsleeping Revel goes sweeping!

Alexander plays a brief instrumental sequence before the next
verse.

Cut to:

Diner One and **Diner Two** in CU.

Diner One

They say he's game for anything!

Diner Two

What have the schoolmasters
been up to with the boy?

Diner One

They're trying to make a
Southerner of him.

Cut to:

Alexander singing.

> ### Alexander's Chorus (continued)
> One dancing band
> shall be all the land
> led by the Clamour-king
> the revel route fills the hills.

Cut to:

Flash shot of **Heiphaestion,** sitting upright on his father's couch, listening intently; but anxiously.

Cut to:

Alexander singing.

> ### Alexander's Chorus (continued)
> O' trance of rapture,
> when, reeling aside
> from the Bacchanal rout
> o'er the mountains flying
> one sinks to the earth,
> and the fawn's flecked hide
> covers him lying.

Cut to:

Philip in anger aside to **Parmenion.**

> ### Philip
> If he still has a girl's voice,
> must he tell the world?

Cut to:

Alexander singing.

Alexander's Chorus (continued)
With its sacred vesture,
wherein he hath chased
the goat to the death
for its blood – for the taste
of the feast raw reeking,
when over the hills
of Phrygia; of Lydia,
the wild feet haste,
the Clamour-king leads,
with his 'Evoe' thrills,
our hearts replying!

Cut to:

Diner Three and **Diner Four** in **CU**.

Diner Three
No endless verses for you to
bray like the stricken goat.

Diner Four
We'll have a good singsong
yet, you see!

Cut to:

Alexander singing.

Alexander's Chorus
Flowing with milk is the ground,
and with wine is it flowing,
and with nectar of bees.

Alexander indulges in another rippling instrumental piece before the final verse.

Cut to:

Lysimachos in **CU.**

Lysimachos
Enchanting

Ptolemy

Off.

He's as good as that fellow from Lesbos
who played a few months back.

Lysimachos
Better. He could be the young Apollo.

Cut to:

Alexander singing.

Alexander's Chorus (final)
And the smoke,
as of incense of Araby, soars,
and the Bacchant,
uplifting the flame
of the brand ruddy glowing,
waveth it wide,
and with shouts,
from the point of the wand
as it pours.

Cut to:

Philip, glowering, flushed and angry.

Alexander's Chorus

Off.

Challenging revellers,
on-racing, on-dancing,
on, on, on,
ever-on.

Cut to:

Lysimachos in **CU**, looking very pleased.

Alexander finishes the virtuoso performance in a flourish of notes.
There is some uneasy, sporadic clapping.

Lysimachos

Clapping enthusiastically.

Good, very good.

Cut to:

Alexander giving **Lysimachos** a brief smile, before looking down impassively at **Philip,** who slams his flagon down on the table between him and **Parmenion.**

Philip

Good?! You call that music for a man?
Leave the kithara for Corinthian hetairas
and Persian eunuchs.
You sing well enough for either.
Never make such a show of yourself again.
You should be ashamed.

During **Philip's** tirade, the room has fallen silent. **Alexander** looks at his father with his typical steady, impassive stare, although he flushes, slightly, before turning on his heel and walk-

150

ing quickly towards the King's door. As he reaches it there is a crash of bronze cups and bowls, and a thump.

Cut to:

Attalos and his cronies gathered around **Pausanias**, who has passed out, drunk, amid the debris. They pick him up and they follow **Attalos** towards a nearby exit.

Cut to:

Ptolemy stands impatiently at the end of his supper couch. **Lysimachos** sits, dithering, on the edge of his. In the background, **Heiphaestion** hurries towards the King's door. Everyone else is intent on continuing with supper.

Ptolemy
Small wonder you have never taken your
man, Lysimachos. You'll wear that cord
of dishonour until you die.

Lysimachos goes to stand up, then reaches towards the fruit bowl.

Lysimachos
I think I'll just …

Ptolemy
Just nothing! Come on, you know
how quick he is.

Lysimachos leaves the fruit bowl, gets up quickly, and hurries after **Ptolemy** towards the main entrance, which **Hephaestion** is just going through.

Cut to:

45. INT/The Main Guardroom of the Palace/Night

The guardroom is effectively lit by four oil lamps. Six off-duty men are either cleaning and sharpening knives or lying down on leather and wood beds. The **Guard Commander** sits at a table in an alcove near the door, which is flung open and **Attalos** enters. The **Guard Commander** gets up and goes up to him. His attitude is the respectful familiarity of shared campaigns.

Guard Commander
An early end to the King's supper,
General?

Attalos
For some, Sarissophoros, for some.

The cronies carry in the still unconscious **Pausanias** and sling him across the nearest bed.

Attalos
Creature comfort for the off watch
moments. With my compliments.

The men grin lewdly.

Guard Commander
The comfort of royalty, no less!

Attalos
Huh! He'll go with anyone. No
payment required.

Attalos walks out to the sound of laughing.

Cut to:

46. EXT/A Companion Calvary Camp in the Mountains/ Early Morning

An Hipparchia of the Companion Cavalry is breaking its overnight camp beside a mountain stream. The **Hirpachos** and three officers, holding the reins of their horses, are being petitioned by **Oileus**, who has his **Ilarches** (squadron commander) beside him.

Oileus
My father won't see this full moon.
I must get to him before Chiron.

The **Hiparchos** looks to the **Ilarches**, who nods.

Hiparchos
Very well, Oileus, you may go.
Do whatever you have to, and return
to the ranks immediately.

Oileus
Immediately, Hiparchos.

Oileus prepares to mount, as the other officers move away.

Ilarches
If you value your pay, Oileus, you'll be
back with us before the sickle moon.

Oileus
Grinning.
Of course, Ilarches. What is there to
life; but pay and the cavalry?

Oileus leaps astride his sturdy mountain horse and walks from the campsite.

47. EXT/The Muzzle of a leopard cub sniffing a Man's Body/Early Morning

The muzzle pushes at the man's back, and a paw enters the shot and drags the body over. We see it is **Pausanias**. The leopard pulls back, and we see that it is collared and, on a lead, held by a slave. **Olympias** and her retinue stand in a half circle looking at **Pausanias**, who lies in a gutter beside the palace wall.

Hyrminia
Pausanias, my Lady.

Olympias
So! The favoured minion. Is he
minion still, I wonder?

A **Female Slave** approaches **Olympias**.

Female Slave
Lord Alexander's horse has gone.

Olympias
You're sure of this?

Female Slave
The stall is empty. A slave-groom heard
a single horse leave while it was still dark.

Hyrminia
I saw Pausanias with the King
yesterday afternoon.

Olympias
To be with Philip is to be on a crest one
moment, and in a trough the next.
Bring him. We need to talk.

Members of the entourage go forward to pick up **Pausanias**.
Olympias walks out of shot, followed by the slave and the cheetah.

Cut to:

48. EXT/A Forest Clearing/Noon

Oileus sits on a fallen branch, in a sunlit clearing of lush grass surrounded by living oak, birch and larch, and in the lichen covered
dead wood of a virgin forest, which man has passed through but
not yet despoiled. He is snacking on bread, softened in the sparkling stream, and a lump of cheese. His tethered horse is grazing avidly, when suddenly its head goes up, and it nickers gruffly, pulling against the rope tether. **Oileus** puts down his food
and reaches for a sheathed sword lying beside him in the grass.

A skewbald pony trots into view and **Alexander's** cheery greeting carries brightly across the clearing.

Alexander
Good day to you, Oileus.

Oileus
Alexander!

Oileus lays aside the sword and finishes his bread and cheese. **Alexander** dismounts, lets the horse drink, and invokes the spirit
of the stream. Three times he scoops water, and lets it run from
his hand held at arm's length. Then he drinks himself, restrain-
ing the horse from drinking too much, before tethering it to a
branch, so it too can graze.

Alexander is tousled and grimy from having slept out. There are pine needles in his hair. He wears a light cuirass over his, faded, homespun tunic; hunting boots and a long, slender hunting knife, slung from one shoulder. He opens one of his saddle bags.

Oileus
Is no one with you?

Alexander
You are now.

He walks over to **Oileus**

Alexander
Here, have an apple …

He tosses one of two to **Oileus.**

> … I thought I should catch up with you
> around noon.

They both start munching on the apples.

Oileus
Are you lost? Were you out hunting?

Alexander
I am hunting what you are hunting.
That's why I'm coming with you.

Oileus
What!? But … Why? You don't know
What I'm about.

Alexander

Of course I do. Everyone in your Ile
knows. It is time I got my sword belt.
I have come out to take my man.

Oileus

At twelve?

Alexander

I need a war. Yours will do very well.

Oileus

My family needs me. For the vendetta.
It's not right what you have done. Now I'll
have to leave them to their troubles and
take you back.

Alexander

No! You have eaten with me. We are
guest friends. It is wicked to betray a
guest friend.

Oileus

You should have told me first. I must
take you back. You are only a child.

Alexander gets up and goes over to his horse. **Oileus** starts
up; but seeing that he is not untying the animal, he relaxes back
down again.

Oileus

If harm came to you the King
would have me crucified.

Alexander

He won't kill you if I get back. If I die
you'll have plenty of time to run away.

Oileus throws his apple core to his horse. He notices a bit of
cheese in the grass and eats it. We see **Oileus** in **CU** scavenging for crumbs

Alexander

Voice off.
> Either way, I doubt he'd kill you. But if
> you try and send me home before I'm
> ready.
> If you ride back or send a message,
> I will kill you...

There are a few moments of silence. **Oileus** finds and eats another crumb or two. Suddenly he stiffens and whips round, to
find himself looking at the leaf-like, blue blade of a javelin that
Alexander is pointing steadily, just three feet from his throat.

> ... Of that you can be sure. Stay just
> as you are Oileus, and do not move.
> You know I'm quick. Everyone does ...

They face each other. **Alexander** stands with the first two fingers hooked into the throwing thong of the javelin, which lies
poised along his forearm.

> ...I don't want you for my first man. It
> would not be enough. I should have
> to take another in battle. But, you
> will be, if you try to stop me.

Oileus holds up his left hand.

158

Oileus

Now wait. Alexander. You don't
mean that.

Alexander

No one will ever know. I'll leave your body
for the wolves and kites.
You will never be given the rites to set you free.
The shades of the dead will not suffer you to
join their company.

Oileus

What I have done to deserve this, the
Gods alone know.

Alexander

Well, what's it to be? Will you pledge yourself?
I cannot stand like this all day.

Oileus

What do you want me to swear to?

Alexander

Not to send word to Pella. Or to tell
anyone my name without my leave. Not
to prevent me going into battle, or get
anyone else to.
Swear to all that, and call down a death-
curse on yourself if you break your oath.
To leave these woods alive you will have
to swear.

Oileus

What will become of me afterwards?

Alexander runs across to his horse, he unhitches a leather game bag, and runs the few yards back to **Oileus.**

Alexander
If I live, I'll see you right. You must chance
my dying, that's war. Do you have respect
for oaths before the gods?

Oileus
For the gods, yes.

Alexander takes a lump of meat from the game-bag and slaps it down on the fallen branch beside **Oileus.**

Alexander
This is a haunch of sacrifice.
Repeat the oath after me.
When it is done, we can go
on as friends.

Fade to:

49. EXT/A Mountain Track/Afternoon

High on the side of an open, mountain ridge, **Alexander** and **Oileus** approach a three-way track junction. To their left, the ground slopes away steeply to the valley floor, with a broad, dirt road, and a swift-flowing river. Close above them can be seen the melted vestiges of the snow line; a gorge and surrounding rocky outcrops amid the trees.

CU of the pair reining to a halt at the junction.

Oileus
Pointing.

Akromeneos. My village. There, near
the head of the valley.

Alexander

And Ephyron?

Oileus

Pointing.

Beyond the far ridge.
Your grandfather's military road
goes past it. So, does that track
through the gorge.

Alexander

Is the pass useable at this time
of year?

Oileus

Could be; but we'll go downhill.
On the valley road we can reach
Akromeneos before dark.

Alexander

No! I will know if the pass is clear.

Alexander urges his horse straight up the hillside, heading for
the gorge. **Oileus** follows more slowly.

Cut to:

Overhead shot of **Alexander** riding through the short, narrow, boulder-strewn gorge. We see the hostile village of Ephyron some distance further on. **Alexander** turns and rides back
towards **Oileus.**

Dissolve to:

Alexander and **Oileus** are about a mile from Akromeneos on the mountain track. **Alexander** slows to let **Oileus** catch up. He calls back.

> **Alexander**
> Oileus! When I've taken my man, you
> will be my witness at Pella.
> The King did not take his man until
> he was fifteen. Parmenion told me.
> He was with him.

> **Oileus**
> I will …

They ride on.

CU of **Oileus** raising his eyebrows, dismayed, and looking sky-wards.

> May he live!
> By all the gods
> may he live!

Cut to:

Alexander stopping beside a skull, and the bones of a pair of hands spiked to a lone tree, just a quarter of a mile from the village.

> **Alexander**
> Who was that?

> **Oileus**
> A son who killed his father, when I
> was a child. I forget the details.

A dog starts barking in the nearby village, and a horn is blown. From **Alexander's POV** we see women and children running from their hovels. Three men armed with spears start towards them, spreading out as they advance.

Alexander

These are your kinsfolk, Oileus.
It is no use claiming I'm your kin.
Say I am your commander's son,
come to learn about war.
No one can accuse you of lying.

Riding towards the approaching trio, **Oileus** waves. He and **Alexander** dismount, where the track spreads out and becomes the general approach into the village, a huddle of some eleven hovels.

Oileus

The pair to the left are my cousins,
Elatrios and Echatos. The Ephyrons
killed their father, and another
of my uncles.
The third man is our Headman.

Leading their horses, **Oileus** walks forward, spreading his arms to embrace **Elatrios.**

Dissolve to:

50. EXT/The Forecourt of a Country Mansion/Evening

King Philip embraces a tall, thin and vigorous old woman with iron grey hair. He steps back. behind him are **Parmenion, Antipatros** and **Eumenes.**

Vigorous Old Woman
The house is dedicated to the muses.
It is yours, if you want it, Philip.

Philip
So, our world of competition no longer
finds favour with the Muses.

Vigorous Old Woman
Mieza is a beautiful place to live.

Philip
I'll send word if I have need of your
beautiful Mieza.

He strides away along the drive. **Parmenion** and **Antipatros**
on either side of him.

We see him in **CU**, with a formal garden beside the drive.

Philip
If the boy doesn't come back,
I'll have no need for the old hag's house,
nor, indeed, for another old hag.

The three laugh together.

Antipatros
The prince's academy will be here, at Mieza?

Philip
Yes. As I say if he returns.

Philip points to the blossom of an orchard beyond the garden.

Here amongst Mieza's famous apples
And away from all Court distractions.

Parmenion
Do you believe the Queen is behind
his disappearance?

Philip
Unofficially, no. He's headstrong.
This latest escapade smacks of
hurt pride and self-will.

They walk away from the camera, through the orchard, and towards the Companion Bodyguard waiting with the horses at the end of the drive.

Cut to:

51. INT/Akromeneos – Inside the Headman's Hovel/After dark

In an atmosphere smoky from cooking, the faces of **Alexander, Oileus, Elatrios, Echetos,** and the **Headman**, are illuminated in the flames of the cooking fire. They drink wine, and eat from a large bowl of dried figs. The **Headman's** wife and son clear up the debris of the goat meal.

Headman
Is it true the King has done away with
the Epirote Queen, and taken a new wife?

Oileus splutters on a fig and replies hastily and too loudly at first.

Oileus
Lies! Lies and gossip! Nothing more.
Queen Olympias stands in the highest

regard as the mother of the king's heir.
He er, er, is a credit to both his parents.

Alexander grins at **Oileus** and turns to the **Headman**.

Alexander
Tell us about the feud.

Headman
Things are bad. They killed again two
days ago.
Two sons of the widow Brattos, out
hunting deer, were ambushed by four Ephyrons.
The youngest crawled back here to die.
We reached his brother's body while
the vultures were still gathering.

Elatreos
Their old headman can no longer control
his three sons. They have to be stopped
before they kill again.

Oileus
As soon as it is light, we will cross
the hill and look in on Ephyron.

Headman
Now it is dark we should rest.

Alexander

Quiet; eager but essentially to himself.

To be fresh for battle

They stand up. **Oileus, Elatrios,** and **Echatos** move towards the door. **Alexander** goes into the gloom beyond the cooking fire.

Dissolve to:

52. EXT/The Sleeping Village/First Light

Several large guard-mastiffs pad between the silent hovels, whose only movements are wisps of smoke from damped down cooking fires. An howl hoots in the valley. A tethered goat bleats half-heartedly. In the animal stockade beside the village, cattle and horses stir and stamp. A fitful breeze mutters through the village. A mastiff runs to the thorn and stake fence, peers out, and abruptly sits down to scratch. The clanging bray of a donkey breaks the silence. Dogs growl. The descant hiccups to a close.

Cut to:

53. INT/Inside the Headman's Hovel/First Light

CU of the bed of the **Headman's** son.

Alexander sits bolt upright, his eyes tight closed. Beside him, the **Headman's** son lies holding the verminous blanket up over his nose. His eyes are wide open, looking at **Alexander**, not seeing the shade of **Herakles** appearing to **Alexander**

Alexander
Herakles!

All around **Alexander** appears the shade of a youthful Herakles. The god of the Pella garden statue, clean shaven and wearing the lion mask. The ghostly figure fades as it speaks to **Alexander** in his dream.

Ghost of Herakles
Get up lazy boy. I have been
calling you this long time.

Alexander opens his eyes, and the **Headman's** son snaps his closed. **Alexander** gets up, takes his cloak from the bed and he heads for the door.

Cut to:

54. EXT/Akromeneos Village/Early dawn

Alexander leaves the **Headman's** hovel. A guard-mastiff pads up to him, and he stands still while it sniffs him before turning away. He rounds the corner of a hovel, walks past a well, and on towards a mound topped by the twisted trunk and gaunt, stunted limbs of an ancient olive tree. He climbs the mound and into the branches of the olive.

In **CU** we see him scrutinising the valley below.

His eyes widen in wonder, and he jumps from the branches. Standing on the mound, he flings his arms out and up in a gesture of pure delight and excitement. He runs down and through the village.

At the **Headman's** hovel, **Alexander** seizes the horn hanging at the doorway. He gives a practice toot and then a single blast, which sets all the dogs barking. He runs back towards the well and jumps up on the wellhead. The villagers start to appear, some half-dressed, others holding a blanket round their nakedness. The **Headman** and his wife approach the well, and **Oileus** from another direction.

Alexander
Shouts.

War! It's war! I have come to fight
your war. The god has called me.

The gathering villagers look at one another in some surprise.

Alexander
I am Alexander, King Philip's son.
Oileus knows who I am.

Oileus and the **Headman** exchange looks, **Oileus** shrugs.

Villager One
The witch's child!

Villager Two
Son of the Epirote!

CU of **Alexander** pointing.

Alexander
Ephyrons! On the valley road.
Nineteen riders. Listen to me.
Before sun-up we will make an
end of them.

He beckons **Oileus** and the **Headman** towards him.

Cut to:

55. EXT/The Valley Road/Dawn

CU shot of the trotting legs of an Ephyron's horse.

We **pull back** to a **Steadicam shot** of the straggle of horses trotting through the frame, both singly and in pairs. The coats of the horses are rough from winter and muddied from living outside.

The Ephyron raiders are armed with a variety of rusting swords, hunting knives and spears. Some wear leather helmets and cuirasses, others are bareheaded and wear leather jerkins.

Cut to:

Ephyron raiders riding **away from the camera**, over a rise of the valley road, and out of sight.

Cut to:

Ephyron raiders turning off the valley road, on to a single file track, leading up the mountainside towards Akromeneos. They slow to a walk.

Cut to:

56. EXT/Akromeneos Village and Animal Stockade/Dawn

A young girl pipes the Akromeneos goats away from the stockade and up the mountain to the grazing area. Four villagers thin out the thorn brushwood gate. **Oileus** runs up to them.

Oileus
Leave the rest.
They must not suspect
that we lie in wait.

They run across to the village.

Cut to:

The first three riders of the Ephyron column which still straggles its way upwards, but with Akromeneos now much closer.

Alexander jumps down from the wellhead. Nearby, the **Head-man** points to the hovel nearest to the stockade, and directs a man carrying a bow.

Headman
On the roof. Keep out of sight
until they are inside the village.

The man runs off, and **Oileus** runs into the frame. Mounted Ephyrons approach from various directions. A woman draws some water from the well, whilst another gathers up a child and takes it indoors.

Alexander
We must get our horses, Oileus,
and form the battle line.

They hurry away. The **Headman** points one of his riders towards a position behind one of the hovels, before following them.

Cut to:

Long shot of the leading Ephyrons reaching the level of Ak-romeneos on the mountainside, still some half a mile away. The three leaders wait in line abreast. Their compatriots come up in turn, and halt behind them.

The leading raider is a **Helmeted Ephyron**. His fellow leaders and brothers, on either side of him, are a **Black-bearded Ephyron** and a **Red-bearded Ephyron**. The pair are wearing greasy leather war-bonnets with crudely stitched cheek pieces. All three are armed with a spear and a sword.

The goat herd can be heard faintly piping on the hill. They start to ride forward at a walk.

Cut to:

Alexander on his horse, alone, beside the gnarled lookout olive tree. He looks towards the approaching Ephyrons and speaks to himself with fierce intensity.

Alexander

Why have you forsaken me?

The shade of the lion–clad Herakles appears amongst the gnarled limbs of the olive tree.

Ghost of Herakles

I left you to make you understand
my mystery.
Do not believe others will die, not you.
It is not for that I am your friend.
By laying myself on the pyre I became divine,
and to know how death is vanquished.
Man's immortality is not to live forever;
that wish is born of fear.
Each moment free from fear makes
man immortal.

The ghostly shade dissolves. In the silence that follows, **Alexander** looks around him. At the villagers on their horses, waiting in twos and threes behind their hovels. At the approaching Ephyrons. His eyes flash with excitement, and he raises his two javelins above his head.

Alexander

I am not afraid!

He rides off the mound. A child screams and is abruptly silenced. An artful woman begins singing a simple song.

Cut to:

The Ephyrons slow down and bunch up just one hundred yards or so from the animal stockade. From **their POV**, there is no visible movement in the village. The lone woman singing can be clearly heard.

Black-bearded Ephyron
The cattle are still penned.

Helmeted Ephyron
The goats are out on the hill.

Black-bearded Ephyron
They suspect nothing.

Helmeted Ephyron
Let's help ourselves.

Red-bearded Ephyron
Yes!

The three Ephyron leaders ride forward towards the animal stockade. Three other others dash past them, heading for the village.

Fourth Ephyron
We'll have the women first.

The singing stops. A cock crows. The three Ephyrons ride towards us, and laughing, they dismount near the first hovel. Beyond them, we see the rest of the Ephyron raiders dragging aside the stockade barrier and riding in amongst the animals.

Alexander's high-pitched yell, like some wild girl's, drowns out every other sound, and roots the Ephyrons where they stand. There is a moment of silence and stillness. One of the Ephyrons in the village shrieks and grasps his leg, stuck by an arrow from the bowman on the roof. Six Akromeneos villagers ride into view from behind a nearby hovel. Yelling like banshees, and accompanied by barking snarling guard-mastiffs, they ride at the Ephyrons. Two try to remount. All three are hacked and bludgeoned to death.

Cut to:

The main body of the villagers sweep into the animal stockade. Individual fights break out amidst the milling, lowing cattle, and spare horses. Two, five-a-side, mini battle lines start to form. One of the Ephyron riders pitches from his horse, a spear sticking from his back.

Alexander confronts the **Helmeted Ephyron**. To focus the man's attention, **Alexander** throws back his head and gives another wild girl yell and kicks his horse forward. He hurls his first spear, and hits, another Ephyron rider. At his approach, **Helmeted Ephyron** lunges with his spear. **Alexander** swerves, his horse is wounded in the neck. Then he buries his second spear in **Ephyron's** throat. Holding on to the spear shaft, **Alexander** is almost dragged from his horse, before riding on, exultant. **Oileus** and another, nearby villager give him a cheer.

The cheering becomes general, and we see the Ephyrons, in ones and twos, are trying to flee the stockade. The villagers are letting them go.

At the far end of the stockade from the gate, **Alexander** in **CU**.

Alexander
This is not victory!

Alexander urges his horse through the cattle, shouting as he goes.

Alexander
Cut them off!
Head them at the pass!

Cut to:

An **overhead, and gradually widening, overview** of the Ephyron retreat. Only eight of the raiders are hurrying away from the stockade. Some twice that number of villagers are forming the pursuit, riding both from the stockade and the village. A single rider overhauls the fleeing Ephyrons. He reaches a track junction first, and the Ephyrons veer away, turning abruptly downhill. The line of villagers riding from the Akromeneos, start to cut the corner to intercept them. The remainder continue to follow.

Cut to:

Medium shot of the last of the Ephyrons reining in his horse and dismounting. It is the **Black–bearded Ephyron** leader. He draws his sword and waits in the middle of the track. Two of the first four pursuing villagers slash at him as they ride him down, and leave him lying, bleeding, on the track.

Cut to:

Alexander approaches the fallen Ephyron leader. Two of the villagers return, leading his horse.

First Villager
Here's the little lion.

Second Villager
Our lucky captain.

Oileus and two other villagers ride up and join the group.

First Villager
Does this whore's bastard live?

A **Third Villager**, who arrived with **Oileus** dismounts. Squatting down he grabs the wounded Ephyron leader by the hair and jerks his head back. He screams. The **Third Villager** draws his hunting knife.

First Villager
Finish him off.

Alexander
No! he was brave, like Patroclus
With Achilles armour. Let him go.

The villagers laugh.

Third Villager
He's no sacred hero.

First Villager
He steals cattle, and would have
our women.

Alexander
He took his stand for the others.
If you kill him, I swear by my
father's head I'll make you sorry.

The laughter peters out in uncertainty.

Fourth Villager
He's our battle prize.

Alexander

You can have the horse
of the man I killed instead.
Now get him mounted.

Oileus

You had better do as he says.

Alexander

Oileus help them.

They plonk the groaning Ephyron onto his horse, point it downhill, and whack it on its way. The animal trots off, with the
slumped rider clinging to the stubby mane.

Alexander

Now, I must find my man.

Alexander and **Oileus** mount up and trot off, back towards
Akromeneos.

Dissolve to:

A woman of Akromeneos helping her man from the animal
stockade. They have their arms around each other. His left leg
is red with blood. The cattle have been driven from the stockade to graze on the hill. The women are stripping the bodies of
the Ephyrons or mourning their own dead. Three women, in
different parts of the stockade, are beating their breasts, tearing
their hair and flinging themselves across bodies. They all shriek
loudly. Children play, quite unconcerned by the carnage. Dogs
size up the possibilities for food. Bigger teenage children carry
a body to the village.

Alexander and **Oileus** reach the stockade, dismount, and walk
in. **Alexander** surveys the scene keenly.

Alexander

This is what it is like. A soldier
Must get used to the sights and
smells of the battlefield ...

Oileus, the experienced soldier, smiles, saying,

... There!

Alexander runs across to the dead body.

Alexander and **Oileus** in **CU**.

The **Helmeted Ephyron** lies stripped of all but his kilt.
His beard juts skyward from an already livid face. The single
wound has not bled excessively.

Alexander

I have taken my man, Oileus,
I must show a trophy.

Female Voice

Voice off, very close and intimate.

Let me take the head off for you,
little warrior. I know the knack.

Alexander turns, and starts back in horror, at an old, dirty, gap-
toothed hag leaning close toward him. Her arms are coated to
the elbows in congealed blood and flies. In her hand she holds a
bloody hatchet. **Alexander's** face drains of colour. The **Headman** and two other villagers walk up and join the group.

Oileus
They only do that in the back
country now, Alexander.

Alexander
I had better have it, there's
nothing else.

Oileus
Old customs are good enough for
a king's son, I have no doubt.

Leering, the Old Hag leans forward and grasps the beard.

Alexander
No! No, I'll do it. Oileus fetch
my game bag.

Oileus walks out of the frame.

Headman
That's the way Little Captain,
you do it.

Cut to:

A youth of the village stands beside a woman wailing over a corpse.
He straightens up from a headless corpse, holding the head by the
forelock. He walks over to the group with **Alexander**, reaching
them as **Alexander** drops the head of the **Red-bearded Ephyron** into his game bag, and stoops to wipe his bloody hands on
the ground. **Alexander** straightens up, and the **Village Youth**
thrusts a black-haired head towards him.

Village Youth
Here's another to show your father.

Alexander recoils. His face is ashen, and he struggles not to throw-up.

Alexander
I never killed that man.

Village Youth
Yes. The javelin-throw before we
closed with them.

An Akromeneos Man
I saw it too. Little Lord. He crept about a
bit before hitting the ground; but he was
dead before the women reached him.

Grinning broadly, the **Village Youth** again holds out the ghastly head.

Village Youth
Two at your first blooding would be
something to tell the grandchildren.

CU of **Alexander** staring in horror at the bloody face of violent death, one eye half closed, and its face set in a rictus of a smile. **Alexander's** voice rises and he backs away.

Alexander
I don't want it! Take it away!
I didn't see him die. You don't
know what happened.
Take it away! Take it away!

Cut to:

Oileus in an aside to the **Headman**

Oileus
He's only twelve.

Headman
Surprised.
> Twelve! And such spirit. What father
> would not be proud of such a son.

Cut to:

The group dispersing. The **Headman** puts his arm around **Alexander's** shoulders.

Headman
Come, Little Captain.
A drop of wine before you
and cousin Oileus leave us.

Together with **Oileus,** they walk towards the gate of the stockade.

Fade to:

57. EXT/The Palace Garden/Morning

Alexander stands between **Philip** and **Olympias** facing a hero-shrine to Herakles, in a paved, secluded corner of the palace garden. The open square, formed by those present and the little alter, are: **Lanike,** with the seven-year-old **Kleopatra, Hyrminia, Lysimachos,** and **Leonidas**, to the left of **Olympias**. **Eumenes, Ptolemy, Parmenion,** and **Philotas** standing to the right of **Philip**.

Eumenes steps forward and hands **Philip** a gleaming red-brown, leather sword belt with a golden buckle. **Alexander** half turns to his father, who buckles the belt around his white chiton. **Alexander** turns to his mother, who takes a golden chalice from **Hyrminia** and hands it to him.

Alexander steps up to the little alter, on which are the glowing embers of a small, wood fire. He holds the chalice up to the bust of Herakles.

Alexander

As you have been to me, so remain.
Be favourable to me in what I shall
henceforth undertake, according to
my prayers.

He tilts the chalice, and pours a slow, sparkling stream of gum Arabic on to the embers. **Alexander in increasing CU**, as the fragrant blue smoke billows up and around him on the clear air. He continues to pour.

Leonidas

Off; severe sounding.

Do not waste precious incense,
Alexander, till you are master
of their homelands.

Still pouring, while being increasingly enveloped in drifting smoke, he looks up.

Alexander

Very serious.

Yes. Yes, I will remember.
Nothing for the gods can
be wasted.

Fade to: White

A hazy image of the Sphynx materialises as a backdrop for the words:

Proclaimed Pharaoh — as the conqueror of Egypt —
in an ironic gesture, some ten years later, Alexander will
order a 'ton' of incense to be sent back to Leonidas.

Fade in:

Three years later

58. INT/Chariot Shed in the Royal Stables 341 BC/Early Morning

Alexander and **Hephaestion** (both aged fifteen) clamber about the dusty mass of old leather, shafts, wheels, wooden cars and bronze fitments, all illuminated by two dust-laden beams of early morning sunlight, from the only two windows.

Alexander
I know who father wants as
the new tutor. In case he is
unbearable we must make a plan.

Hephaestion
You can count on me, even if you
do decide to drown him.

Alexander
He was a student of Plato. Father
says you can come to the lessons.

Hephaestion
I'd hold you back.

Alexander

No, Sophists teach by disputation.
He's been told to teach me things
I can use.
He says a man's education
should be suited to his needs,
which doesn't tell us much.

Hephaestion

At least he can't beat you.
Is he Athenian?

Alexander

No, from Stagira. His father was court
physician to my grandfather. I don't know
how good he was; but my grandfather
died in bed, which is rare enough in our family.

Hephaestion

So, what's this son called?

Alexander

Aristotle.

Hephaestion

Is he old?

Alexander

Not for a philosopher.
They live forever.

CU of **Hephaestion** dragging back a heavy, moth-eaten blanket. Balancing on the jumble, he holds on to a wheel for balance, and looks down intently.

Hephaestion
He is in Athens at the moment?

Alexander
Off.

No, Assos. He left Athens because Plato
chose his nephew, not him, to run the
Academy. Father had just burnt Stagira
to the ground, so he couldn't go home.

Hephaestion
Excitedly.

Alexander! Quick!
Come and look at this.

Cut to:

Alexander jumping across the jumble. Reaching **Hephaestion**,
he puts an arm around him for support.

CU of the two looking down at a little chariot.

Hephaestion
A two-horse racer.

Alexander
A Synoris. For dismounters …

Alexander steps down and crouches beside the little chariot.
The delicate walnut and pear wood inlay gleams if dully, in the
murky, dust-filled light. He grasps the bronze handrail.

… For our chariot-borne heroes, who
rode into battle to fight on foot.

Hephaestion
We've got one in a barn at home,
somewhere, not as well preserved
as this one.

Alexander
Bring it! …

He jumps up beside **Hephaestion** and puts one hand around the
back of his neck, speaking excitedly.

… I'll get the Royal Charioteer to restore
them, and we'll run them behind
Venetian ponies.
Leaping from them in mid-flight
will give us some real Homeric
exercise. Now, we must prepare
for the annual Pella Horse Fair.

He moves quickly towards the door. **Hephaestion** flings the
blanket back over the synoris and follows.

Cut to:

CU of **Alexander** standing at the door.

Alexander
I know why Aristotle was chosen. He
is with the tyrant Hermeias at Assos, and
the King wants an alliance with Hermeias.
Leonidas came for politics too.
Only Lysimachos … old Phoenix,
came for *me!*

He runs from the chariot shed.

59. INT/A Palace Corridor/Morning

Dressed for riding, and both carrying whips, **Philip** and **Parmenion** stride **towards the camera**, along a corridor of the palace. Rounding a corner, they almost collide with **Olympias**, who is accompanied by **Hyrminia** and two of her staff. The ladies are cloaked.

Philip is at his most affable; **Olympias** aloof, and at times scornful.

Philip
Ladies at the spring horse sales?
Now that would be a break with custom!
I willingly accept commissions on your
behalf, madam.

Olympias
My son will see to any such needs
of mine. That son you would banish
from the Court

Philip
The philosopher asked …

Olympias

Sneering.

A philosopher no less!

Philip
… For an Academy away from Court distractions.

Olympias

Where he can pervert young minds,
free from the proper influence of
their mothers and the gods.

Philip

The Prince will be accompanied by
his Companions.

Olympias

Including your Philotas, Parmenion?

Parmenion

Hesitant.

The King has given his gracious
permission, yes.

Olympias

And the Antipatros brat?

Philip

I do not discriminate between
my friends.

Olympias

You know Alexander and
Kassandros cannot tolerate
each other.

Philip starts to move on.

Philip

If they are on bad terms, now is
the time to mend them …

Walking faster, he glances back

... It is an art that kings must learn.

CU of a smiling **Olympias.**

Olympias

Quietly to herself.

> The god may try his hand at being King
> sooner than you think!

Cut to:

60. EXT/The Spring Horse Fair/Noon

Antipatros and his son **Kassandros**, accompanied by two slaves on foot, ride slowly through the fair crowd. An easy-going throng of buyers and sellers, nearly all with horses of all shapes, colours and sizes. The morning saw a brisk trade in sturdy little work-horses for cavalryman and farmers. Most of these are still about the ground, tethered, prior to being taken away. The dealers are concentrating on gaily decked-out thoroughbred racers, or heavier battle-chargers, all with attendant slave-grooms.

The fairground itself, is a broad, clear area south west of Pella. Cleared originally for the military to exercise cavalry and the phalanx, the area is free of all buildings, other than a flat stone platform, some thirty feet square, and a little over half that in height, with all four sides comprising fifteen long stone steps. The platform overlooks the whole area and stands where the flat area drops in a wide, open sweep to the Pella lagoon.

Antipatros

I have a few scores to settle from last
Royal Sales Day. Dealers to catch up with.
Seek out the Companions. I intend to
ask the King for your place at the
Prince's Academy.

Kassandros

Whining, sulky.

No, Father, don't make me go.

Antipatros

You are going. Your success in life
depends on it.

Antipatros halts his horse first; they both dismount.

Kassandros

I want to be a soldier, not a sophist.
Everyone knows philosophy skews
the mind.

Antipatros

Soldiering can come later. Learn first
to be a man, and work hard at the
Academy. Stir up trouble and I'll flay
you. And be wary of Alexander.

Kassandros

Sneering.

He's just a little boy!

Antipatros gives his reins to the slave, and he waves him away.
He rounds on **Kassandros**.

Antipatros

Try not to be a bigger fool than you were
born. When you're both grown up the age
gap will disappear.
Remember, that boy has his father's cunning
and, if he doesn't prove as bad to cross
as his mother, then I'm the Great King's
eunuch. Now, off you go.

Philip on foot, moving against the men and horses towards the platform. Followed by seven members of the Companion Bodyguard, he greets old soldiers and acquaintances with a wave of his whip, and a smile. There is no bowing or ceremony. A nearby **Dealer** indicates his pair of racers.

Dealer
From the fabled Nisaian strain of the
Persian kings.

Philip
Smiling.
Of course.

Dealer
To the king, the pair for ten talents.

Philip
I'm in the market only for a warhorse.

Dealer
Less than half the price of your Olympic winner.

Philip walks on still smiling.

Philip
A winner is without price.

Cut to:

CU of **Alexander** and **Ptolemy** examining a horse close to the platform.

Ptolemy
Always examine the hoof thoroughly.

Alexander
Xenophon writes, 'a thick horn makes
for sounder feet than a thin one'.

Ptolemy
Yes. The horn should not be flattened,
like this one, but high front and back.

Alexander
'And ring like a cymbal when it strikes
hard ground', as Xenophon has it.

Cut to:

Very close shot of a pair of jet-black fetlocks, with high, polished brown hoofs, pounding the ground. They lift up and out of shot.

Cut to:

A great black stallion rearing up, its forelegs pawing the air. The groom, **Irus**, clings to a leading rein attached to the heavily barbed bit and bridle. The owner-dealer, **Akroneos**, steps in, grabs the stock whip from **Irus**, and lashes the horse across the exposed belly. The horse appears to reach for him with its front hoofs, almost like a boxer.

Cut to:

Philip, appreciably nearer the platform, looks carefully at four battle-chargers, each held by a groom. He shakes his head at the Dealer, and heads for the platform. **Akroneos** walks into shot and intercepts him.

Philip
So, Akroneos, where is this fabled beast
which had you writing to me from Larissa?

Akroneos
Some fool let slip the halter, and being
in prime fettle he was hard to catch.

Philip
Well, bring him when you are ready; but
at three talents a sale is unlikely.

Akroneos
He is all I wrote you ... and more.

Philip sees **Lysimachos**, strides across to the platform, and he
puts an arm around his shoulders.

Philip
What has coaxed you from the
bookshelves, Lysimachos, horseflesh
or my son?

Lysimachos
The most beautiful of all animals, Lord.
The horse. I come every year.

Cut to:

Akroneos grabs one of his slaves from the crowd.

Akroneos
Tell Irus to bring it now, or I'll have
his guts for picket lines.

Slave

Irus says he can bring him, sir, but …

Akroneos

By all the gods! Not but! Now! Now!
If I miss this sale you and Irus won't
have skin enough between you for
a pair of sandal soles.

The **Slave** hurries away through the crowd, leaving **Akroneos** chewing his nails.

Cut to:

The Companions, **Hephaestion, Philotas, Harpalos,** and **Kassandros,** near the platform; but they are some way away from **Alexander** and **Ptolemy.**

Philotas

I shall need a bigger horse soon;
but father's leaving it till next year
when I'm taller.

Harpalos

Alexander rides mmmmen's horses,
and he's a hand shshshorter than yyyyou.

Kassandros

Sneering.

I expect they train them specially.

Hephaestion

He's taken his man and his boar. Do
you think they were specially trained?

Kassandros

The boar was set up, always is.

Hephaestion

Flushed, angry.
> For you perhaps. Alexander killed a
> rogue tusker with his knife. Ask Ptolemy.

The companions smirk, and exchange knowing glances. **Hephaestion** begins to look uncomfortable.

Kassandros

You know, Hephaestion has a look of
Alexander about him.

Harpalos

They're nnnnnot really alike.

Philotas

With your colouring you could be
his big brother.

Kassandros

You hear that, Hephaestion. How well
does your mother know the King?

With a single blow to the mouth, **Hephaestion** puts **Kassandros** on his backside.

Cut to:

Philip and **Lysimachos** on the lower steps of the platform. The bodyguards are at each end, and on the top of the platform. **Akroneos** hurries up.

Akroneos
King. He is on his way.

> Cut to:

The crowd parting, and the great black stallion, **Bucephalus**, led by **Irus**, approaching the platform. The crowd falls silent watching the vigorous approach. **Alexander** and **Ptolemy** move nearer the platform to get a good view. **Philip** and **Lysimachos** step down to grass level. **Bucephalus** and **Irus** reach the open space before **Philip**. The horse rolls his eyes, snorts, and paws the ground.

Lysimachos
He's very beautiful.

Philip
Beauty isn't everything.

> Cut to:

Alexander, his look a mixture of awe and pure greed, and **Ptolemy** look admiringly at the horse.

Alexander
Ptolemy look! A perfect horse.
He's perfect everywhere.

Ptolemy
He looks vicious to me.

> Cut back to:

The group centred around **Philip**.

Akroneos
There sir! A mount fit for a monarch.

Philip
Yes, I like his looks, let's see
him move.

Akroneos walks towards **Irus**.

Akroneos
Irus, take Thunder …

Immediately, **Bucephalus** squeals like a battle-trumpet, and rears
back on his hind legs. **Irus** steps back, paying out the halter rope.

Akroneos
Bastard!

Akroneos moves back towards **Philip**, an uncertain smile on
his face.

Akroneos
You could train a horse like this to
rear up and strike the enemy.

Philip
Unimpressed.
And show its belly? A sure way to
get it killed under you …

He beckons to a weathered, leathery little man standing at the
end of the platform, and carrying a whip.

… Will you try him, Diocles?

Cut to:

Alexander and **Ptolemy** are looking hard at **Bucephalus.**

Alexander

Look at the barbs, his mouth must
be torn to shreds.

Ptolemy

And even that bit cannot curb him.

Alexander

Still he's got his head up.

Cut to:

CU of **Diocles** with **Irus** and **Bucephalus**.

Diocles

Hold him until I'm up.

Diocles closes with **Bucephalus**. The sunlight catches the Ox-head brand on the shoulder, which matches the shape of the small white blaze on the forehead.

Diocles

Soothingly.

All right, now, all right. Steady boy,
steady now, steady, Thunder.

At the sound of the name, **Bucephalus** shies to his right, whirls around, and lashes out at **Diocles** with both rear hoofs. **Diocles** jumps for his life. He and the king exchange glances. **Philip** raises his eyebrows; **Diocles** turns down the corners of his mouth and widens his eyes, before trying to close the horse once more. As he does so, **Bucephalus** swings round through his own shadow, and rears up again on his hind legs.

Cut to:

Alexander, looking at **Bucephalus** with a mixture of anguish and longing.

Alexander
He isn't going to buy him.

Cut to:

Alexander and **Ptolemy** together

Ptolemy
Who would!
Certainly not your Xenophon.
How does it go?
A nervous horse will hurt you,
but not let you hurt the enemy.

Alexander
Nervous! Him? He's the bravest horse
I ever saw.
Look where he's been beaten across
the belly.

Philotas walks into shot and joins them.

Philotas
Diocles has had enough.

Alexander
He should have realised he shied at
the name or the dealer's voice.
Or his shadow.

Philotas
He's got the king's life to think of.

Ptolemy

You wouldn't ride a horse like
that to war.

Alexander

I would. To war most of all.

Cut to:

Philip, with **Akroneos**, and then **Diocles** and **Bucephalus**
beyond.

Philip

If that is the pick of your stable, Akroneos,
let us waste no more time.

Akroneos

He's just lively, sir, from corn and too
little exercise.

Diocles

For three talents the King can buy
something better than a broken neck.

Akroneos

My Lord, a special price.

Philip

There are others, Akroneos.

Philip approaches **Lysimachos** standing on the bottom step of
the platform. **Alexander** speaks loudly, his clear voice made strident by urgency.

Alexander

Voice off.

What a waste!
The best horse in the fair!

Philip does not turn around. He and **Lysimachos** look at each other.

Lysimachos

Quietly.

A colt too full of corn.

Philip

Quietly.

No lesson so good as the one
we teach ourselves!

Cut to:

The Companions backing away, leaving **Alexander** to face **Philip** alone, but closely watched by **Lysimachos**, and opposite him, **Akroneos,** and **Irus** with **Bucephalus**.

Philip
Diocles here has been training
horses for twenty years.
And you, Akroneos, how long?

Akroneos
Ah well, King, I was reared to it as a boy.

Philip
You hear that, Alexander. But you
think you can do better.

CU of **Alexander** looking eagerly and with longing at **Bucephalus**.

Alexander
With this horse I could.

CU of Philip.

Philip
And if you cannot, what are
you staking?

Cut to:

Overall shot, including some of the fairground crows in the background, and the Companions, with **Hephaestion** in front, looking anxious.

Alexander
If I cannot ride him, I'll pay
for him myself.

Philip jeers. **Akroneos** looks pleased.

Philip
At three talents?! It will take your
allowance for the next two years!

Akroneos
King, I'll …

Philip waves him to be silent.

Alexander
Only if I cannot ride him.

Philip
I hope you mean it. I certainly do.

Alexander and **Hephaestion** exchange glances.

> **Alexander**
> So, do I ...

He looks at **Philip**, gives a challenging, vigorous battle smile, and starts towards **Bucephalus:**

> ... The bet's on then, Father. He's
> mine, and the loser pays.

Some of the crowd in the background laugh and applaud. **Akroneos** hurries over to **Alexander**.

> **Akroneos**
> You will find, my Lord ...

Alexander speaks firmly; but without raising his voice. He does not take his eyes from the horse.

> **Alexander**
> Go away.

> **Akroneos**
> But my Lord, when you ...

> **Alexander**
> Go away, Downwind. Now! And
> where he cannot hear or see you.

Alexander stops and turns his unblinking, silent gaze on **Akroneos**, who looks back for a moment, and then slinks away as he is told.

> **Cut to:**

Bucephalus watching, blowing, wary. **Alexander** steps across beside **Irus**.

Alexander
I will take him. You need not wait.

Irus
My Lord! When you are up, or he will
hold me accountable.

Alexander
No. He's mine now. Give me his head
without jerking that bit …
Bucephalus snorts and paws the ground.

… Give me the lead rein. Now!

Alexander takes the lead rein and slowly moves in close, speaking quietly.
… Go behind me.
Don't cross his light.

As **Irus** walks forward out of the frame, **Alexander** steps right up to **Bucephalus**, and runs his hand along the gleaming, black neck, to the brand on the shoulder.

Alexander
Oxhead! Bucephalus!

He pushes the great horse round to face the sunlight. **Bucephalus** snorts, stamps, then swings his head down, and pushes the boy in the chest with his muzzle, before stepping away a couple of paces.

Cut to:

Ptolemy and **Harpalos** standing on the edge of the Companion group.

Ptolemy
The king may be sorry he set
him on this.

Harpalos
He was bbbbborn llllucky.
Want a bbbbet?

Ptolemy laughs without taking up the suggestion.

Cut to:

CU of **Alexander** working his hand along **Bucephalus's** neck. Then across the white ox head-shape blaze to the muzzle, the frothed lips tinged red with blood. The horse backs away.

Alexander
Easy now, Bucephalus. Easy now.
You and I don't run away.

Bucephalus throws up his head and blows hard. **Alexander** goes to his left shoulder, and pushing his fingers through the mane, smooths the broad back. He moves him forward at a walk.

Alexander
All right, all right, all in good time.

Alexander takes three running paces, grabs the mane at the shoulder, and vaults across the broad back. **Bucephalus** immediately stops, quivering. Almost as if he is standing tiptoe.

Alexander
Steady, steady now. Steady.

Remember we are
Alexander and Bucephalus …

Alexander eases the horse round to face the sloping ground down to the Pella lagoon)

… Easy. That's it. I'll tell
you when.

Cut to:

Overview. Alexander and **Bucephalus** stand alone in an arena made by the platform on one side, and a swathe of fairgoers, curious, silent, and still increasing. The only way out is a broad swathe of grass, leading down towards the lagoon.

Cut to:

Flash shot of **Lysimachos** standing next to **Philip**.

Lysimachos
Man cannot master him; but he
will go with the god.

Cut back to:

Slow zoom in on **Alexander**, sitting upright and relaxed. He holds the reins loosely, his thighs gripping **Bucephalus**, and his legs straight down. Relaxed below the knees. Slowly he leans forward.

Alexander
Now!

Bucephalus explodes forward, in a bound, and in three strides is at full gallop. The crowd breaks out into laughter, clapping and cheering.

61. EXT/The Ride by the Lagoon/Same afternoon

Very long-distance Steadicam shot of **Alexander** and **Bucephalus** at the moment they come over the crest of the slope. No one else is in the shot. Just the blue sky, the forest on each side, and the long sweep of grass.

The pair race down the slope, at an angle which takes them out to the left of the frame, by the halfway mark. Near the edge of the forest, they start to drift back across the frame, and as they near the bottom of the slope, and approach the reeds and the water's edge, they are at the right of the frame.

Still at full gallop, they swing right-handed to run parallel with the lagoon side.

Cut to:

Very long-distance Steadicam shot of **Alexander** and **Bucephalus** as they appear from behind the trees and begin a long straight run along the shore. On they come straight towards us, on, and on. We see waterfowl scatter, and water spraying from the pounding hoofs.

On they come, until the pounding **Bucephalus** fills the screen and gallops **out of the top of the shot.**

Cut to:

62. EXT/The Ride through the Forest/Same afternoon

Alexander's POV, as he turns **Bucephalus** right, and they gallop towards a game trail leading into the forest. The trail takes them beneath low hanging branches, over streams, through sunshine and shade, down inclines, and up steep banks. They jump fallen tree trunks, and swim one deep river. Finally, the game trails bring them out on a narrow, dirt roadway, and they gallop the four hundred yards to the fairground.

Cut to:

63. EXT/On to the Fairground

Alexander walks **Bucephalus** through the crowd, and up to the platform. **Philip** goes over to him. **Alexander** swings his right leg over the horse's neck, and slides to the ground.

Philip

Slightly tearful.
My son! My son!

They embrace and kiss.

Alexander

Smiling.
Thank you, Father, for my horse. I am
naming him Bucephalus.

Bucephalus stands still beside **Alexander**, sweating, foam-flecked, blowing. The Companions, the Bodyguard, and the nearby crowd, applaud.

Cut to:

64. INT/The Queen's Apartment/Evening

In the room overlooking the palace gardens, and filled with evening sunshine, **Olympias** sits dictating letters to a scribe. By a window, **Kleopatra** is weaving at a small loom. **Hyrminia** stands at the table unpacking a bundle of cloth newly arrived from Athens.

Olympias

Next.

To Molossia's King, at Epiros,
my own dear brother, Alexandros.

Begin: Dearest brother.
You will be surprised at another letter so soon;
but you must know the good news. The one-eyed
oaf of all Macedon has been publicly humiliated,
at the Great Spring Fair.
By my beloved son and a horse, no less!
The eye lighted on a beautiful; but vigorous
Black Stallion. The war-horse of legend was his
for the buying; but the upstart's body
was not up to the peasant's lust.

Six times he tried to mount, and six times was he
frustrated, despite the presence of dealers, slave-
grooms, the Royal Bodyguard, and the land-owning
elite of Pella.

I am told that the infamous temper was in no way
improved by the ease with which the beast was
then tamed by our own son of the god ...

There is a rap on the door. Before **Hyrminia** can respond, **Kleopatra** has run across and opened it to **Alexander**. She seizes his
hand and pulls him over to her loom.

Olympias

Continues dictating.

... Your namesake, my own beloved
Alexandros.

Dismissing the scribe.

Now go. I will summon
you again later.

She waves away the scribe, who gathers up the tablets and stylos. We start to follow her from the room, and then **dolly in** on **Alexander** and **Kleopatra**.

Alexander
Beautiful. Patra you are very good.

Kleopatra
It's called egg and dart. It's easy.

Olympias
Voice off to **Alexander**.

They say the ship sent for the
Sophist is on its way back.

Alexander
So, I hear …

He draws **Patra** towards him

… No, really, you are very clever.
It is beautifully done.

With his arm around her, **Alexander** kisses his sister on the
forehead.

Olympias
Voice off.

When he arrives, I shall receive
him in the Perseus Room.

Alexander does not look up and replies with his lips still close
to **Kleopatra's** forehead.

Alexander

I shall receive him Mother.

Olympias

Voice off.

Of course, you must be there,
I say so.

Cut to:

Alexander moving to the centre of the room, where he looks
at the smiling, and still seated **Olympias.**

Alexander

No, Mother. With Father away,
it is for me to do.
I shall present Antipatros, as Regent,
then bring Aristotle of Stagira
here to meet you.

Olympias stands up. Both children are mesmerised by her glare,
and the edge that her voice takes on. **Alexander** is uncertain
about taking on his mother and is a little sullen as a result.

Olympias

Are you saying to me Alexander,
that you do not want me there?

Alexander

It is for little boys to be presented by
their mothers.
I shall start with this Sophist in the way
I mean to go on.

The voice of **Olympias** becomes quiet and menacing.

Olympias

Did *he* put you up to this?

Alexander

In some surprise.

No, no. I didn't need him to
tell me. I am a man.

Olympias

Glaring, fierce.

So! you, are a man!
And I am the mother who bore you,
suckled you, and fought for you when
the king would have discarded you
like a stray dog.
I have lived for you each day of my life,
since before you saw the light of the sun.
Have gone through fire and darkness for
you, and, yes, into the house of the dead.
Now! You plot to treat me like a peasant wife.
Now! I can believe you are his son.

Alexander continues to look wide-eyed at **Olympias**. The silence is broken by the clatter of **Kleopatra** dropping her shuttle on
to the tile floor. Frightened, she looks at **Olympias** and gabbles.

Kleopatra

Father's a wicked man. I don't love him.
I love Mother best.

Alexander and **Olympias**, with their grey eyes locked together, ignore her.

Olympias

You will look back upon this day.

Alexander's voice is not far from breaking, and his reply ends in a squeak.

Alexander
I will.

Olympias
Is that all you have to say?

Alexander takes a long, deep breath, and he swallows hard.

Alexander
I'm sorry, Mother. I have done my tests
of manhood and must live like a man.

Olympias throws back her head, and her fighting, jeering laugh rings around the room. It is the first time that she has treated **Alexander** like **Philip**.

Flash shot:

Olympias jeering at **Philip** in the bedroom scene with **Alexander** aged five.

Cut back to:

Alexander rooted to the spot and flinching, but he still confronts his mother.

Olympias
Jeering; strident.
Your tests of manhood!
You silly child. Talk to me of your
manhood when you have lain
with a woman.

Kleopatra breaks this moment of stunned silence by bursting into tears. Again, she is ignored. She runs from the room. The door slams behind **Kleopatra**, and **Olympias** flings herself back into her chair, and breaks into shrieking sobs. After a moment of surprise, **Alexander** hurries forward and throws his arms around **Olympias**. She weeps on his chest, and he kisses her hair.

Alexander
I love you, Mother.
You know how much.

CU of **Alexander**, with **Olympias** leaning her head against him, no longer crying.

Olympias
Darling heart! the cruelties!…
The indignities I suffer from that man.
If you were to turn against me
they would become unbearable.

Alexander
Never! I love you. I will always be there
for you.

Cut to:

65 INT/ At the Foot of a Palace Stairway/ Evening
CU of a weasel playing with the end of a boy's girdle. **Hephaestion** has removed his, and wriggles it back across the floor towards him, like playing with a cat.

Hephaestion looks back up the staircase and sees **Alexander** looking down at him. They exchange smiles. **Alexander** runs down the stairs. The weasel runs for cover. Together, they run from the Palace.

Cut to:

66. EXT/A Forest Glade/Evening

Hephaestion sits down with his back against the trunk of an ivy-infested great oak. **Alexander** sits back against him, nestling in the curve of his left arm. For a moment they watch, in silence, the sun sinking towards the far hills, and a kite wheeling high before them.

Alexander
Quietly musing.

I made her cry.

Hephaestion
She cried too when you were born.
That too had to be.

Alexander
They claim to love you, while at the same
time trying to eat you raw!
The problem is the child belongs to them;
but the man has to grow up.
To move on.

Hephaestion
My mother says she wants me to grow up.

Alexander
The Queen needs a man to stand up
for her, because the King slakes
his lust with boys and girls ...
With young wife clauses in his political
treaties. But you know all this.

Hephaestion
Of course, everyone does.

Alexander
She knows I will always be her
champion; but I realised today, that when
my time comes, she thinks I will let her
rule for me.
We did not speak of it in so many words;
but she knows I told her; No …

Alexander twists round and looks up at his friend.

…You remember the other thing
we spoke of?

Hephaistion
About who is your father? Yes.

Alexander leans forward, looking into the glade, clasping his
hands around his knees.

Alexander
Last night I dreamt I caught a
sacred snake, and tried to make it talk.
It kept turning away. Escaping.

Hephaistion
Perhaps it wanted you to follow?

Alexander
No. She promised to tell me everything.
One day she says one thing, next another.
Sometimes I think I'll go mad.

Hephaistion
Never think that. You've got me. Do you
think I will let you go mad?

Alexander

I can always talk to you, as long as
you are around.

Hephaistion

I promise you before the god I will
always be around.
As long as I live, I'll always be
there for you.

Alexander looks around at **Hephaistoion** then leans back against him. The kite stoops against the still blue sky.

Dissolve to

67. EXT/Blue Sea/Morning

CU of the wake on the blue sea, between swirl pools left by the oars of a manoeuvring galley. The camera pans up to reveal a Macedonian war galley entering Pella harbour. Still under sail and oars, the galley spins through ninety degrees, and pushes stern first towards the unloading bay wall.

An **on-board shot** shows sailors letting go of the sheets of the triangular sail and swinging the yard to lie against the stubby mast. The **background view** shows **Alexander** standing on the edge of the unloading wall, watching, his thumbs hooked into his leather sword belt. Looking up at him from the nearing galley is **Aristotle**, standing in the stern sheets, surrounded by the bustle of sailors and slaves, stacking his collection of boxes and bags, ready for unloading.

Aristotle is small and thin, with a protruding, wrinkled forehead, and domed head of thinning hair. His short beard is trimmed neatly, and he is elegantly dressed, with good costume jewellery and finger rings. His piercing deep-set eyes record ceaselessly; but without judgement.

Two sailors leap ashore with heaving lines attached to mooring ropes. **Alexander** leaps between them into the stern sheets of the galley, and with barely a check, walks up to **Aristotle.**

Alexander
You are Aristotle of Stagira,
the Philosopher.

Aristotle
I am he.

Alexander
May you live happy.
I am Alexander son of Philip
Welcome to Macedon.

They exchange smiles. Something which both do well. **Aristotle** speaks with a slight speech impediment

Aristotle
I thank you. It has been
sometime. I was about your age
when I left Pella.

Alexander
A lifetime ago.

Aristotle
Certainly, progress wwwwill have destroyed,
or hidden, what was once familiar.

Alexander
King Philip is campaigning in Thrace.
I will introduce you to our Regent

Alexander puts one foot lightly on the gunwale, and springs up on to the jetty. He turns and proffers a hand; but, with a friendly gesture, and another smile, **Aristotle** indicates the gangplank being put in place. **Antipatros** walks up as **Aristotle** steps ashore. They embrace as acquaintances, if not as close friends.

Alexander

Surprised.

You are friends?

Antipatros

We have corresponded ever since
the time the King entrusted me
with our Peace Mission to Athens.

Alexander

And what of Queen Olympias,
Philosopher, do you and
she correspond?

Aristotle

Your renowned mother's dddddislike
of philosophy is well known, Prince.

All three laugh.

Alexander

Today you will meet, at least.
Before we go on to Mieza.

Aristotle

And the students?

Alexander

Already there. Except for myself
and Hephaestion, my close
Companion. Son of Lord Amyntor.

Alexander indicates Hephaestion, standing a short distance away, with the Prince's six-man Companion Cavalry escort. Hephaestion holds Bucephalus as well as his own horse. Mistaking Alexander's gesture towards him, he releases Bucephalus, who immediately trots across to Alexander, and, with a soft nicker, nuzzles his back. Aristotle watches intently, and with surprise. Alexander reaches to stroke the horse, without taking his eyes off Aristotle, saying,

Alexander
We are the youngest. There are
to be no children, no matter
how high born. Just as you asked.

Aristotle
Excellent. We shall have some
interesting and valuable ddddebate
and discussion.

With Aristotle continuing to watch intently, Alexander turns to Bucephalus, and taps the horse lightly on the back. Bucephalus sinks his crupper on to his haunches for Alexander to mount. Astride the saddle cloth, and a further, light tap on the neck and the horse stands up.

Alexander
Mount up, Aristotle, son of
Nichomakos.
I would be in Mieza before
this sun sleeps.

All becomes activity. Hephaestion approaches Alexander. The companions mount, and the slaves ride over with horses for Antipatros and Aristotle, and for the Philosopher's two attendants. They mount. Alexander and Hephaestion lead off from Pella harbour.

Fade to white:

68. EXT/A Forest Clearing in Deep Snow/Early Morning

Four heavy, black hunting dogs snap and bark at a small buck which they have cornered against the towering roots of a fallen oak, its outline softened by the thick blanket of snow. To stop the buck escaping, the dogs feint in and back from different directions. The breath of their excited baying spurts in rapid puffs on the freezing morning air.

Cut to:

Ptolemy and **Philotas** running towards the clearing on a narrow game trail. They each carry a single hunting spear, and wear leather leggings and shoes, Macedonian hats (the petasus), and long hunting knives slung from the shoulder beneath fur cloaks.

Ptolemy
They've stopped running.

Philotas
No roaring, only barks. It
cannot be much.

Ptolemy
Enough for breakfast, I hope.
I'm ravenous.

They break cover near the dogs. Seeing the humans, the buck turns in despair for the trees; but is headed off by two of the dogs. It turns again, and **Ptolemy** kills it with a spear thrust to the heart. **Philotas** whistles off the obedient; but reluctant, dogs.

Cut to:

69. INT/The Specimen Room at Mieza Academy/Early Morning

Aristotle and his trained slave, the youthful **Charaxus,** are bent over some notes on a neat; but cluttered table. **Charaxus** is taking dictation. The whole room is a wealth of scrolls, notes and drawings, birds, insects, and animals, all in various stages of skinning, dissecting, curing, and being preserved in clear honey.

Aristotle

Dictating.

> Our first season at Mieza is ending with the coldest
> weather that even the oldest of the local grannies
> can remember.
> Herd boys and cattle have dddied on the lowest slopes
> of the traditional winter grazing,
> just twenty miles away, in Pella, wolves came dddown
> at night to scavenge the capital's watch dogs.
> Here, at night, young Chawaxus and I dddoubled-up …

He strokes the youth's hair

> … For warmth. So too did the students, although, so I
> understand, the Prince only agreed after Hephaestion
> said that if they dddid not, 'people might suppose
> they had quarrelled!'

Cut to:

The Companions are breakfasting at the head of a snow filled valley above Mieza; chewing at joints of meat from the small animal they are spit roasting. **Harpalos** kicks snow over the embers of their cooking fire.

Aristotle

Continuing to dictate. Voice off.

> Alexander has them out at cockcrow, and in all
> weathers, hunting for their breakfast, and specimens
> for my Enquiry into Animals, which some ddday
> I will codify ...

Alexander throws his bone to a hunting dog, and walks towards the horses, tethered amongst the trees. The camera begins a slow zoom in on Mieza, which we can see down in the
valley beyond him.

> ... A new kitchen, dddining hall, and
> Slaves quarters were completed ddduring
> the summer. Now, a detachment of the
> King's army, from my Thracian
> homeland and well used to extremes
> of temperature, are putting the finishing
> touches to a gymnasium complex ...

Cut to:

In the Mieza gardens, snow and ice blanket the paths and bowers,
the stone seats and archways. It covers little rustic bridges taking pathways across runnels and conduits, and on beside streams,
with their now silent jets and fountains. We glimpse an occasional briar rose tangle, a lichen covered rock, and hear the tinkle
of water in the fountain-house. Otherwise, all is hidden and silent under the monochrome of winter. The zoom ends with the
gymnasium, where the soldier-builders are at work, and we hear
the sound of horses entering the nearby stable yard.

Aristotle (continuing voice over)

Off.

... The Companions of the Prince use the
gymnasium's conversation hall to read, or
to write and dddraw. And for music practice.
For our morning's esoteric lectures, when
we talk of ethics and politics, we walk in the
gardens. Frozen or not.
Together, we may discuss the nature
of pleasure, justice and the soul, or
consider virtue, love and friendship.
In the afternoons, villagers sometimes join us
for our exoteric lectures. Then we talk of ...

We hear an eager **Harpalos** interrupting **Aristotle.**

Harpalos
Voice off. Mimicking Excited.
> PhPhilossophpher!

Cut to:

70. INT/The Mieza Specimen Room/Early Morning

Carrying in both arms a cloth bundle from which a furry tail
protrudes, **Harpalos** limps up to the table where **Aristotle** and
Charaxus are sitting.

Harpalos
We've brought you the
world's oldest ffffox.

The Companions straggle in after him, with **Alexander** and **Hephaestion** bringing up the rear, by some appreciable way. They
are reading a letter, which **Alexander** holds, and **Hephaestion**
reads from behind, a hand resting on **Alexander's** shoulder. **Aristotle** stands up, as **Harpalos** dumps the bundle on the table,
and begins to throw back the edges of the cloth.

Aristotle
What's this? What's this?
World's oldest!

Harpalos
There! White wwwwith age!

Kassandros
Like a philosopher.

Aristotle
The world is white with cold, and you
think this animal turned white with age!

Ptolemy
My grandfather's white with age.

Harpalos
Mine are bboth dead.

Kassandros
Mine's bald with age; but his beard
Is white.

Aristotle
Such inability to reflect dddoes you no credit.
Zeus dddoes not send rain to ripen corn;
But because vapour, as it rises, cools.
When cooled, it turns to water, and so
must fall.

Alexander
And the fox is a hunter who must
hunt to live.

Aristotle
Precisely! So, he changes his coat in
winter to be inconspicuous.

Kassandros
This spring all foxes will turn green.

The Companions, apart from **Alexander**, laugh. **Aristotle** is
not amused, as he ushers them to the door.

Aristotle
After your music period, we will
consider the function of the colour
green in nature.

CU of **Alexander** and **Aristotle.** The Companions start leaving the room.

Aristotle
Will you play for us this morning?

Alexander
No.

Aristotle
With mere listening, half the ethical
effect of music is lost.

Alexander
I learned all about the ethical effect
of music when I was twelve.
The experiment is not for repeating.
I will never play again.

Aristotle
As you will.

Aristotle leaves the room. **Alexander** strides quickly across to one of the windows to join **Hephaestion**. The two talk, standing close together. Through the window we see a file of twelve cavalrymen issuing from a wood, some distance away, on the open eastern approach to Mieza. **Alexander** watches intently.

Alexander
When he is not being as wise as a god,
he can be silly as some old hen-wife.

Hephaestion
Kassandros is still envious of your
private lessons in statecraft.

Alexander
Shrugs.

I thought they were going to be more
interesting; but he wants to fit me out with
answers to everything in advance.
What would I do if faced with this or that?
When I say, I would decide at the time,
happenings are made by men and circumstance,
by place and conditions, which to decide one
needs to know, he thinks I'm being obstinate.

Hephaestion
Would the king let you drop the subject?

Alexander
No, it is my right. And besides,
disagreeing makes one think.
The trouble is he thinks of kingship
as a kind of science, like putting a
ram to an ewe and getting a lamb.

Every time.
But in war, no two conditions will ever
be the same again. Not the ground,
the weather, the mood of the men,
or the degree of surprise.

Alexander points at the approaching cavalrymen.

Hephaestion
Another letter from the Queen?

Alexander
Men are what make an army, and a city.
Men with hearts to use what comes
to hand. Look! Kleitos!
Those men are from the King, quick!

Alexander is halfway to the door before
Hephaestion moves to follow.

Cut to:

71. EXT/The Mieza Stable/Morning

As **Kleitos** and the eleven cavalrymen ride into the stable yard,
Alexander, carrying a sheathed sword in his left hand, races into
view from the opposite direction.

Alexander
Kleitos!

Kleitos
Alexander!

Kleitos dismounts. They embrace and kiss each other on the cheek.

Alexander
What's happened? Why are you here?
Where's the king?
Has he captured Doriskos?

Kleitos
Laughing.

He had not when we left.
His Majesty asks if you would like
a change from sitting about
with philosophers. He invites you
to his headquarters.

Alexander
Shouts.

Yes!

Alexander goes quickly down the two lines of cavalrymen, looking intently at each in turn. The men dismount as he passes. Reaching the last pair, he looks back at **Kleitos**, with a smile.

Alexander
You were in no hurry to reach us,
Kleitos. You all look very fresh.
We'll leave at first light tomorrow.
We must not miss the assault
on Doriskos.

Cut to:

72. INT/The Mieza Stables/First Light

Alexander, Hephaestion, Ptolemy and **Kleitos** enter the stables together. They split up, heading for their various horses. **Alexander** restrains **Hephaestion** with a hand on his arm. They walk together to a stall at the far end of the line. Behind them is all the activity of others arriving, and horses being readied and led out.

Alexander
The gods made only one Bucephalus;
but, for you, a strong, good tempered
fleet Thessalian mare.

They go around the corner of the loose box, where a slave-groom holds the headstall of a rich brown horse, with a pale cream, spikey mane, and flowing tail. **Hephaestion** looks excitedly at **Alexander**, before going forward and running his hand along her neck and flank.

Hephaestion
She's beautiful! And fast you say?

Alexander
Yes, and she's a stayer. I rode her back
from Pella on my last visit to the Queen.

Kassandros
Having paid a good, strong Thessalian
price, no doubt.

Hephaestion reaches for a nearby dung fork. **Alexander** shakes his head and turns to confront **Kassandros**.

Alexander
In battle, the cost of the horse is not
its most important feature.

Kassandros
Sneering.

So says Xenophon?

Alexander

Smiling.

To some of us it's obvious.

Alexander walks away quickly, as a slave-groom brings **Kassandros** his horse.

Cut to:

Hephaestion leading the mare hurriedly past **Kassandros**, on their way to the doorway.

Kassandros

Really, Hephaestion, I'm very pleased
for you. All the sucking-up is beginning
to pay off.

Hephaestion

Kassandros, I'll …

Kassandros

Not in front of the escort! Our
princeling would not like it!

His echoing laughter follows **Hephaestion** out of the door.

Cut to:

73. EXT/A Wooden Bridge across the River Strymon/Day

Steadicam shot of a straggle of peasant families clomping across the bridge. Beyond the ragged children and dogs, some fifteen adult men and women, leading three carts and another six laden donkeys, we see the small, fortified town of Amphipolis, nestling beneath the snow-capped peak of Mount Pangaion. The lower sides of the mountain are scarred by open-cast mining. Smoke from the smelting works drifts away northwards on the otherwise clear air. Two grandfathers ride side by side on donkeys. Most of the men carry staves. The breath of man and beast puffs as smoke on the cold morning air. The sounds are of the slap and thump of bare feet, and unshod hooves, on loose planking.

From out of shot, comes the sound of a male voice duet singing a wistful, haunting song, to the accompaniment of a single flute.

Cavalry Song – Verse One
And youths in the flower of their beauty,
to the flute's clear voice replying
with voices as clear as lovely, in order
due shall sing.
Of thee, and where thou goest, to the
place of bitter crying,
Deep in the earth's abyss, where Hades
sits as king.

Cut to:

The POV of the peasants coming off the bridge. The dirt road-way winds away into grass-covered sand dunes which surround the mouth of the river. Beyond them the Strymonic Gulf is clearly visible. **Kleitos's** advanced guard of four cavalrymen ride into view, and the singing gets louder, the whole party joining in the chorus.

Cavalry Song – Chorus
And yet, for all this, Beloved,
I am nothing in thine eyes!
Shameless, thou hast deceived me,
Like a little child with lies.

Cavalry Song – Verse Two

To thee my Love for ever
am I given wings to praise thee
to fly the wide world over.
To cross the infinite sea,
Swift as a thought laid lightly
on the lips of men that praise thee,
At every feast and revel
in the midst thou too shall be.

The four cavalrymen ride up the crown of the roadway, forcing the peasants to move to the sides. They bawl out a chorus as they approach the bridge. All are armed with fighting spears and swords, and are identically clad in Macedonian/Thessalian helmets, with nape and cheek pieces, and high bulbous, forward-pointing bronze crests and close-fitting cream coloured vests and leggings. Their blue chitons, red chlamys and hymations, billow out behind them, and are fastened at the throat with the starburst insignia of Macedon. Their regulation sword belts and boots are of red leather.

Cavalry Song – Verse Three

Thou shalt not lie forgotten,
Not even in the grave,
winging forever over,
the teeming, tireless wave.
Riding, not upon horses;
but on the pennant of the Muse,
In a song that will sound forever,
till earth and sun lie dead.

Cut to:

The two **Grandfathers**, riding on donkeys, pass **Kleitos** and the five Companions (**Alexander, Hephaestion, Ptolemy, Philotas** and **Kassandros**) as they ride clear of the sand dunes.

Grandfather
Where's the party, soldier?

Kleitos
What party?

CU of the gap-toothed, cackling laugh in the grizzle-bearded face.

Grandfather
The wedding party!
Tell us where the bride lives,
We'll be there.

The Companions laugh. They halt for a moment. **Kleitos** is serious. The rear four cavalrymen are heard singing the final chorus.

Kleitos
The Son of the King goes to war,
not a marriage bed.

The **Grandfather** looks closely at **Alexander** as the chorus comes to an end.

Grandfather
He can marry my granddaughter.
She's beautiful too.

Ptolemy
Cheerily.
He would always be away with Hephaestion.
Better me for your granddaughter, Old Man.

Kassandros
You already have five children by five
different mothers.

Ptolemy

Laughing.

> And still I have love for more!

Kleitos waves to the leading cavalrymen, and the first pair start across the bridge, followed by the others.

Cut to:

Kleitos and the Companions, in a close group, walking their horses across the bridge.

Kleitos

> Fifteen years ago, it was all Thracian
> tribal land beyond this River Strymon.

Kassandros

> You had better watch your blue-painted
> friend, Alexander.
> Lambaros may decide to take it back,
> while we're after King Kersebleptes.

Alexander

> Is that so? They have always
> honoured their pledges.
> Lambaros invited me to visit him
> during the summer.

Kassandros

> I'm not surprised, your head would
> look good stuck on a pole outside
> his mud hut.

Alexander

> As you said, Kassandros, he is my friend.
> Perhaps you can remember that.

Hephaestion
And shut your mouth.

Kleitos

Pointing

Philippi.

Philotas
And the famous gold mines of
Mount Pangaion.

Kleitos
That's right.

They reach the end of the bridge and stop. We see **Alexander** in **CU**.

Alexander

To himself.

Gold! …

Kleitos

Voice off.

We must keep moving if we are
to reach the army in eight days.

Alexander

To himself.

The mother of armies …

As they ride forward at a walk. **Alexander** pushes forward eagerly.

Alexander
… Five, Kleitos! We will do it
in five.

Kleitos
We took eleven to reach Mieza.

Alexander
Laughing.

Never mind Doriskos, if we take
that long, the King will be
halfway to the Hellespont.

Ptolemy
You will have to make do with a
drink in every other fort
we pass, Kleitos.

The laughing group break into a trot, riding on along the coastal path.

Dissolve to:

Kleitos and the Companions on a steep part of the track, on a
low coastal hill. At the bottom of the steep slope on their left,
several tracks meet on an open, valley floor. Philippi and the gold
mines are still clearly visible across the valley.

Kleitos
I first joined the army during the
Summer we took Philippi,
Klenides, as it then was.
It was a time for celebration.
Your father, Philotas, had just defeated
the Illyrians, and you, Alexander, came
into the world, 'with a great shout',
so, we were told.

Ptolemy
And on the night when the Temple
of Artemis, at Ephasaus, was burnt
to the ground.

Kleitos
And king Philip's horse had just won
at Olympia.
He decreed we should all have a
double issue of wine. I don't know
why he didn't make it treble.

Alexander
I do. He knew how much you could take,
before passing out.

Alexander kicks **Bucephalus** forward over the edge of the track.
The horse tucks his rump underneath him, and the two slither
and bound down the slope in a cloud of dust and stones. They
canter gently on towards the crossroads. **Hephaestion** catches
up, and they go forward together.

Alexander
I've been hearing that story since
I was three!
He nearly always told it when he
visited his sister in the nursery.

Hephaestion
Lanike?

Alexander
Dear Lanike, yes. And always with
the same ending!

The two ride down, and splash through a substantial stream, the water lapping the soles of their winter boots.

Hephaestion
I expect he's telling the others that
The Persians drank this stream dry
when they invaded Hellas.

Both laugh.

Alexander
And that we are near the Nine Cross Ways,
Where Xerxes buried alive nine boys and
nine girls to placate his gods.

Hephaestion
Much good it did him!

Alexander
Very intense.
It is important to show respect for the
gods. Diviners and omens have their place
in settling the troops. But the victory is to him
who is best on the day. The best man at the
head of the best army!

Cut to:

74. EXT/Farm Buildings near Doriskos/Sunset

CU of hairy, bare forearms and a pair of hands holding a pile of steaming, dripping entrails. The hands are removed, and we see them splosh on to a stone threshing floor. They stay together in a quivering pile, and then begin to ooze outwards. That they are being observed, is clear from the half circle of sandaled feet, beneath hairy shins of various hues.

Diviner

Voice over and ecstatic.

> Perfect! Magnificent! Wonderful!
> Exquisite! Absolute perfection!

Cut to:

Overall shot of the group, which comprises **Philip** and **Parmenion,** surrounded by some twelve junior commanders. The **Diviner** faces **Philip**. Behind the group a beautiful, red sunset is developing, and illuminating a group of horsemen, too far away to be identified.

Philip

Drily.

> Well? Are the signs propitious for
> an assault?

Diviner

Unctuously.

> Wait no longer, King.
> Attack at once.

Philip turns to his commanders, and they open their ranks to let him through, accompanied by **Parmenion**.

Philip

Tell your men the entrails
are with us.

As **Philip** and **Parmenion** walk clear of the junior commanders, a stooping eagle crashes into the scrub a short distance ahead of them, and lumbers into the air, a hare clutched in its talons. **Philip** looks at his friend with a wry smile.

Philip
The augural bird does not need
entrails, Parmenion.

Cut to:

75. EXT/The Assault on Doriskos/Just Pre-Dawn

A single, blazing arrow arcs across the screen, and disappears behind the walls of Doriskos. The dark outline of the walls is just visible against the lightening, eastern sky. Above them is a sickle moon and a few wisps of cloud. There is a flaring, as something catches fire in the town, then a rush of arrows, and a sudden blare of trumpets, followed by shouts and yells from both besiegers and besieged.

Cut to:

Low level shot of two lines of men running towards the camera, with a rough wooden scaling ladder, held on shields above their heads.

Cut to:

Medium shot of three scaling ladders being slammed against the walls. Immediately the besiegers begin to climb in files of three. The men grouped at the base of the ladders hold their shields above their heads, and overlapping, in a protective screen. On the left-hand ladder, a leading climber throws up his hands and he falls backwards on to the shields below. His body slowly slithers across them to the ground, where it is lost in the press of men waiting to climb. On the right-hand ladder, a step breaks halfway up, and some five files fall backwards on to the men below. We **zoom in** on the defenders pushing the now half full ladder away from the wall. As we get in close, the ladder reaches the vertical. Two of the defenders lunge forward with their spears and push

241

it over. From the struggling mass below, the ladder is reinstated, and men in threes begin to climb once more. A non-human series of loud, staccato shrieks breaks out, **off camera.**

Cut to:

A wheeled battering ram is dragged up to the main gates. The shrieks come from the wooden wheels and axles, as it is jerked forward three feet at a time, by two grass ropes attached to the front, and led through pulleys fixed into the ground close beneath the walls. Those at the pulleys are not so lucky, and several bodies lie around, amongst engineers crouching beneath their shields. As the ram jerks closer, we see an enormous boulder poised above the gates. A loud cheer goes up**, off camera**.

Cut to:

We **dolly up** to the level of the top of the wall and see that four of **Philip**'s men have established a small bridgehead and are defending themselves vigorously against a half-circle of defenders. The shouts and yells, and the clash of weapons is considerable. Other attackers scramble on to the wall. The besieged begin to give ground, backlit by fires that are beginning to take hold at many points in the town. A rhythmical thumping of wood on wood **off camera.**

Cut to:

CU, low level shot of the ram beginning to thump and pound the gates. It is just light enough to make out the various eyes, beasts heads, eagles and the starburst of Macedon, that have been painted on to the strips of leather, that cover the framework supporting the ram.
After a dozen or so thumps, there comes a splintering sound and cheering.

The main gates are beginning to splinter and give at the centre. An opening is made by the ram, and immediately yelling and cheering soldiers rush forward to fight their way through. We **dolly up** to the level of the top of the wall, where figures struggle with iron bars to lever the massive boulder over the edge of the wall. A single figure races along the top of the wall towards the boulder. Without being able to clearly identify the figure as **Alexander**, we see him kill two of those at the boulder with rapidly thrown spears. We hear an enormous crash and an extra loud cheer, from **off camera.**

Cut to:

The gates collapsing inwards, and **Philip's** men pouring through the breach, into the burning town.

Cut to:

CU of the helmeted figure of **Hephaestion** putting his foot on a dead man and pulling a spear from his chest. He runs towards the great boulder. He passes the two men speared to death moments before, and a third, killed with a sword thrust. He turns towards a small gatehouse by the boulder, and above the main gates. A narrow stone staircase leads down from the gatehouse to the street level below.

Cut to:

Hephaestion running down the narrow steps into the gatehouse. The atmosphere is smoky, from the embers of a brazier set against one wall, and a single spluttering torch in a wall sconce above it. **Alexander** stands in the centre of the little room, his face calm but triumphant. Across a table behind him, a man lies dead in a spreading pool of blood. Behind and to his left, lie a sword and a severed arm. In a corner beyond, a second man lies dead with a stab wound in the throat. **Alexander's** shield rests against the table. The sword in his right hand is red with blood and appears like an extension to the seeping sword cut on his upper arm. He grins broadly at **Hephaistion**, removes his helmet, with its white, horsehair crest, and places it on the table, before running his fingers through his damp hair.

Hephaestion is already overwrought, his face flushed, and his voice a little too strident.

Hephaestion
You're hurt! I will
stop the bleeding.

Alexander lays his sword on the table. **Hephaestion** tears a strip of cloth from the tunic of the dead Thracian and wipes the blood from **Alexander's** arm.

Hephaistion
Scolding
You should have waited, and not
gone dashing on alone from the
fight at the ladders.
You know you run faster than anyone.
You should have made sure we were
with you.

Hephaistion tears off another strip of cloth and binds the wound.

Alexander
Smiling, calm
They were going to drop that
great rock.
I knew you would follow.

Hephaistion

Loudly, his voice rising
> You would have gone on,
> rock or no rock.
> It is only luck you're still alive!

Alexander

Still calm; fierce, then thoughtful,
> It was the help of Herakles...
> and hitting hard before they could
> hit me...
> It was easier than I thought it
> would be.

Hephaistion

> These Thracians are dull peasants.
> Cattle thieves. Not trained soldiers.
> Your father's men would have cut
> you down.

Alexander

Sharply!
> Wait till it happens, then tell me!

Hephaestion

Shouting; near to tears.

> You went in without me!
> You didn't even look!

Still relaxed and smiling, **Alexander** reaches for his friend's
shoulder.

Alexander

> Patroclus reproached Achilles
> for *not* fighting!

Hephaestion

Quiet; looking away.

>At least Achilles listened.

Above the sounds of the looting and burning town, a woman shrieks and shrieks. The sound stops as abruptly. **Alexander** walks to the doorway.

Alexander

>He should call the men off.
>There is little else worth having
>in Doriskos; but even so …

Hephaestion joins him in the doorway.

Hephaestion

>Alexander don't be angry. When
>you're a general … when you're king,
>you won't be able to do it.
>Your father's a brave man, but he doesn't
>risk his life unnecessarily.

Alexander turns, and fixes **Hephaestion** with his intense, full gaze.

Alexander

>I can never *not* do it. That I
>know. It is the gods' truth.
>It is at that moment I feel …

A panting, sobbing young **Thracian** Woman, in a torn, dirty and bloody dress, reaches the top of the steps, and runs past them towards the wall. **Alexander** runs after her, and as she puts a foot on the ledge to jump off, he grabs her right arm.

Thracian Woman
No! No! No!

With a scream she swings around to claw at his face with her free hand, and he catches hold of that also. She looks at him, and then wrenches free, and kneeling, clutches him around the knees.

Alexander
Come on stand up.
We won't …

Alexander looks to **Hephaistion** for help. He touches her on the shoulder.

Hephaistion
Shaking his head.
We won't……

He makes a universal raping gesture, followed by a vigorous negative. The **Thracian Woman**, looks at **Hephaistion** and then lets go of **Alexander**, and rocks back on her heals, moaning softly, and tugging her hair.

Footsteps pound on the gatehouse steps. All three look towards them. A sweating, helmeted **Kassandros** pants into view. The **Thracian Woman** screams, and rushes behind **Alexander**, clutching him from behind with both arms, as if he were a shield. She is several inches taller. As **Kassandros** moves forward from the top step, we see his face is scratched and bleeding.

Kassandros
I can see you. Come here
you bitch, you are mine…

Alexander plants his feet apart, and, hooking his thumbs into his sword belt, looks at **Kassandros** with disgust

…She's mine! You don't want her.
She's mine! Mine!

Alexander
No. She's a suppliant.
I have pledged her.

Thracian Woman
Murderer! Murderer!

Kassandros
She's mine, I tell you. I caught her.
She got away before I could …

Alexander

Icily.

So! You lost her and I found her.
go away.

Thracian Woman
Murderer! Murderer!

Kassandros
Don't interfere. You are only a boy.
You know nothing of these things.

Hephaestion
Don't you call him a boy!
He fought better than you.
Ask the men.

Kassandros
He was looked after. They would follow
him into stupidity. He's the king's son,
or so they say.

As **Kassandros** reaches to draw his sword, **Alexander** springs forward, and taking him by the throat, lays him on his back.

CU of Kassandros pinned to the ground by the throat, despite the struggling kicks and blows. A three-legged stool swings down through the shot. Missing **Alexander** by inches, it smashes into the face of **Kassandros. Alexander** rolls clear and stands up. He and **Hephaistion** watch the **Thracian Woman** belabour **Kassandros** with the stool, smashing it repeatedly into his face and upper body.

Thracian Woman

She repeats quietly in time to the blows.

Murderer! Murderer! Murderer!

Kassandros raises an arm to shield his face and tries to roll clear. The arm breaks under the stool with a sharp crack. **Hephaistion** breaks out in a fit of hysterical laughter.

Hephaistion

Almost weeping with laughter

She'll finish him off!

Alexander

Very matter of fact.

He murdered her child.

That's its blood on her dress.

Hephaistion

If he dies she will be stoned.

The King couldn't

refuse as you pledged her.

Alexander

Smiling

Who will know, except you and me?…

He steps forward and grasps the woman's arm. He gently takes the stool. The **Thracian Woman** lets go, grabs **Alexander** and sobs on his shoulder. He looks at **Hephaestion.**

> ... It is said that when a town is
> taken all its gods depart.
> We'll find someone reliable,
> and get her to safety. Away from
> Doriskos, for the time being.
> Fetch the weapons.

Cut to:

76. INT/A Sitting Room Fireside at Mieza/Evening

Harpalos, Philotas, Nearchos, and **Ptolemy** lounge about, reading, in the gloom of an early evening, broken only by the flames of a single fire. They look towards the door at the sound of approaching footsteps. The door opens. **Alexander** and **Hephaestion** walk in together, their hair damp from a recent bath.

Philotas
Welcome back.

Harpalos
It's rrroast duck for supper.
You're just in time.

Alexander
Thank you. Where's Aristotle?

Ptolemy
He went to his room early this morning,
after reading a letter taken to him in the
specimen room. He looked dreadful.

Alexander
Bad news?

Philotas
Shrugs.

Is Kassandros with you?

Hephaestion
Aggressive.

No. Why do you ask?

Philotas
Shifting; uncomfortable.

I wondered, er I've been asked,
… uhm, why he doesn't come back.

Alexander
Laughing.

If you're asked again, say he fell
in love with war and forsook philosophy.

Hephaestion
Laughing.

He could hardly have come with us.
Not with all those broken ribs!

Harpalos
Have you seen Lambaros?

Alexander nods affirmative, while looking intently at **Philotas**.

Alexander
Has your father been asking
about him, Philotas?

Philotas reddens and avoids **Alexander's** stern gaze. At that moment, the door opens, and three slaves enter. Two go around the room lighting the wall sconces from handheld lamps and tinder sticks, while the third closes the shutters, and draws the wool curtains across the four windows. The boys return to their reading. **Alexander** and **Hephaestion** move together to a wall alcove, where **Alexander** reads quietly from a scroll he has been carrying.

Alexander

The same toils do not bear equally on the
general and the common soldier.
The honour of the general's rank, and his
knowing that nothing he does will go unnoticed,
make his hardships lighter to endure.

Hephaestion

Do you think Xenophon makes Kyros
too like himself?

Alexander

The Persian exiles at Pella used to say that
Kyros was a great warrior and a noble king.

Hephaestion puts his left arm around **Alexander**, and points to the text with his right hand.

Hephaestion

He trained his Companions not to spit
or blow their noses in public; not to
turn around and stare.

Alexander

The Persians must have been pretty rough
in his day. To us, a bit like Kleitos the Black
would seem to an Athenian ...

They laugh together.

> ... I like to think of Kyros at mealtimes,
> Selecting special pieces of food
> for his friends.

Hephaestion
Oh, don't remind me, I'm starving.

Cut to:

The three slaves, about to leave, stand aside to let **Aristotle** enter. Looking tired, drawn and grim, he walks towards the fireplace.

Aristotle
Accusingly to **Alexander**.

> So, you are back; in time to go to
> Aigai for the Dionysia.

CU of **Harpalos** rolling his eyes and leering – hamming it up.

Harpalos
For the gggirls! For hillsides
carpeted with gggirls! Hurrah!

Nearchos
No girgirgirl would let you catch her, Lefty.

Alexander moves swiftly to the fireside, to face **Aristotle**.

Harpalos
I resent that.
Unless of cccourse you bbback your
cheap tttongue with a handful of obols?

Alexander

Directly to **Aristotle.**

> Come and sit by the fire. Nearchos,
> a chair. Tell us, who is dead?

Aristotle

His voice thin and tired.

> My friend; my father-in-law.
> Hermeias of Atarneus.

Aristotle sits in the chair brought by **Nearchos**, and stares into the fire, holding out his hands for warmth. The boys draw round him.

Aristotle

> A Hellene has served his Barbarian
> master well. It was Mentor the Rhodian.
> King Ochos's general …

Aristotle draws his hands back into his lap. The wood fire spits. **Harpalos** grabs the fire tongs and throws a piece back

> … Mentor knew Ochos coveted the lands,
> and hated the popular example of Hermeias,
> so, pretending a friend's concern, he held
> a council.
> Hermeias went, as a guest-friend. Mentor
> sent him in fetters to Persepolis. Then, fixing
> the official seal to forged orders, Mentor took
> over all the strongpoints of Atarneus.

A slave enters with a tray of wine cups. Only **Alexander** does not take one.

Alexander

What happened to Hermeias?

Aristotle

King Ochos wanted to know if he had made
any secret treaties, so he sent for men
skilled in such things, and told them to make
him speak. After a day and a night, he was
still alive, so they hung him on a cross.
In Athens they are saying he died, finally, with
the words: Tell my friends I have done nothing,
weak or unworthy of philosophy.

Looking embarrassed, the boys make sympathetic noises; but
they say nothing. **Alexander** puts an arm around **Aristotle** and
kisses him on the cheek.

Alexander

I am truly sorry. If ever I take those
who did this to your friend, he shall
not go unavenged.

Aristotle drains his wine cup and holds it out to be taken by
the slave. He stands up, some colour back in his cheeks, and his
voice firmer.

Aristotle

Some of you will command in war.
Some may even have the ruling of
conquered lands.
Always remember that just as it is the
body's function to labour, that the mind
may live, so also with the Barbarian slave, that
the Hellene may progress mankind.
Nothing exists without its function.
that is theirs.

As **Aristotle** turns and walks from the room. The gong goes
for supper.

Harpalos
Ssssupper!

He limps immediately after **Aristotle**, followed by **Ptolemy, Philotas,** and **Nearchos. Alexander** turns, and stares into the fire.

CU of him watched by **Hephaestion**.

Alexander
Thoughtful; musing.

It's as if grief had warped his mind.
Imagine calling the Great King – the
successor to Kyros, Artaphenes and
Darius – a Barbarian, simply because
he was born a Persian!

Hephaestion
Do you think Mentor set up a treaty with Hermeias?

Alexander
At the prompting of my father,
I have no doubt; as he well knows.
What must he be feeling!

Hephaestion
At least he knows his friend died
faithful to Philosophy.

Alexander
Let's hope he believes it. A man dies
faithful to his pride, If ever I lay hands on
Mentor, I will crucify him.

Hephaestion looks at the stern, yet serene and beautiful face, and shudders at the remark.

Hephaestion
You had better go in, they cannot start
without you.

Alexander
Instantly brisk and smiling.

> And you, dearest Hephaestion are
> hungry! One should learn to do
> without. It is useful in war ...

He puts a hand around the back of **Hephaestion's** neck.

> ... But I should find it very hard to
> do without you.

Cut to:

77. INT/The King's Study at the Ancient Palace of Agai/ Morning

CU of hands bandaging a thigh. The bandage is being neatly crossed over on the front of the thigh, so as to leave a perfect row of vees. We see a young body-slave dressing **Philip's** wound. He rests his scarred and hairy right leg on the desk. **Eumenes** walks **into shot**, and whispers in his ear.

Philip
Tie that and get out.

The body-slave does so. **Eumenes** walks out of shot.

Alexander
Voice off.

> Did you get that at Kypsela?

Philip
My boy!

Laughing, **Philip** stands up. The body-slave walks **out of shot**, and **Philip** limps a couple of strides to embrace **Alexander**. He thumps him on the back.

Philip
Not all the Kypselians succumbed to
the blandishments of our golden donkey,
so, we had to force our way in. Like at
Doriskos …

Laughing, he limps back to his chair and sits down

… But my people recovered most
of the gold!

Alexander
Did you go in from the river side?

Philip
I tried a sap there; but the ground was
too soft, so I started to build a tower.

Philip picks up a stylos, and searches in vain for a clear tablet.

Alexander
Here!

He runs to the fireplace and gathers a bundle of kindling wood. As he returns, **Philip** clears two swathes on his desk, with a sweep of each forearm. Eagerly, the two begin constructing Kypsela with bits of wood and scrolls of state, from opposite sides of the desk.

Alexander
Here's the river line.

Philip
My siege tower near the western gate.

Alexander
And the outline of the walls.

Philip
Leaving them to mull over the tower, I
began to sap the north-east corner, here.

Alexander
Catapults! Ladders! We need them.

Alexander dashes back to the fireplace.

CU of him gathering up the fir cones lying about the hearth.

Philip
Voice off.
My plan was for Parmenion to ...

Philip stops speaking. **Alexander** freezes, looking down into the
fireplace. We hear light footfalls entering the room. They stop,
and **Alexander** swings round. From **his POV**, we see the su-
perb, statuesque figure of **Olympias** filling the screen. Dressed
in a floor length, draped, purple robe, edged in white and gold,
with gold sandals, her heavy, henna-red hair is bound with a gold
filet. Both gleam through a wafer-thin veil of pure white byssos
silk. Her smouldering gaze is for the traitor alone.

Olympias
When you have finished playing,
Alexander, I shall be in the Queen's
Apartments. Do not hurry. I have waited
these past six months, so what are a
few hours more?

Without so much as a glance at **Philip**, she turns and walks from the room. **Philip** gives **Alexander** a wry, conspiratorial grin, and fiddles with the model.

Alexander
Excuse me, Father. I had better go.

He throws the fir cones back into the fireplace and strides for the door. **Philip** looks across sharply.

Philip
You can stay, I suppose, until I
have finished speaking?

Alexander stops and faces **Philip**.

Alexander
Yes. What is it?

Philip
Sit down.

Alexander
I'm sorry. I must see Mother now.

He turns away again.
Philip
Angry.

Come back here …

Alexander looks back from near the door

> Do you mean to leave this mess
> On my desk? You put it there.
> Clear it up.

Alexander strides quickly to **Philip's** desk. Quickly; but very precisely, he picks up the sticks, takes three strides towards the fireplace, and flings them into the hearth. With a prolonged glare at **Philip**, he leaves the room.

Cut to:

78. INT/The Door of the Queen's Apartment/Same morning

The door is opened inwards, **away from the camera**, and out steps a beautiful, seventeen-year-old girl. She has long, shining, raven-dark hair, and an olive complexion. Some five foot ten inches tall, and deep breasted, she is dressed in white, with a red girdle, red arm-rings, and red leather sandals. She walks to the head of the stairs. As she starts down, **Alexander** comes around the corner and starts up towards her. She looks down as they approach each other, but **Alexander's** eyes never leave her.

CU of the two standing together on the same steps. She is noticeably the taller.

Alexander
Is my mother there?

Dark-haired Girl
Yes, my Lord …

Alexander smiles.

... Shall I tell her, Alexander, that you
are here?

Alexander
No. She expects me, and you
are on an errand.

Averting her eyes, she goes on down the stairs. **Alexander** walks
sideways to the top of the stairs, watching her until she is out of
sight. He waves to the sentry, some distance away, runs to the
door, raps on it, and throws it open.

Cut to:

Alexander and **Olympias** alone in a small sitting room, less
sumptuous than the Queen's Pella apartments.

Olympias
So! You finally decided to come.

Alexander
Not a day passes; but I think of when
we shall be together.

Olympias
You have returned a man, and faithless
like a man. How soon you have learned
to make your life without me.

Alexander
Mother, how shall I be anything without
learning war? He is my general.
Why offend him without a cause?

Olympias

And now you have no cause.
Once, you had mine.

Alexander

What is it? Mother tell me.
What has he done?

Olympias

Why should I trouble you? Go and enjoy
yourself with your friends. Hephaestion
will be waiting.

Alexander

I can see them at any time. I only wanted
to do the proper thing. For your sake
as well. You know that.

Olympias

Once I counted on your love. Now,
I know better.

Alexander

I love you more than life itself, always.
And true friends share everything,
except the past before their friendship.
Tell me, what has he done?

Olympias

It is nothing. Except to me.

Alexander

Mother! one would think you
hated me!

Olympias goes forward and lays her cheek against his.

> **Olympias**
> Never be so cruel to me again.

CU of **Alexander's** face over her shoulder. His eyes blur with tears. He breaks free and runs from the room.

> **Cut to:**

Alexander takes the flight of fourteen stairs from the Queen's Apartments two at a time. Rounding the corner of the passageway at the bottom, he canons into the **Dark-haired Girl** coming back from her errand. He holds her arms to steady them both.

> **Dark-haired Girl**
> I'm sorry, I'm sorry, my Lord.

> **Alexander**
> No, no it was my fault. I only hope
> I did not hurt you.

> **Dark-haired Girl**
> No, I'm not hurt.

She smiles at him, and then looks down demurely. **Alexander** gently releases her arms. She walks around the corner and out of sight. **Alexander** feels his cheek to check that there were no tears, then walks on.

> **Cut to:**

79. INT/A Gold Inlaid Iron Dagger on a Workbench/ Morning

CU of a man's hands holding the dagger and cleaning it with a makeshift brush – the teased-out end of a stick. The inlay depicts four men with shields, spears, and a bow, hunting two lions. One lion has downed a man, while the second flees towards the point of the blade. The stick breaks.

Pulling back, we see **Hephaestion** break off the end of the stick and stub it on the bench to start fraying the end. He tries a couple of times, then he gives up, throwing the stick under the bench.

Hephaestion
To himself.
> That'll have to do.

He sheaths the dagger, and hangs it, with a second, on a peg on the wall behind him. They hang together with his own sword and helmet, and those of **Alexander**. Most of the helmets on the shelf running the length of the wall, have coloured stripes, and crests of different colours. **Alexander**'s helmet is of burnished metal, and has a white plume flowing from a metal spigot on the crown. It is flanked by two smaller white plumes, one above each ear, and has inlaid cheek pieces, and upturns to a small, pointed peak at the rim, which allows a clear view of the wearer's face.

As **Hephaestion** heads for the door, **Harpalos** enters.

Hephaestion
Have you seen Alexander?

Harpalos
You?! Are asking mmmme?

Hephaestion grabs him viciously by the throat.

Hephaestion
Yes! I am asking you.

Harpalos
All right, all right. I saw him abbbout
half an hour ago.

Hephaestion
Where?

Harpalos
Near the libbbrary.

Hephaestion thrusts him away and walks out, leaving **Harpalos** rubbing his throat as he watches him go.

Cut to:

Hephaistion walking into a small, square room, with shelves, and a floor to ceiling wooden ladder in one corner. **Lysimachos** leans against a shelf, reading.

Hephaestion
Have you seen Alexander? Lysimachos.

Lysimachos looks up, and raises an eyebrow in surprise, before replying.

Lysimachos
I have, as it happens. He's up there,
in the archive room.

Lysimachos points upwards, and **Hephaestion** goes towards the ladder. A large, black hunting dog, chained to a ringbolt at the foot of the ladder, growls and stands up. **Hephaestion** offers the back of one hand, which the dog sniffs. He rubs its head and then he climbs the ladder.

Low level shot of **Hephaestion** coming through the open hatchway in the floor of the archive attic-room floor. The room is cluttered with wooden boxes, cloth bundles, and loose scrolls, all covered in dust and cobwebs. There are three low, window alcoves letting in the sun. In the one furthest from the ladder, **Alexander** lies, curled up, reading, like a small animal in its lair. His long hunting knife rests against his leg, and three scrolls lie on the floor next to him. Stooping slightly, and stepping over boxes and bundles, **Hephaestion** goes over to him.

Hephaestion
What are you doing?

Alexander
Reading.

Hephaestion
I'm not blind. What is the matter?

Alexander looks up at him for the first time. His look is fierce and secretive. He does not reply. After a moment, **Hephaestion** squats down beside him.

Hephaestion
I've never seen this room before.

Alexander
It's the archive room.

Hephaestion
So Lysimachos said. What shall we do
tomorrow. After the sacrifice?

Alexander
It is unlucky to lay plans for
the Dionysia.

Hephaestion
Do you want me to stay?

Alexander
I just want to read.

Hephaestion straightens up, and looks down at **Alexander**, who
has returned to his reading.

Hephaistion
What are you? …

He turns and picks his way over to the step ladder, without looking back.

Cut to:

80. INT/The Menagerie Room at Aigai/Evening

Olympias, accompanied by **Hyrminia** and two attendant
slave-women, stands looking at three black puppies; in a cage
which stands on a workbench, near a variety of ornate daggers.
Close by, a Thracian slave sharpens a sword with a curved blade.
Other animals and birds are in cages about the room.

Animal Keeper
All three, Lady?

Olympias
Yes. Bring them to my apartments with
the snake baskets and the thyrsae.

Cut to:

The **Dark-haired Girl** leaving the Queen's Apartments. She closes the door behind her, and drawing a thick, oatmeal coloured cloak around her flimsy white dress, walks away down the stairs.

Cut back to:

Olympias standing beside the **Animal Keeper**, in the doorway of the menagerie room, looking out on to a small grass compound, where a number of tethered sheep and goats are grazing.

Olympias
The big ram, and the black goat.

Animal Keeper
Thank you, Lady.

Olympias
Have them cleaned, oiled and collared,
And outside the Queen's postern
three hours before dawn.

Animal Keeper
Yes, Lady.

Cut to:

Alexander looking out of his lair in the archive room, over the Falls of Agai, to where the sun is in the first stages of a blood-red setting, over the distant mountains. He gets up, stretches, and picks up his scrolls and his hunting knife, and makes for the stepladder.

Cut to:

Philip sitting at his desk, now with **Parmenion** and **Antipatros** standing on the other side of it. Two scribes sit on stools to **Philip's** left.

Philip

In assaulting a town, men scaling the
walls on ladders are too vulnerable.
We need more flexible siege towers.
The workshops are producing a light
weight tower, which I want Admetos's
Phalanx to try out the day after tomorrow.

Parmenion

Grinning.

That should clear a few heads after
the Dionysia!

Philip

Yes, and every other phalanx can do
the outer ring first thing that morning.

Antipatros

The full twenty miles?

Philip stands up, and limping slightly, makes for the door as he speaks.

Philip

The full twenty. And, Parmenion, detail
four hundred of the Silver Shields to
go round with me, Kleitos and the
Companion Cavalry. Full fighting
order. It will be trotting pace all the way.

Cut to:

Flash shot of the **dark-haired Girl** leaving the main gate of Aigai Palace.

Cut to:

81. EXT/An Orchard Near Aigai Palace/Evening

The hallmark sound of the whole area is the sound of the water crashing down the Falls of Aigai. Here, the sound is louder. **Alexander** picks violets in an orchard between the falls and the palace. Already he has a considerable bunch in his left hand, and he straightens up, sniffing their scent. Some distance off, he sees a pale figure moving between the fruit trees. He picks up the telamon of his hunting knife, and slips it over his right shoulder, so that the knife hangs on his left-hand side.

Quietly and swiftly he runs from tree to tree to intercept the figure.

Cut to:

Alexander stepping out on to the track in front of the **Dark-haired Girl**. She stifles a scream.

Dark-haired Girl
You frightened me!

Alexander
I won't eat you. I came to say Hello …

Dark-haired Girl

The **Dark-haired Girl** mumbles.

Good evening, Lord Alexander

Alexander
… And may I ask your name.

Dark-haired Girl
Anactoria

Alexander
Hesitant and also slightly shy.

Smile for me, Anactoria, and, and …

Alexander looks at the violets and he divides the bunches into two.

… and you shall have flowers.

Anactoria gives a fleeting, bashful smile, and looks down. **Alexander** looks from one to the other of the two bunches, and then puts them both together and holds them out.

Alexander
Here.

Alexander steps forward and brushes her cheek with his lips. She shakes her head, and, opening her cloak, slips the flowers between her breasts.

Anactoria
Whispers.
They are beautiful, thank you.

She runs off through the trees. **Alexander** looks towards the last rays of the setting sun. A wolf howls, and a woodman's axe pounds above the sound of the falls. A second wolf, nearer than the first, replies. **Alexander** looks across the empty orchard. He takes the sheathed hunting knife in his left hand and walks away through the trees.

Dissolve to:

Beneath the walls of Aigai Palace, **Four Soldiers** practice a few steps of a phallic dance, in preparation for tomorrow's festivities. Nearby, a **Fifth Soldier** tends to chunks of meat cooking in the embers of a fire. Beyond the throw of the fire it is now quite dark. As one, the dancers stop, and peer out into the gloom. One edges backwards to where their spears and shields are piled beside the fire. The remaining three speak in stage whispers.

First Soldier
Wolves?

Second Soldier
No... too big ... too noisy.

First Soldier
Lion?

Second Soldier
Man, I reckon.

The **Fifth Soldier** moves from the fire, and stands behind the three.

Third Soldier
I didn't hear anything.

Fifth Soldier
Come on, it's nothing.
The steaks are nearly done

The Fifth Soldier turns and collides with the **Fourth Soldier** bringing the spears.

Cut to:

Alexander, in the early evening darkness some fifty yards from the **Soldiers**. From **his POV** we see the two **Soldiers** come together. The other three turn round. **Alexander** hurls a large stone some way beyond the five, who immediately look towards where it crashes into the undergrowth. A grinning **Alexander** runs swiftly and silently towards the wall of the palace, and a small postern gate, in the opposite direction from where the soldiers are looking.

Cut to:

82. INT/Inside the Palace/Night

Steadicam shot down twelve steep, narrow, stone steps to the postern gate. **Alexander** comes in, closes the gate behind him, and runs up the steps. The **camera follows** him through a heavy wooden door at the top of the steps, into a colonnaded passageway. He takes four strides along the passageway to his right. He hears a girl's breathless giggles and he moves silently behind a column immediately to his right.

Alexander looks out from the column. Two columns further on, **Anactoria** edges into view. A man's arms is round her waist. His other hand massages her breasts clear of the filmy dress. Drooping violets spill on to the stone floor. She giggles with pleasure, throwing back her head. The hand on her waist slides downwards. **Anactoria** reaches back and pulls the man's head into view. He nuzzles her ear, and she drops her hand. It is **Philip**.

We **dolly in** on **Alexander**. His face is drained of colour; but shows no emotion. He walks away along the corridor.

Dissolve to:

Alexander entering his bedroom. A **Thracian Slave** has lit one wall sconce and is moving to light a second. **Alexander** throws his hunting knife on the bed and opens a chest.

Alexander

Get out. Now.

Without speaking, the **Thracian Slave** leaves the room, **Alexander** bolts the door behind him. He turns, reaches for and pulls on his hunting boots. We hear **Hephaestion** speaking to the **Thracian Slave**.

Hephaestion

Voice off.

       Is Lord Alexander there.

Thracian Slave

Off.

       Yes, Lord.

Hephaestion

Voice off.

       Alexander? Alexander! It's me.

The door handle is rattled, and **Hephaestion** knocks several times.

Hephaestion

Voice off.

       Please let me in. We should talk.

Alexander walks swiftly across the room to a curtain on the far wall. Drawing it aside reveals a second, smaller door. He opens it and goes down the narrow stone staircase to the Prince's Postern.

Fade to black/
Fade up to:

83. EXT/The Sacrificial Dancing Floor above the Falls of Agai/Dawn

An **over-view** of the sacrificial dancing floor, which is over-looked by distant peaks, and the nearby forest of cedar and rowan, myrtle, arbutus and broom. It forms a hidden crescent beside the falls. It cannot be overlooked from the far side of the gorge, which is lower. A stone alter has been built at the northern end, and halfway along the western side, a small outcrop of rock rises higher than the tallest tree, above the falls. Mist and a fine spray rises from the gorge, like early morning smoke.

The steady drumming of the falls is punctuated by individual cockerels crowing in the valley below. From a distance, a dog barks. The altar smokes, from the burning of small, sacrificial animals, and flares, from resin flung on torch butts in offerings to the god. A fire also burns before the altar, its flames flickering without smoke. The lone figure of **Olympias** stands in front of the fire, watching a line of twelve **Maenads** dancing towards her. Everyone holds a pine-cone-topped thyrsus. Wolves howl, then fall silent.

We **zoom down and in** behind the **Maenads**, and approach **Olympias** from **their POV**. The six **Maenads** in the centre of the line wear white dresses and fawnskin capes, and the three on each end of the dancing line, coloured dresses and fawnskins. **Olympias** raises her thyrsus.

Olympias

A cry.

Otototototoi!

The **Maenads** stop a few yards away from **Olympias**, who we see framed by the fire and smoke on the altar. She wears an ivy tiara, in which a snake is entwined. Her lustrous hair flows free down across one bare shoulder. A fawnskin covers the other. The front of her flowing white dress is dappled with blood.

Maenads

Halting, the **Maenads** cry in unison.

Ototototoi

Olympias

Repeating the cry.

Ototototoi!

Hyrminia walks into shot and takes the Queen's thyrsus. As she walks out of shot, **Olympias** raises her left hand and points to the first, white-clad **Maenad**, on the right of the line.

Cut to:

The **Maenad's** line from **Olympia's POV.** The **Maenad** pointed at drops her thyrsus. It is **Anactoria**. All the other **Maenads** lay down their thyrsae. Nearby, a single lyre begins a slow, twanging rhythm. The sound galvanises **Anactoria**, and as hands reach out to grasp her, she turns and sprints towards the gorge, in the direction of the outcrop of rock. **Maenads** wearing coloured dresses, two from each end of the line, give chase.

Some twenty yards from the gorge side, **Anactoria** stumbles and falls. Although she is up in a moment, it is not quick enough, and she is caught in the next few strides. The four **Maenads** start to run **Anactoria** back to **Olympias**.

Cut to:

The rocky outcrop in **CU**.

We see **Alexander** lying in a crevice, amongst the rocks and scrub, his chin resting on the scabbard of his hunting knife. We watch **Anactoria** and the four **Maenads** running towards **Olympias**. From **Alexander's POV**. **Anactoria** stops running; but with her legs trailing, the **Maenads** run on, holding her by her arms and shoulders.

Cut to:

Hyrminia handing **Olympias** a long, narrow bladed dagger, with a gold hilt. The **Maenads** drop **Anactoria** face down before **Olympias**. The lyre, which has been twanging throughout, stops.

Anactoria begins a series of high-pitched shrieks. Two **Maenads** jerk her upright onto her knees. **Olympias** steps forward and rips the flimsy white dress from her left shoulder. She places the point of the dagger against the left of **Anactoria's** neck, just inside the collar bone.

Cut to:

CU of **Alexander**, who has remained in the exact same position. The series of shrieks suddenly stop, leaving only the sound of the falls. **Alexander's** eyes brim with tears, which then flow down his cheeks.

Fade to black:
Cut to:

84. EXT/Somewhere in the Forest Below the Dancing Floor/Noon

Hephaestion walks through the forest searching for **Alexander**. He carries a bag slung over one shoulder. Several boys and girls, laughing, chase one another, either across his path or amongst the trees nearby. The sound of the falls is loud.

Hephaestion

Calling.

Alexander! Alexander! …

… Alexander! Alexander!

Hephaestion follows a narrow game path, which takes him to the edge of the river, downstream from where it leaves the gorge. He quenches his thirst with handfuls of water, then throws back his head and yells.

Hephaistion
Alexander! … ander … ander … ander!

The gorge throws back a multiple echo. **Hephaestion** looks upstream towards the source of the echo, and sees a lone figure, on the opposite bank, sitting on a rock with his back against a tree. **Hephaistion** splashes into the river, crossing, sometimes on rocks and sometimes almost waist deep in water. He runs along the bank to where **Alexander** is sitting.

Hephaistion
What's happened? Have you
hurt your head? Tell me.

Alexander is dirty, and scratched, the blood recently dried. His clothes are torn in several places. He looks at **Hephaestion** blankly, with strained, sunken eyes. His speech is slow and slurred.

Alexander
Why are you running about on
the mountain? Are you looking
for a girl?

Hephaistion
No, of course not. I've been
looking for you. Since sunrise.

Alexander
Look up on the dancing floor.
You'll find one there, but she'll
be dead.

Hephaestion
Did you kill her?

Alexander
I didn't no. She was beautiful. My
father thought so. My mother too.
Beauty is truth, a gift from the gods.
But without good fortune a deadly
Blessing. A curse even. We'll watch
out for her. She'll pass by on the stream.

Alexander draws up one knee, and wrapping his arm around it,
stares listlessly into the river. **Hephaestion** takes a round, pint
sized flask of wine from his bag.

Hephaestion
I'm sorry you were a witness.

Alexander
Xenophon says, a boar's tusk
scorches violets.

Hephaestion
Hair. A boar's tusk scorches hair.
Drink some of this, you've been
up since yesterday.

Alexander
Xenophon says …

Hephaestion
Are you sure you are not hurt?

Alexander
Giggling.

Oh no! I didn't let them catch me.
I saw their game.

Hephaestion
Sharply.
>Look at me! Now drink this.
>Do as I say. Drink! …

Alexander takes a couple of mouthfuls, with **Hephaestion** holding the flask.
>… You should not have followed
>the Maenads. Everyone knows it's
>unlucky. No wonder you feel bad.
>And look, you've got a thorn in your leg.

Alexander takes the flask. **Hephaestion** pulls out the long thorn from his right leg. A trickle of blood flows, and **Hephaestion** scrapes some moss from the rock. He slides down and soaks it in the river, and squeezing it out, climbs back, and cleans the wound.

Alexander
I've seen worse on a battlefield.

Hephaestion
Yes. We have to get used to blood.

Alexander
One should be able to look at anything.
I was twelve when I cut off the head
of my first man. He was dead.

Hephaestion
I know.

Alexander leans back against the rock and turns his face to the gorge. While he speaks, he gradually drains the wine flask.

Alexander
"She came down from Olympus walking
softly", *Homer says*, "with little steps like
a quivering dove. Then she puts on the
helm of death!"

Hephaestion
Everyone knows you can look
at anything.
Alexander, are you listening?

Alexander
Be quiet. They are singing.

Hephaestion
Look! It's finished. Over.
You are with me. I promised
I would always be here for you.

Hephaestion holds out his hand. **Alexander** drains the last
drops from the flask. The wine brings the colour back to his face.
He looks at **Hephaestion**, and after a moment, reaches out and
touches his hand. Then he grasps it and puts both their hands on
his upturned knee.

Hephaestion
You mean more to me than
anything. I would give my life
for you. I love you.

Alexander relaxes his grip. His expression relaxes, and he re-
verts to looking merely dirty.

Alexander
The wine was good. I'm not so very tired.
To be able to do without sleep is useful in war.

Hephaestion

Smiling.

> Next time we'll stay up together. Come
> on, let's swim and wash off the dirt.

They leave the rock and start to undress.

Dissolve to:

85. EXT/The Pella Stadium Games Track/Morning

Philip has a Phalanx practising with his new four-at-a-time scaling ladders placed against scaffolding. The whole track is taken up by twisting lines of soldiery, four abreast, shuffling towards one of the four ladders, and stirring up clouds of swirling, choking dust, which clings to the men, hangs on the still air, and glistens in the hot sun. Smeared and streaked with dust, **Philip** is near one of the two middle ladders, happy, and relaxed amongst his army. He reaches for a young soldier, who, although just two files away from climbing, has his back to the ladder.

Philip

Kindly.

> Never look away. Look up.
> Then if the god is kind you may survive
> the hail of death, and live.

The young soldier nods dumbly. **Philip** turns away from the ladders, and pushes his way through the press of men, who try to make way for their King. Confronted by an 'inadvertent' spear point, he pushes the blade upright from his belly, and, holding the shaft, snaps at the owner.

Philip

> Save this for an enemy,
> not the back of a friend.

Moving on, **Philip** is confronted by the grinning veteran, **Delphos**.

Delphos
Give us a real assault, King,
where there is less dust and
more women.

Philip
There'll be plenty of wine
when you finish here.

Delphos
And one of your women?

Philip

Laughing.

Get one of your own, Delphos
– when we take Perinthos.

Cut to:

Philip confronts a dour, grizzled veteran near the back of the crowd.

Philip
So, 'Makos!
You survived Doriskos?

'Makos
I was with Alexander on the wall,
my King.

Philip
Victories would not be ours
without you, 'Makos.

284

The Royal Bodyguard, mounted, with one holding **Philip's** horse, grouped beside **Parmenion**, as he watches the Phalanx at work. **From their POV** we see **Philip** walk clear of the crowd, and gesture for one to join him. **Pausanias**, and the one holding **Philip's** horse, respond at once.

Philip
Has Prince Alexander returned
from Aigai?

He strides across towards **Parmenion**.

Pausanias
Yes, but he rode out as it was
getting light.

Philip
Find my son, Pausanias. Have him
join me after the manoeuvres ...

Philip takes the reins of his horse and a spear from the bodyguard. He looks at **Parmenion**

... Drive this lot hard, Parmenion. At
best they're too slow.

Philip drives the butt-spike into the ground and uses the spear as a support to vault on to the horse's back.

Parmenion
Many have been with us since you lost
the eye at Methone.

Philip
Then they should know enough to do
better. If the young ones go on like that,
their first siege will be their last.

Cut to:

86. EXT/The Woods Around Pella/Morning

Hephaestion is ahead of **Alexander**, as they ride along a narrow game trail.

Alexander
I came across a book of
Plato's at Aigai.

Hephaestion
In the Archive Room?

Alexander
Yes. Aristotle never showed
it to us.

Hephaestion
What's it about?

Alexander
Listen to this. Plato says,
"Love makes one ashamed of disgrace,
and hungry for what is glorious.
Without love, neither a people nor
a man can do anything great or fine."

Hephaestion
What a glorious idea.

The game trail drops down into sunlit glade. **Hephaestion** stops.
They both dismount, and tether the horses loosely to trees, and
in shade.

Alexander

Later he writes,
"Suppose an army were made up of
lovers and beloved. Each one rivals
for honour, and despising infamy. Even
a few, fighting side by side, might
conquer the world."

Hephaestion

Why do you suppose Aristotle
never showed us that book?

Alexander

Plato was a soldier when he was
young, like Aeschylus.
I expect Aristotle was envious.

Hephaestion

Let's walk.

Cut to:

The pair moving through the trees, down slope**, towards the
camera. Alexander** leads, moving more quickly than **Hephaestion**.

Alexander

Only the Thebans have ever founded
a Lovers Regiment, and no one has
ever defeated their Sacred Band …

They reach a low escarpment in the forest and look across to the
Pella Lagoon.

> ... Socrates, perhaps, ends it, when he
> Says "The best, the greatest love
> can only be made by the soul."

Hephaestion

His tone both hurried and dismissive.

> Well everyone knows he was
> the ugliest man in Athens.

Alexander

Smiling.

> The beautiful Alcibiades
> threw himself at him.

Hephaestion

Triumphant.

> Only because Socrates saved
> his life at Potidaea.

Alexander

> They say Alcibiades saved him
> at the battle of Delium ...

Alexander touches **Hephaestion** lightly on the forearm.

> ... To make love with the soul is
> the greatest victory. Like the triple
> crown at Olympia.

Hephaestion looks out at the Lagoon, and replies slowly, closing his eyes.

Hephaistion
It would be the greatest victory
to the one who minded most …

Alexander looks thoughtful. **Hephaestion** suddenly turns to him, excited and eager.
… If you mean that?!
If that is what you really want?!

Alexander raises his eyebrows and grins, tossing back his hair.

Alexander
I'll tell you one thing.

Hephaestion
Eager.
Yes?!

Alexander
If you can catch me!

Alexander is ten yards away before **Hephaestion** starts to run after him. One after the other they run into the trees and out of sight.

Cut to:

Hephaestion looking down at a bend in the low escarpment, to where **Alexander** lies crumpled beside some rocks, his left leg at an odd angle. **Hephaestion** climbs down beside him.

Hephaestion
Is your leg broken.

Alexander lies without moving, his eyes closed, as **Hephaestion** checks his arms and his legs for broken bones. After a moment, **Alexander** opens one eye.

Alexander

Grinning.

Shhh. You'll scare the foxes.

Hephaestion
I could kill you!

He flings himself down, close against **Alexander**, and they lie back against a rock in silence. The sun glints on a heavy gold brooch on **Alexander's** chiton, and he manipulates the bright spot across a patch of lichen.

Hephaestion
What are you thinking?

Alexander
Of mortality and death.

Hephaestion
Such thoughts leave me feeling sad.
As if the vital spirit has drained away.
I don't like it, but wouldn't have it
any other way. Would you?

Alexander
No, I wouldn't.
True friends should be everything
to one another.

Hephaestion
I cannot bear you to be sad.

Alexander
It soon passes. It's the envy
of some god perhaps.

Hephaestion
Envy! It makes me think of the
King's Squires, with their bitchy intrigues,
and endless jealousies.

Alexander reaches up, and gently pulls **Hephaestion's** head down to rest against his shoulder.

Alexander
Their insolence.

In **CU**, we see silent tears flow down the face of **Hephaestion** and drip on to **Alexander's** throat. **Alexander** strokes his friend's hair.

Cut to:

87. INT/Outside Philip's Study at Pella/Noon

Nine of the King's squires stand about in groups, talking in low voices. They fall silent, and stand staring at **Alexander**, as he reaches the top of the stairway landing, and walks through them towards the doors of **Philip's** study. **Menestas** is one of the two guards on duty at the doors.

Alexander
Smiling.
I am expected, Menestas.

Menestas
And welcome, Basiliskos

Sub-title: Little King.

Alexander looks sharply at his soldier-friend, as the doors are swung open. **Philip** gets up from his desk. **Alexander** walks briskly into the room, looking **Philip** straight in the eye, as is his custom. Father and son embrace.

Philip
I thought you were behind with your
beard; but I see you are not.

Alexander
No, Father.

Philip
Together with several of your young
friends, you have been shaving!

Alexander
Yes, Father.

Alexander is very polite throughout; but gives his father just the hint of a look of amused tolerance, his head tilted slightly to the left, in a characteristic pose.

Philip
Gruffly.
Effete Southern practises! The beard
Is proper for a son of Macedon.

Alexander
Yes, Father.

Philip gestures towards a stool and moves over to the campaign model on his desk. **Alexander** adjusts the stool closer to the model, and looks at it closely, sitting with elbows on knees and his chin cupped in his hands.

Philip
We are well forward here,
as you well know. Perinthos will be
tough to break into …

Philip points to the places as he speaks.

… Byzantion will support them, either
openly or not. So, will the Great-King,
who, from what I hear, is in no fit state
to make war; but will send them supplies.
His treaty with Athens allows for that.

With his finger still pointing South, in the direction of Athens,
Philip is lost for a moment in thought. **Alexander** looks at the
familiar, beautiful, bronze statue of Hermes inventing the lyre,
by Polykleitos. He looks from the slender, athlete's figure and
sombre expression, to the thoughtful, scarred features of **Philip**.

Alexander
Eager.
Well then, Father, when do we march?

Philip
Parmenion and I, in three days' time.
You, my son, will remain here.

Alexander sits bolt upright, his face tense and fierce.

Alexander
Here?! At Pella?
What do you mean?

Philip
Grinning broadly.

You look like that horse of yours,
shying at its own shadow. Don't be so
quick off the mark, you won't be idle …

Philip pulls from his finger, the signet of sardonyx, carved with
an enthroned Zeus, carrying an eagle on his fist. The Royal Seal
of Macedon. He tosses the ring into the air and catches it in the
same hand.

… You will be our Regent. You will be
the keeper of the Seal …

Alexander looking only slightly placated.

… You have had a good grounding in war.
In two years, I'll promote you general.
Meanwhile, you must learn administration.
It is futile to push out frontiers, when the
realm is in chaos behind you.
I had to organise Macedon before dealing
with the Illyrians inside our borders. They
could return at any time. You will have to protect
my lines of communication. The Regency
is serious work.

Alexander
I understand, Father. Thank you.
I will not give you cause to regret
the appointment.

Philip
I'll leave you Antipatros; but it will be
up to you whether you consult him or not.
The Seal is the Seal.

88. EXT/A Mountain Valley in Northern Macedonia/ Afternoon

In a **wide-angle, long distance shot**, we look down across a field of ripening corn, and a narrow, but boisterous river, with forested hills beyond. From the darkness of the trees a man runs, carrying a blazing torch. Like an athlete with the Olympic flame.

We **slowly zoom from a long distance to a medium shot**, with the man as the focal point. As we do so, he splashes across the river. From the darkness behind him, other torch carriers follow on either side of him. They begin to torch the standing corn, which ignites quickly in the brisk wind. The **zoom stops** with billowing smoke and blazing corn filling the screen. Through it, the men can be seen running back towards the river, and the woods beyond.

Dissolve to:

89. INT/Inside a Dingy, Cluttered Jeweller's Workshop/Day

CU of **Lapidary** showing **Alexander** how he has reduced the finger size of the Seal. In the background can be heard the tramp of infantry and cavalry, whinnying horses, and the shriek of wagon wheels.

Lapidary
I have melted a fine slip of gold
into the hoop of the signet.
It will be more comfortable than gold
wound around the hoop,
besides being invisible when
the ring is worn.

Alexander

Thoughtful.

> And the symbols are magical,
> both in perfection and in defect.

Lapidary

> Should the finger of a king
> prove broader, Lord,
> then I can always restore the hoop
> to its original size – or bigger.

Alexander pushes the ring, with some difficulty, on to the middle finger of his left hand.

Alexander

> Secure enough for the most
> violent fighting.

He places two coins on the workbench and takes three strides across to the little window. He leans against the window frame; looks briefly at the seal ring gleaming on his finger in the bright sunlight, before looking out at the indistinct figures of marching men and horses, passing in swirls of dust. Philip's field army are moving out.

> **Fade to swirling dust:**
> **Fade up to:**

90. EXT/A Village in Northern Macedonia/Afternoon

CU of a mother breastfeeding her baby. She sits on a wellhead, her left hand cradling the infant's head.

Medium shot of the tiny village of five hovels. Chickens scavenge, small children play in the dust. Two women are tending vines and vegetables between the dwellings and a strip of olive trees.

Cut to:

POV of a woman tending the vines. We see the woman breast feeding. Beyond her is an animal stockade, where a man is bridling a stocky horse. Beyond them, the ground slopes upwards to a ridge line, across which grey-black smoke is billowing. The man mounts with the aid of a spear and rides out of the stockade towards the crest line and the smoke.

Cut to:

91. INT/Philip's Study at Pella/Day

Olympias sweeps unannounced into the Study. **Alexander** is standing at the campaign model on the great desk. He waves away the scribe seated on a stool nearby and greets his mother with obvious pleasure. She offers her cheek, and he kisses it affectionately, but then moves aside a little, looking at the campaign model.

Olympias
My Darling, there is a little thing
you must do for me before the
King returns.
You know how he crosses me
in everything.

Alexander
Mmm.

Olympias

Deinias has done me so many kindnesses;
looked after friends, kept me warned of
enemies, coming injustices, and so on.
Out of spite, your Father has held back his
son's promotion. Deinias would like him to
have a squadron.
Deinias really is a most useful man.

Alexander

Is he? Where's he serving?

Olympias

Slightly reproachful.
Serving? No, no, Darling, it is
Deinias who is useful!

Alexander turns and gives his full attention to **Olympias**.

Alexander

Yes, yes of course. Sorry!
What's the son's name?

Olympias

Heirax.
He is here in the Garrison.

Alexander

Heirax! He wants *Heirax*
to have a squadron.

Olympias

It is a slight to a distinguished man,
and he feels it.

Alexander

He feels it's the right time to ask!
I expect Heirax asked him.

Olympias

And why not? The King has taken
against him for my sake.

Alexander

No, Mother. For mine …

Olympias looks at **Alexander** imperiously. Her fierce gaze explores his face.

… I have seen Heirax in action,
and I told Father what I saw.
He resents those who are quicker
thinking than him, and when he's wrong
he tries to shift the blame.
Father transferred him to the Garrison.
I'd have demoted him myself.

Olympias

Since when is it Father this and
Father that?
Am I no one to you now that he has
given you that stupid ring to wear?
You take his part against me?

Alexander

No, my Darling. I take the men's part.
They may have to be killed
by the enemy; but that is no reason
to have them killed by a fool like Heirax.
If I gave him a squadron, they would
never trust me again.

Olympias
You are growing absurd.
What do you think it means, that thing
stuck on your finger? You are
no more than the puppet of Antipatros.
That's why Philip left him behind.
You know nothing of men.

Olympias looks fiercely at an expressionless **Alexander**, whose face breaks suddenly into a roguish grin.

Alexander
Very well then, little boys should
leave matters of state to the men,
and not interfere ...

Olympias continues to glare at **Alexander**, who moves closer to her.
He slides his arm around her waist, and drawing her to him, kisses her neck.
　　　... Dearest Mother. How much I love you.
　　　Now! Leave all this to me. You are not
　　　to be troubled, I will see to the father.

After a moment, **Olympias** relaxes, and she begins to straighten **Alexander's** hair with her fingers.

Olympias
Cruel boy! What *shall* I tell Deinias?

CU of the two smiling at each other.

Cut to:

92. EXT/A Track Junction in Northern Macedonia/Evening

On the track leading downhill from the junction, twelve horse-men, riding in pairs, pass **out of shot** around a tree-lined corner.

Cut to:

Reverse, Steadicam shot of the track winding downhill to-wards the junction. The horseman who rode from the village in the previous scene, rides into shot. He turns to his right at the junction, and we follow him into the village. The five hov-els are all on fire. The children and dogs lie dead. Of the wom-en and the chickens there is no sign. The man jumps down from his horse, and peers quickly into each of the five hovels. He re-mounts, and gallops on out of the village.

Cut to:

93. INT/ he Workshop of the Royal Chariot maker, Pella/ Day

Alexander, Hephaestion and **Antipatros**, attended by the **Chariot Maker**, stand looking at the two nearly restored, Syn-oris cars. Without wheels, they rest on a workbench surrounded by tools, wood shavings, paints and stains, and assistant crafts-men, at work on other jobs.

Chariot Maker
We've had to replace the axle, and the spokes
of both wheels, on your family synoris,
Hephaestion; and the spokes from both wheels
of the Royal car.

Alexander
Where are the wheels?

Chariot Maker
At the forge. I expect them
any day now.

Alexander
Tell me the moment they are ready. Having
to stay close to Pella, I'm short of exercise.

Alexander starts towards the door.

Cut to:

94. EXT/The Pella Street, Outside the Chariot Workshop

Alexander comes out of the workshop in conversation with
Antipatros. They turn left along the street. **Hephaestion** follows, and a handful of dismounted Regent's Bodyguard close
up behind them.

Antipatros
I was tipped off about a threatened
rape charge this morning.

Alexander
Involving the Garrison?

Antipatros
Yes. I only bother you with it, because
it could lead to a blood-feud. I'm inclined to
believe him about her willingness.
His case is well argued.

Alexander
Who is he?

Antipatros
Sotion, a Silver Shield recruit.

Alexander stops in the doorway of an armourer's shop and turns to **Antipatros**.

Alexander
Sotion! When he's sober, he will talk his
way out of a bear trap, as anyone in his
phalanx will tell you.
When he's drinking, he wouldn't know
a farrow sow from his sister, and either
will do as well.

Alexander leads the way into the shop. At the far end of the street, we see a hurrying **Harpalos** wave, as he limps into view.

Cut to:

95. INT/The Armourer's Shop

Alexander, Antipatros and **Hephaestion** stand around an unfinished cuirass on a dummy torso. Beyond, six men work in cramped conditions, hammering out shields, and other pieces of armour. The **Armourer** explains the position reached in making the cuirass for **Alexander**.

Armourer
Pointing.
The four metal chest plates, and
those covering the shoulders, are
hinged, to give complete freedom
of movement. Each will be sheathed
in soft leather and finally cloth …

The **Armourer** picks up samples of each from the workbench beside him, and hands them around

> ... The cuirass will be edged throughout
> in gold, and have tripled width gold
> bands here and here ...

The **Armourer** shows gold samples from the workbench.

> ... I have decided on this extensive
> honeysuckle pattern for the gold leaf
> covering the apron flaps.

Alexander

Smiles.

> Hephaestus will surely approve.
> And the side plates?

Armourer

There's a traditional representation of Athena,
in full armour, for the right side, and a
young Herakles guarding the fastening
on the left, as you ordered.

The **Armourer** is interrupted by **Harpalos** shouting excited-ly from the doorway.

Harpalos

The Thracians have invaded
The Northern villages!

Alexander and **Harpalos** in **CU**.

Antipatros and **Hephaestion** have not moved.

Alexander
Not the Agrianoi?

Harpalos
No, the old Maidoi.

Alexander from halfway through the doorway.

Alexander
Lambaros!

Then to Harpalos.

Where's the man who
brought word?

Harpalos
With Eumenes in …

Alexander is out of the shop and running.

Cut to:

96. EXT/The Street outside the Armourer's Shop

Alexander, running – **away from the camera** – in the street outside the **Armourer's**, followed, at an ever-increasing distance, by the Regent's Bodyguard.

Dissolve to:

97. INT/King Archelaus Study/Day/A few moments later

Filthy and exhausted, the **Messenger** droops on a stool before the great desk. We recognise him as the rider from the village in northern Macedonia. Beside him, a scribe takes notes with a stylos on a wax tablet.

Eumenes sits back in **Philip's** great chair; but leaps to his feet in guilty surprise as the Study doors are flung open, and **Alexander** strides in.

Eumenes
Under his breath to the Scribe.
> Go! Write up the notes.
> Wait till I send for you …

The Scribe walks out of shot, and a smiling **Eumenes** walks up to **Alexander.**

> … I am having this man's story written
> up for you, Lord Regent.
> We have no further need of him.

Alexander
> Thank you, Lord Chamberlain. I must
> understand for myself what he has to tell …

Alexander claps his hands, and **Aegis**, one of the sentries on duty, hurries into the room.
> … Wine, Aegis, and hurry! …

Aegis hurries away. **Alexander** goes to the **Messenger** and grips him under the left shoulder.

> … You look dead tired, here …

Eumenes watches disapprovingly, as **Alexander** helps the **Messenger** into **Philip's** chair.

> … You did well to bring us word. The invaders
> are the Maidoi? They've never broken
> their oaths of fealty before.

Messenger
Their food gods have failed them.

Eumenes
King Philip is only a name to their young
men. They don't remember his conquest.

Messenger
That's true too. In the hill country they
make no distinction between the loyal
Thracian and the Macedonian settler.
Either will do to blood their spears.

Cut to:

Aegis strides into the room, accompanied by a slave, who carries a flask and a single gold cup on a polished wood tray, and
some bread.

Aegis
Your wine, Lord Alexander

Alexander takes both the flask and the cup from the tray, and
filling the cup, holds it out for the **Messenger.**

Alexander
For you.

Cut to:

98. EXT/Philip's Siege Lines Before Perinthos/Day

A Slave holding a tray with two cups, stands between the horses
of **Philip** and **Parmenion**. Each in turn reaches down and takes
a cup. As they drink, they watch three bolt-firing, spring catapults, each standing some four feet high, and protected by earth-

works, bombarding the walls of the town, some two hundred yards away. Behind each siege piece is a pile of bolts, all chalk marked in Greek. We see the nearest pile in **CU** as the artillery-men reload, and can read From Philip in English, on one round.

The nearest catapult fires, and from **the POV** of its crew, we watch the bolt sail over the walls and into the town. Beneath its trajectory, and amidst cries and shouts of derision, a number of **Philip's** mercenaries are being thrown back from the wall. Of the six scaling ladders, two fall backwards, the men leaping from them as they fall. Two more are cleared by flaming material poured down over them, and one is being systematically cleared of climbers by bowmen on the walls.

As **Philip** watches, the bowmen complete their work of completely clearing the ladder, and with cheers of triumph, actually pull the ladder up on to the walls.

Cut to:

CU of **Philip.** Anguished, then angry.

Philip
No! Don't give up!

Cut to:

Philip, on horseback, turns to **Parmenion**. Beyond the catapult we can see the retreating soldiers.

Philip
Fucking mercenaries!
By the stomach of the god!

Philip hurls a wine cup he's holding at the feet of a nearby slave.

Cut to:

Philip urging his horse across the earthworks, and riding at his retreating soldiery.

Philip

Shouting

> Don't give up!
> Go back! Go back!
> Get up there!

Philip leaps from his horse, and drawing his sword, lays about him with the flat of it, in a vain attempt to stop the retreat. The mercenaries avoid the angry monarch and run faster for the safety of the catapult line. Laughter and whistling breaks out from the walls of Perinthos. A lone figure between the siege lines and the walls, **Philip** sticks his sword into the ground, and grasping his right bicep with his left hand, jerks his fist at the enemy. The laughter and the whistling continues.

Fade out:

99. INT/The King Archelaus Study/Day

Antipatros walks into the room, as **Eumenes** walks out with the **Messenger**. **Alexander** sits in the great chair. He indicates a seat for **Antipatros** in front of the table.

Alexander

Smiling.

> If a good sleep sets him right,
> I'll take him with me as a guide.
> If he dies; then we know everything
> he has to tell us.

Antipatros continues to settle in the chair. He speaks without looking at **Alexander**.

Antipatros
I would gladly have you with me, but it
is impossible for us both to be away from
Pella with the King away on campaign.

Alexander leans back in the chair, and speaks firmly; but quietly, looking straight at **Antipatros.**

Alexander
Of course. I should not think of such a
thing. You will have the seal while
I am gone.

Antipatros looks at **Alexander**.

Antipatros
Alexander! Consider …

Alexander makes a small stopping gesture with his left hand, and **Antipatros** falls silent.

Alexander
Like my father, I fully appreciate how
fortunate we are in having you,
to entrust the realm to …

Alexander stands up and moves clear of the great chair. **Antipatros** also stands, but more slowly. He is noticeably the taller and stands fully erect. **Alexander** tosses back his heavy, wavy fair hair, and stands, feet firmly planted, with his hands resting on his gleaming sword belt. The stance emphasises the youthful, already powerful athleticism.

… Be in no doubt about this,
Antipatros, I am going.

Antipatros

As you will; but think, you're good in the
field, and the men like you, I agree.
But you've never mounted and supplied
a campaign or conceived its strategy.
Do you know the country?

Alexander

By now, the Maidoi will be well down the
Strymon Valley.
Supply, we will discuss at the war council,
in one hour from now.

Antipatros

You realise, that if you lose, all Thrace
will be at our throats? The King's lines
of communication will be cut and I'll be
holding the north-west against the
Illyrian masses.

Alexander

Laughing.

How many troops would you need?

Antipatros

Many more than will be left under
arms in Macedon.

Alexander tilts his head slightly to the left, and looks beyond
Antipatros, becoming fleetingly almost lost in his own thoughts.

Alexander

Also, if I lose, the men won't trust me again,
and I shall never be a general. Then my
father may well say I am no son of his
and I shall never be a king...

After a pause, **Alexander** turns and he looks at **Antipatros.** Smiling, he speaks gently.

> … It seems, I shall just have to win.

Cut to:

Eumenes hurrying back into the room.

Eumenes
He was asleep before I left him. I'll see
how the notes are progressing.
Lord Regent.

Eumenes goes past into the reading cell, and **Alexander** sits back in the great chair.

Cut to:

CU of an indignant **Antipatros.**

Antipatros
What about me?! What will
he say to me for letting you go.

Alexander
If I lose you mean? That I should have taken
your advice. Write it down and I'll sign it.
Win or lose it goes to the King.

Antipatros looks sharply at **Alexander.**

Antipatros
But you would hold it against me later!

Alexander

Blandly.

> Naturally. Place your stake where
> you will, Antipatros. I cannot hedge
> my bet, why should you?

Antipatros

> The stakes are high enough already.

Alexander

> Well?

Antipatros

Smiling.

> Let me know what you need.
> I've bet on worse horses in my time.

Dissolve to:

100. EXT/A hillock overlooking the Strymon Estuary/Day

{*The following series of dissolves provides a glimpse of **Alexander's** lightning campaign of victory over the invading Maidoi. The sequence is narrated by **Alexander** himself in a number of extracts from his campaign report. At various times we cut to the comments of **Philip** and **Parmenion**, as they read the report. The glimpses also illustrate aspects of the nature and the character, which combined in **Alexander** to make him the unique conqueror, and one of the finest, and most humane, of history's generals. Each section of the campaign comprises the descriptive action followed by the narration*}.

CU of a dozen, lightly armed, peltasts erecting the framework of a beacon, and assembling the wood and pitch which will fill the iron cage.

In the **middle distance**, on another hillock on the far side of the river, a second detachment is also building a signal beacon.

In the distance, at the limit of visibility from the top of the hillock, a thin cloud of dust can be seen drifting seaward. All along the edge of the drifting cloud, the sun glints on points of metal. **The camera begins a slow zoom in** on the dust cloud. We hear, faintly at first, the deep beat of a Macedonian marching song. As it gets louder, we make out a column of fast marching heavy infantry. They are in a column of four lines; but the ranks are staggered, so no one man is immediately beside another. All are armed with the twenty-foot sarissa, which two lines carry over the left shoulder, and two over the right shoulder. The swirl of dust and men, and the rhythmic roar of the marching song, fills the screen. The song fades. **Alexander** begins his narration, as contained in his report to **Philip**.

Alexander

Voice off.

My original plan was to march due east to Amphipolis
secure your lines of communication with Pella, and
establish a run of coastal beacons, and look-out posts
to give warning of any attempt by Athens to support
the invading Maidoi from the sea.
At the same time, to move north, on the line of the
Strymon Valley, driving the Maidoi before me.

However, at Lete, a rider met me from my guest-friend
Lambaros; Prince of the Agrianoi, in fulfilment of a vow
taken when he was with us as a hostage at Pella

Cut to:

101. INT/Philip's Headquarters Hut before Perinthos/Day

Philip and **Parmenion** are alone in the rough-hewn hut, the King is using as campaign headquarters for the siege. **Philip** stands with one foot on a table, which is against a wall, on which a sketch map has been pinned. He holds **Alexander's** report in one hand. **Parmenion** stands to his right.

Philip
Guest-friend? Guest-friend? Amongst the
Agrianoi? I'd have bet on them joining the Maidoi.

Parmenion
Didn't he go off on some jaunt to the Agrianoi
on his way back to school after Doriskos?
As I recall, you were not pleased.

Philip
You're right, he did. Well, I don't take
hostages from tribes I think are safe ...

Philip points on the map.

... Now, let's see, he got as far as Lete.

Cut to:

102. EXT/Outskirts of Lete/Morning

Twelve wagons, each pulled by three mules, are drawn up in a line outside the little town. Between them and the nearby forest, **Alexander**, mounted on **Bucephalus**, watches his infantry striding in disorder from every point of the town. With him are **Hephaestion, Ptolemy, Philotas,** and **Krateros,** together with fifty cavalrymen of his personal squadron. As the soldiers reach the wagons, they deposit bundles of kit, spare spears, and heavy helmets. Only the peltasts retain their light, curved shields and leather helmets. Leaving the wagons, they funnel into single file, heading for a track into the forest.

Cut to:

Alexander jumping from **Bucephalus**. He hands the reins to a nearby cavalryman. Followed by **Hephaestion** and **Philotas**, he runs across to a wagon, and deposits his own helmet and one spear. Dressed like his men, apart from the rich gold of his cuirass, **Alexander** runs towards the head of the column of infantry now disappearing into the forest. Behind him, **Bucephalus** whinnies and prances at being left, with **Krateros** and the cavalry.

Dissolve to:

Steadicam shot across a small mountain stream. **Alexander** and three of his soldiers jog down the steep slope towards the camera. Higher up the slope behind them, the head of the main body comes into view, also running. **Alexander** and the guides splash into the stream, stopping briefly, to scoop up a few handfuls of water and to splash their faces, before moving on at a walk of short sharp strides as the trail leads uphill.

Dissolve to:

Alexander

Voice-off.

The word from Lambaros was that the Maidoi
were still on the upper Strymon.
I therefore sent Krateros with our cavalry and
horses east to the lower river, where they
were to unite with Koinos, and his detachment
of Polyperchon's Phalanx from Amphipolis.
With the infantry, I travelled light and fast
up over the game trails of the Krousia Ridges.

My aim was to secure the old fort at Rushing
Gate, before the Maidoi could move through
the gorge, to harry our settlers on the plain,
and loot the silver mines. Although it was
rough going, several of our men are native to
the area. They guided us well, and we reached
the Strymon in sight of Lake Prasia and the
fort, at dawn on the third day.

103. INT/Philip's Headquarters Hut/Day

Parmenion
What? Over Krousia …

He runs his finger across the sketch map, between Lete and Lake
Prasia.

… It must be seventy miles at least.

Philip

Trying to look dismissive.

Yes, well, they travelled light.

Cut to:

104. EXT/The Strymon Valley/Morning

Vultures spiral on warm, mid-morning thermals. Below them
the old fort overlooks the Strymon, where it leaves Lake Prasia,
to plunge through Rushing Gate gorge before winding on south
through its wood-sheathed strath.

The **camera follows** a single griffon vulture in **CU**. It glides
down to land amongst others, waiting and watching with rau-

cous impatience, as a pair of wolves tear at the remains of a deer. One lunges at the expectant birds. They give ground reluctantly. One wolf trots away into the forest.

From a position amongst a rocky outcrop, where they have been observing both the feast and the fort, two of **Alexander's** men watch the wolf pass nearby. They stand up, and hurry away looking pleased and excited.

Dissolve to:

The men of Polyperchon's Phalanx moving along the east bank of the Strymon. They are still marching fast; but now in silence, and, because here the country is overgrown, they carry their great sarissas fore and aft, and parallel to the ground, either on one shoulder or at the trail, in one hand.

A **panning shot** reveals **Alexander's** cavalry moving up ahead of the heavy infantry, on the far west bank of the river.

Dissolve to:

Alexander's mountain men moving forward in irregular lines, to the edge of the trees growing close to the old fort. They gather behind trees, lying and crouching in the undergrowth, to remain unseen from outside the forest.

Cut to:

The fort and its immediate surroundings, from the **POV** of **Alexander's** mountain men: The river flows on the far side of the fort, tumbling over the gorge directly beneath its walls. It is a peaceful scene. Three women are washing clothes in the river. A fourth carries water back to the fort. A dog lies, stretched out in the sun, while a second scavenges beneath the walls. The **camera follows** the water carrier through the door, just long enough for us to see half a dozen Maidoi putting on leather cuirasses, and sword belts, and picking up their gorytos, preparatory to going out.

Cut to:

Steadicam shot through the doorway of the fort, looking across the open ground to the trees. One of **Alexander's** mountain men breaks cover in a sprint towards the doorway. He is halfway across the open ground before others follow, and the dogs bark. One attacks him, and without breaking his stride, he knocks it, yelping, aside, with a blow from the butt of his spear.

Cut to:

Oblique, close-in shot from behind the sprinting mountain man, in the last five strides before he reaches the doorway. One of the Maidoi appears framed in the doorway. The mountain man lowers his spear, and with a yell, thrusts the blade into his face, and runs on, out of sight, with the Maidoi impaled on the spear. **The camera remains outside** the fort, and after a fleeting moment of no movement, **Alexander's** men run past on either side, and fill the doorway with their numbers.

Dissolve to:

Alexander

Voice off.

> By the time we reached the Strymon, the Maidoi
> had overwhelmed the fort, and moved against
> the farms of the middle valley. Others had raided
> the silver mines.
> I reasoned that their best fighters would not have
> missed the chance of loot, simply to protect their
> rear, and so sent five hundred mountain men
> round through the woods to re-take and hold the

fort. I united the rest of my force, now some three thousand in total.

As we prepared to destroy the isolated bands of looting Maidoi, and work the rest north into the trap at Rushing Gate, two of my mountain men reported seeing wolves feeding on a lion's kill. The omen pleased us, and I rewarded the men with gold, before sacrificing to the appropriate gods, and to Herakles.

105. INT/Philip's Headquarters Hut/Evening

Philip
Money well spent.
But he goes on to say that while moving
north he was joined by some Macedonian
settlers, who had sent their families to
safety, and stayed themselves to harry
the invaders.
These he promised a tax-free year. Huh!
You can be sure he never thought to find
out what their tax was worth!

Parmenion
The young never understand where
money comes from.

Cut to:

106. EXT/Rushing Gate Fort Overlooking the Falls/Noon

Alexander stands watching, as six of the Maidoi are seized in turn, and pushed from the walls on to the rocks half obscured by spray, one hundred feet or so below. One shakes free and jumps unaided. A seventh, lying with two smashed legs is the last to go. Dragged to the edge, legs trailing, he is slung head first over the edge, without ceremony. Some of the executioners stand peering down into the mist. Without going near the edge, **Alexander** turns and walks quickly away into the fort.

Alexander

Voice off.

On re-taking Rushing Gate Fort, the mountain
men found our garrison had been butchered,
and wounded villagers maltreated.
My detachment commander, Kephalon – a
most energetic officer whom I commend
highly – isolated the perpetrators.
After they had given each other their rites,
I had them thrown over the cliff, in
accordance with Maidoi custom.

Dissolve to:

Alexander and **Hephaistos** walking from the entrance of Rushing Gate Fort. The one hundred Companions of **Alexander's** personal squadron, already mounted, mill about the open ground before the edge of the forest. **Alexander** takes **Boukephalas** from one of the Companions. The horse lowers its haunches for **Alexander** to mount.

Cut to:

Wide-angle, Steadicam shot through the camp of the heavy infantry, looking back across the Strymon towards the Fort. **Alexander** rides through the river, with the Companions strung out behind him. Reaching the near bank, the horseman turn upstream, and immediately begin to pass twin lines of lightly armed peltasts already marching north on a riverside track.

Dissolve to:

A high, rocky crag overlooking the upper Strymon valley. **Lambaros** sits on his horse, watching the right wing of **Alexander's** army advancing obliquely across an open slope, two hundred feet below him. He turns his horse, and rides from view.

POV of the peltasts at the very point (the extreme right flank) of **Alexander's** advance: The line angles sharply back down the slope to their left, with the result that the advance controls the high ground. They are approaching thick woods beneath **Lambaros's** crag position. Somewhere on the middle of the slope, and without warning, **Lambaros** and his Agrianoi horsemen gallop from the woods. The men immediately at the centre of **Alexander's** line begin to form a phalanx, twelve lines deep. The first six lines have their sarissas pointing forward, while the rear six hold theirs aloft, ready to face in any direction which the tactical situation demands. **Alexander** gallops forward alone, past the phalanx, and straight towards the approaching horseman. As he reaches the leader, both rein-in, and jump from their horses. In **CU** we see **Alexander** and **Lambaros** embrace.

Dissolve to:

Alexander's two lead peltasts in the minutes after sunrise: We move with the second man, on the shoulder of the first, as they move swiftly along a narrow footpath, winding downhill between high rocks. Rounding a rock corner, the two come face to face with six Maidoi moving up the track towards them. Both sides freeze! From behind the camera, **Alexander's** silver and gold figure erupts into the split second of frozen tabloid. Two of the Maidoi stagger under the impact of his throwing spears. As **Alexander** goes in with the sword, the fighting becomes general, and he is obscured by his peltasts pouring forward in support.

Dissolve to:

High overhead shot of **Alexander's** men swarming through a Maidoi settlement: We **zoom in** on the heavy black smoke from torched hovels, as it begins to drift across the whole scene. As the **camera tracks** through the settlement, typical scenes of pillage come at us through the varying density of the smoke, before fading or moving on, like figures in a fog. A fleeing man cut down by a thrown spear. A woman dragged from a hovel, followed by a screaming child; **Alexander**, bleeding from an arm and a leg wound, wrapping his cloak around one of his soldiers, who clutches a half severed arm. A soldier raping a woman.

Alexander separates two of his soldiers who are fighting over a woman with two children. He leads the three away. They are joined by other women. **Alexander** puts his sword at the throat of a soldier who has grabbed at one of the women. The soldier backs away into the smoke. **Alexander**, and the women and children, reach the centre of the settlement, where prisoners, including a few wounded men, sit or lie about under the guard of groups of Companions. From a nearby cart, **Alexander** takes recovered silver, and distributes it among the women and girls.

Alexander

Voice-off.
> Several hundreds of the Maidoi died in our trap
> at Rushing Gate, but most of those with the
> looted silver headed home through a pass
> further to the east.
> To recover the silver and crush the invasion
> totally, I decided to reduce the tribe's home
> settlements by war.
> We moved quickly in pursuit, to deny them time
> to reorganise. Crossing the homelands of the
> Agrianoi, I was joined by a troop of horse led
> by Lambaros and his kinsmen.
> They proved skilled guides, enabling us to
> surprise the enemy in his own high mountain
> passes. In the final battle, they were staunch
> allies, and fought bravely.
> Once we had overrun the last bastion of the
> Maidoi, the mood was to slaughter all those

left alive; even the women and children who had harmed no one. I had them spared, and sent south to Amphipolis, under guard, for you to do with as you will.

Cut to:

107. INT/Philip's Headquarters Hut/Evening

Parmenion
Very sensible. Those strong hill women will fetch a good price. They work better than the men.

Philip
Looking at the report on the table.

What's this? What's this?
Founding a city!

Parmenion
Amongst the Maidoi?

Philip
Somewhere on their land certainly –
apparently he and his guest-friend
have considered suitable colonists
from amongst the Agrianoi; a few
loyal Paionians, some landless
Macedonians tired of army life.
And, listen to this, 'have I any good
men I would like to reward with a gift
of land?' He thinks he could take twenty!

Parmenion bites his lip to stifle a laugh.

Parmenion
Does this city have a name?

Philip
Yes. Alexandropolis!

Philip glares at **Parmenion**, still struggling with his laughter.

Parmenion
The boy's always saying you'll
leave him nothing to do.
He's just taking his chances.

Philip
Yes, well. He and this Lambaros
have only thirty odd years between them.

Parmenion
Blandly.
If that.

Philip scowls more fiercely. Then his face relaxes, and he crashes his fist down on the table.

Philip
Damn me if I'm not proud of him!
Proud of him! We will
see things from this boy of mine,
Parmenion. Mark, I said it.

Parmenion
Why don't we drink to it?

Philip
We will. And, by the stomach
of the god we'll find him those
twenty settlers.

Parmenion

I'll ask around.

Philip

First, I have to rein him in. He
proposes going north to quell
the Triballi, who, he says,
have been massing along
the Istula.

Sub-title: River Danube

Parmenion

Then who? The Hyperborei?

Philip

Laughing.

Beyond the north wind? I won't
compete with him there!

Parmenion walks to the door and claps his hands.

Parmenion

Sosias! Wine for the King.

Sosias appears fleetingly at the entrance. **Parmenion** turns back
to **Philip**, who has sat down at the table, and is drawing a writing tablet towards him.

Philip

His army must return to garrison duty.
Antipatros may have need of them.
Alexander and his Personal Squadron
can pay us a visit ...

Adding with wry sarcasm.

... Maybe this army will respond to
a victorious general!

Parmenion

Growls.

Achilles himself could not breathe
fire into those blood-stained
mercenaries.

CU of **Philip** as he bangs the table and gives his great bellowing laugh.

Philip

Lysimachos reckons Alexander
is Achilles come again. Let's see
what he can do!

Cut to:

108. EXT/A River Crossing Near Perinthos/Sunrise

A river of no great size or depth, flows between two low, sparsely wooded hills. Looking across the river from one hill, we see the one hundred or so Companions of **Alexander's** Personal Squadron – led by **Alexander** and **Hephaestion** – strung out, and riding straight down the slope towards the river. As the two reach the water's edge ...

Cut to:

POV of the Companions riding near the middle of the squadron. **Alexander** takes two throwing spears from his carrying case and, dismounting, hands the reins of **Bucephalus** to **Hephaestion**. The Companions bunch up and halt behind him, as he walks forward into the water up to his knees. He drives the spears into the riverbed on either side of his body, and scoops water with both hands, before holding them wide above his head. The water drips for a moment, and he repeats the gesture twice more, before turning to face the Companions. He jerks the spears from the water, and holds them, point up and at arm's length, above his head. The s respond to his honouring the river god, by raising their own spears aloft and giving a single, low-voiced shout.

Companions
Basiliskos!

Sub-title: 'Little King'

Alexander strides from the water and remounts. As the squadron rides forward to cross the river, we **dolly forward** to cross with **Alexander** and **Hephaestion**, who, like everyone else, pause at times to let the horses drink. At no point is the river deep enough to reach the feet of the riders.

Hephaestion
Are you sorry we did not make
war on the Triballoi?

Alexander
Of course. We were halfway there,
and they will have to be dealt with
sometime …

He grins broadly.

… And besides, I want to see
their country beyond the Istula!

Hephaestion
You're not angry?

Alexander
Disappointed. Nothing more.
He wrote a very generous letter,
although, when I saw it a recall,
I didn't read it thoroughly ...

As they approach the far bank, **Alexander** looks back to those riding immediately behind him

... Krateros, see if you can see
Perinthos from that rise.

Krateros urges his horse past them, spray flying, and heads straight for the low summit ahead.

Hephaestion
He might be angry when he hears
you gave away the silver.

Alexander smiles; but his mind is elsewhere.

Alexander
Only enough for the marriage
dowries of captive girls ...

He suddenly looks intensely at **Hephaestion**

... You see, he must have them all —
if he could! All women are his people ...

He looks ahead to where **Krateros** is waving and pointing with his spear.
... Come on, we are nearly there!
Alexander leads the rush from the river and up the slope. He joins Krateros well in advance of everyone else.

109. EXT/Two Wrestlers in the Siege Lines at Perinthos/ Morning

In **CU**: two soldiers wrestle for a fall. A barking dog runs **into shot** and snaps at their legs. Hit by a stone thrown from **out of shot**, it barks, turns to yelp, and runs off. We watch its progress through a section of the mercenaries' camp behind the siege lines. A few half-interested spectators watch the wrestling. Leather tents are pitched at random amongst sparse trees, tethered mules, the odd cart, and smoke from a number of small cooking fires. The background sounds are pastoral; of the camp, not the fighting. Laughter, a male voice singing, a mule braying, hammering, and a kite mewing overhead.

Dogs run from view behind a tent near the first of the trees. The **camera moves in** on **Seven Mercenary Soldiers** sprawled beside a woman who stands before the tent stirring a heavy iron pot. All are dirty. Four of the soldiers have small wounds bandaged, while one lies semi-conscious and is heavily bandaged and blood stained about the chest. Two have old facial scars, two are missing fingers, and one an eye.

Soldier One
I say do it immediately he arrives.

Soldier Two
Yes!

Soldier Three
No! Every Macedonian cur will
be on the alert, pressing to touch
their child ikon,

Soldier Four
I agree. We need a time when every
one's thoughts are elsewhere.

Soldier Two
During an attack?

Soldier Four
He may not be there.

Soldier Three
When we're feeding then.

Soldier Five
At the afternoon meal! That's it!
With a diversion. We'll need a diversion.
To lure him from the 'gilded trough of royalty'.

Shouts of **Basiliskos**, from **off camera**, carry to the **Seven Soldiers**, with increasing loudness and frequency. Trying to think of a diversion, they look towards the shouts in silence. **Soldier Five** stands up.

Soldier Five
Well, don't just lie about. Go and bow
down before their gilded prodigy.

The **Six** get reluctantly to their feet and straggle **out of shot**.

Soldier One
You're not coming?

Soldier Five
A diversion is essential if we are to
succeed in this. I need to talk with
certain of our fellow Greeks.

110. EXT/Alexander's Arrival at Philip's Camp/Morning

Very close, low level shot of the black forelegs of a horse coming on at a slow, collected canter, across open dusty ground. Throughout the scene, cheers, shouts of **Basiliskos**, and the occasional shout of **Alexander**, rise and fall against the steady, rhythmic thump of horse's hooves.

The **camera jumps back** to fill the frame with a **Steadicam**, a head-on shot of **Bucephalus**, surmounted by the helmeted head of **Alexander**. The men and horses of the one hundred or so members of the personal squadron are a shimmering, colourful blur behind the pair.

Cut to:

Cheering Macedonians of both sexes running to line **Alexander**'s approach route.

Cut to:

Steadicam, head-on shot of **Alexander**, with **Hephaestion** and **Krateros** riding very close on the quarters of **Bucephalus**. All three advance at the slow, collected canter, with the rest of the personal squadron still a colourful blur immediately behind them.

Cut to:

Brief shot of **Soldier Five** greeting a fellow Athenian mercenary at the entrance to an isolated tent. An extra loud shout of **Basiliskos** comes from the gathering of the crowd, **out of shot**; but no great distance away. The two look in the direction of the shout, before exchanging wry smiles, and ducking inside the tent.

Steadicam, head-on shot of **Alexander, Hephaestion** and **Krateros,** with **Ptolemy** and **Philotas** riding close on the quarters of their horses.

Still the same slow, collected canter, and the blur of the other companions riding close-packed behind them.

Cut to:

CU of **Philip** and **Parmenion,** with the Royal Bodyguard arranged close around them, watching **Alexander**'s approach along the broad corridor of **Philip's** yelling Macedonians. **Philip** gives **Parmenion** a wry smile.

Cut to:

Alexander's approach from **Philip's POV.** He looks up a gradual slope of open ground, flanked by men and women from the field army, in two untidy lines, and interspersed with the few trees left in the immediate area, which the besiegers have not yet felled for fuel. At the far end of the rough funnel of soldiery, **Alexander's** personal squadron advances towards **Philip,** in a tight arrowhead formation. Closely packed, and sloping back from the gleaming back horse, and the glittering figure of their sixteen-year-old leader, they come on at a slow, collected canter, from an initial distance of some eight hundred yards.

Cut to:

Alexander, and those at the point of the arrowhead formation, passing close in front of a section of enthusiastic Macedonians. As we track alongside, the mood changes with a small group of silent onlookers, amongst whom we recognise the **Six Mercenary Soldiers** from the previous scene. The **camera tracks on** to more wildly cheering, shouting Macedonians. The horses, and

Bucephalus above all, sense that they are the centre of attention, and they prance and cavort in their canter. The approach is relentless, the mood both thrilling and cheerful in its reflection and realisation that this is **Alexander's** battle formation for the companion cavalry.

Cut to:

Overhead shot from the rear of the arrowhead, with **Alexander** on his final approach to **Philip**. Stopping in front of him, **Alexander** bounds from **Bucephalus**, and embraces his father. The riders in the arrowhead spill forward until they completely surround the King and his group.

Cut to:

CU amongst the crowd of men and horses: The Royal Bodyguard clear a narrow passage for **Alexander** and **Philip**. Also, the crowd are dispersing, and the personal squadron dismounting. There are still some shouts of Basiliskos, amidst the general chatter, and one or two men and women come forward and touch **Alexander** as he passes. The huts of **Philip's** headquarters are close by.

Cut to:

A flash shot of the southern Greek mercenary **Soldier Seven**, running from the leather tent we saw him enter a few moments ago.

Cut to:

The entrance to **Philip's** campaign hut: The King speaks briefly to a servant. The Royal Bodyguards keep the thinning crowd well clear. The royal couple go inside.

111. INT/Philip's sleeping and eating quarters/Moments later

Philip, followed by **Alexander**, enters the room where we saw him reading **Alexander's** report. He watches as **Alexander** hangs his helmet and shield on wooden pegs, next to those bearing **Philip's** weapons, helmet and cuirass. The King is wearing a belted, red chiton, and the sword, which he is never without, on a telamon slung over his right shoulder. **Alexander** hangs up his sword, and they chat as he removes his cuirass.

Alexander
This camp is taking on a permanent
feel, father. It's unlike you to spend
so long over a single town.

Philip
You are right. The siege has not gone
well. The Athenians are using their fleet
to supply Perinthos, and we are powerless
to stop them ...

Sosias leads in four slaves, two carrying bread, wine, water, cups and spoons, and each of the rear two, a steaming bowl of fish stew.

... Making an example of Olynthos has cut
both ways. This lot have decided to die
rather than face slavery. They fight well.

Alexander
The word is that you are employing a
number of southern mercenaries.

Philip moves to the head of the rough wooden table and indicates to **Alexander** the place on his left. **CU** of the two talking, as they suck up the hot stew, watched by **Sosias** in the background.

Philip
Needing the numbers, I had little choice.
But they're a poor lot, despite fair pay, tents
and regular rations. I had to get rid of an
officer for bathing in hot water, if you please. In
Macedon even our pregnant mothers bathe
In cold water.
I would back a single Macedonian against
any three. And they don't like the sarissa.

Alexander
They don't have to, to take this town.

Philip
True.
When I've marched with our men, they
are staying here. We'll see how they get
on with the short spear.

Alexander
Eager and anxious.

You're moving on! You are going
to cross the Hellespont?!

Philip
Laughing.

No! Not yet at least. First, we have
to secure the north shore along its
entire length.

Alexander

At this rate, I swear, you'll leave
me nowhere to conquer.

Philip

Don't concern yourself with conquest.
There are many lands beyond
Macedon's borders …

Angry shouting breaks out some distance away. **Alexander** stops
eating and listens. **Philip** goes on speaking

… For now, master what it means to rule.
The duties, the demands, the needs
of a single country.
Already you have left Antipatros
to his own devices for too long.

Alexander

Listen.

They both stop eating and look in silence towards the direction
of the noise. The angry shouting gets louder, swollen by more
voices, rather than getting closer. **Philip** stands up.

Philip

Zeus strike them! What now? …

His good-natured, bellowing laugh echoes about the room.

… Cock fighting? Dice? Is the prize
Boy too pretty? …

He laughs again, and walks towards the door, shouting,

… Sosias, keep mine warm.

Standing up, **Alexander** points at their accoutrements on the pegs. **Philip** pauses at the door.

Alexander
Go fully armed. They sound rough.

Philip
And inflame things, when it may
be nothing?

Alexander
I'll come with you.

Philip
Roughly.
I don't need you. Stay and eat.
I'll be back before you've finished.

As **Philip** leaves, **Alexander** goes across to the door.

Cut to:

112. EXT/The Headquarters Camp Behind the Siege Lines/Moments later

Watched by **Alexander**, **Philip** strides away from his headquarters hut. Next door, the Royal Bodyguard are at the door and windows of their quarters, looking at the crowd, some three hundred yards away, and still increasing in noise and size. Individuals run in from all directions to see what is going on. None of the bodyguards accompany **Philip**.

A cavalryman, riding up to see what the noise is about, is summoned by **Philip.** The man gives him a leg up, and he rides forward into the throng.

Cut to:

From **Alexander's POV**, we see the horse disappear amongst the crowd, and for nearly a minute or so, we can make out **Philip's** head, as he moves towards the centre of the row. The horse whinnies and rears up. **Philip** moves forward again; but only for a brief moment, before the horse, still shrieking, rears up almost vertically, and crashes sideways out of sight.

Cut to:

CU of **Alexander** shouting to the bodyguard.

Alexander
Get armed! All of you. Quick!

Cut to:

Alexander runs into **Philip's** headquarters hut. He grabs his shield from its peg on the wall and slides his left forearm behind the back-strap to grasp the outer lanyard. He reaches for his sword, and draws it with a swift jerk, sending the scabbard and telamon slithering across the floor. He transfers the sword to his left hand, so that it is held against the inside of his shield and runs from the room.

Cut to:

Alexander sprinting towards the crowd. Beyond and behind him, none of the bodyguards have appeared. Reaching the edge of the crowd, he takes his sword in his right hand.

Alexander
Make way ... Mind yourselves.
At first the crowd comprises curious, and he makes easy progress. Then he reaches the more involved, Macedonians, and so favoura-

ble to him. We see him thrusting forward with his shield, in a collage of fleeting faces, bodies, arms, shoulders, and turning heads.

Alexander
Let me through. Let me through
to the King.

Suddenly, in still clarity, a southern mercenary confronts him. Mocking. We recognise the bulky figure of **Soldier Two** of the seven who were conspiring during **Alexander's** arrival amongst **Philip's** army.

Alexander
Come on, let me pass ... I want
the king.

The grinning, mocking face of **Soldier Two** fills the frame.

Soldier Two
Look! Here's miracle child.
He wants his dad!

The grin changes to a gape. The eyes bulge. He retches, chokes, and then slumps forward, blood oozing between fingers clutching at a wound made by **Alexander's** mortal sword thrust to the throat. In his death throes, **Soldier Two** pitches forward, on to the ground. A space opens beyond him, revealing **Philip** lying on his right side, pinned to the ground by the dead horse, hamstrung and its throat cut. He too could be dead.

Cut to:

Alexander jumps over the dead body and runs forward to the King. He puts one foot on the horse's quarters, and points round the circle of hostile mercenaries with a now red sword blade. In the surge and press of the crowd, men struggle to keep away from him. Isolated voices begin to chant; Kill him! Kill him! Although all those around him are armed, there is uncertainty.

Alexander
This is the king. I will kill anyone who
touches him.

The crowd look towards the bearded, giant figure of **Soldier One** facing **Alexander** across the dead horse. His chanting of Kill him turns to a mumble. Uncertain, he pushes back against the crowd.

Alexander
Are you mad? Get back.
All of you.
                                                    Cut to:

A section of the crowd behind **Alexander**: **Soldier Five**, carrying a spear, is easing his way to the front row of the crowd, immediately behind **Alexander**.

                                                    Cut to:

CU of **Alexander** confronting those around **Soldier One**, across the figures of **Philip** and the dead horse.

Alexander
Kill me, and the King, and you'll never
get out of Thrace alive.

Soldier One
We've got out of worse places.

Alexander
You're surrounded by our men, and the
enemy holds the harbour.
Are you tired of life?

There is a drawn out, silent confrontation between **Alexander** and **Soldier One,** watched with increasing tension by the immediate crowd. Abruptly, **Alexander** whirls round, and we see **Soldier Five** seemingly towering above him, with upraised spear. Before the spear blade so much as moves, **Alexander** buries his sword in the throat of **Soldier Five**. With a deft jerk **Alexander** frees the sword, and **Soldier Five** crumples backwards, the gasps of the crowd mingling with the hissing cry of the death-wound. **Alexander** turns back to face **Soldier-One**, and from his **POV**, we see **Hephaestion**, together with members of the Royal Bodyguard, thrusting through the crowd, that has spread out to form a ring around **Philip** and **Alexander. Hephaestion** moves to cover **Alexander's** back.

Hephaestion

You're not hurt?

Cut to:

A fearless, triumphant looking **Alexander**, his face glowing, glances towards **Hephaestion**

Alexander

Quiet smiling.

None of them laid a finger on me.

The **camera draws away**, showing **Alexander**, lost in his own thoughts, a point of calm amidst the surges of the crowd. Macedonians roughly disarm and drag away the remaining mutinous mercenaries.

Cut to:

CU of Macedonians at the back of the crowd, straining to see what has happened, and voicing their concerns for both their King and their Prince.

Several Voices

The King's dead? ... Have those bastards
killed Alexander too?

Cut to:

CU of **Alexander**, still motionless.

Alexander

To himself.

Praise Herakles.

Pausanias

Close by; out of shot.

Sir! Sir! Are you all right?

Alexander brings his concentration back to the scene around
him. He looks down at the king.

Alexander

Father?

Cut to:

The horse being dragged off the still motionless **Philip**. **Pausanias** crouches beside the King. Members of the Bodyguard look
on. **Alexander** kneels and puts a hand on **Philip's** heart.

Alexander

He's stunned. Pausanias,
a big shield ...

Pausanias stands up and beckons to a Macedonian leaning on
a big round shield with a prancing boar motif. He hands it over

> ... He's stunned from the fall and
> that head wound ...

Alexander stands up.
> ... Lay him on it gently.
> I'll hold his head.

Philip is placed on the shield. **CU** of **Alexander** pulling back one eyelid. **Philip's** eyelids flutter, and he looks up at **Alexander** before immediately closing his eyes again. Four of the Bodyguards pick up the shield. A fifth holds **Philip's** legs, and with **Alexander** supporting the blood-stained head, they start walking away through the curious crowd.

> **Dissolve to:**

113. INT/Philip's Headquarters Hut/Evening – Moments later

Philip is carried into the bedroom of the hut, and laid on the leather double bed, which is set low, on square, sturdy legs, and occupies much of the floor space. Members of the Bodyguard, **Alexander's** companions, **Sosias, Eumenes**, and two of **Philip's** body-slaves crowd into the remaining space around the walls of the dimly lit room. The shield bearers settle **Philip** on the bed, and the body-slaves cover him with a fur blanket. **Alexander**, leaning down with his hand still beneath **Philip's** blood-stained head, looks along the length of the bed to **Krateros**.

Alexander
All Perinthos was up and gaping at us,
Krateros. Have the catapults volley them
off the walls. That may encourage them
to do other than jeer like furies.

Krateros nods in confirmation and moves immediately towards the door. **Alexander** adds.

> … And have the Heralds proclaim the
> King is alive and well…

Philip groans and opens his eyes. **Alexander** straightens up, and looks at his blood-stained hand and wrist.

> Sosias, water and a sponge.

Pausanias
It was your son, King.
Your son saved you.

Philip's response is weak, and he barely glances at **Alexander**.

Philip
So? Good boy.

Cut to:

Eumenes standing on the opposite side of the bed to **Alexander**. We see also a slave enter the room with a dish of water.

Eumenes
Did you see which of them struck
you down, King?

Philip
No. I was struck from behind.

Alexander
Well, I hope I killed him. I
killed one there.

Philip

Good boy. I remember nothing till
I woke up here.

Alexander looks sharply at **Philip**. The slave reaches him with
the water. **Alexander** stops him from going to **Philip**, and taking the sponge from the ceramic dish, decorated with boys fishing, he carefully cleans the blood from his right hand. The slave
looks at him in surprise, and then at **Philip**. **Alexander** drops
the sponge back in the water.

Cut to:

114. INT/Alexander's Bedroom at the Headquarters/Night

The room is identical to **Philip's** and lit by moonlight only. **Alexander** lies on his back in the double bed, his hands behind
his head, and his eyes wide open. A single, multi-coloured wool
blanket covers the lower half of his body, and, like his eyes, his
muscled torso gleams in the moonlight. From outside come camp
noises. A dog barking, a shout and a scream, a burst of laughter,
and the rasp of a sword or spear being sharpened. We become
aware that a bell is being rung at intervals (by the night watch
of Perinthos) ding-ding, ding-ding. Immediately after one double ring, comes a double rap on the bedroom door, followed by
a scratching and a single tap. **Alexander** smiles, and folds back
the bedcovering with his left hand. The action exposes the side
of his left leg, and leg and reveals that he is naked.

Cut to:

CU of **Alexander's** upper body, and the pillows stretching the
width of the bed. We hear the sound of soft, sandaled footsteps in
the room. They stop beside the bed. **Alexander** moves over to
one side of the bed, and takes his gold, eagle's head-hilted dagger
from beneath the unoccupied pillow and slides it beneath his own.

Clothing is dropped quietly to the floor. **Alexander** plumps the pillow beside his head. A naked figure stretches out beside him, and like him, leaves the upper body uncovered by the blanket. Another watch bell rings close by. The two exchange smiles, and we recognise **Hephaestion**. They speak together in low tones.

Hephaestion
They'll wear out that
watch bell.

Alexander
The attempt to kill the king has unsettled
everyone. Us and them. But where, I
wonder, did it all start?

Hephaestion
Behind the walls of Perinthos?

Alexander
At Pella? … At the Parthenon?

Hephaestion
Loudly.
Pella? …
Whispered.
… What is it?

From the left shoulder we see **Alexander** in **CU**, looking away. He turns and looks into the eyes of his friend, speaking in a fierce whisper.

Alexander
He says he remembers nothing!
But he'd already come round when
we laid him on that shield.

Hephaestion

Casual whisper.

He won't remember what
happened to him.

Alexander reaches out and digs the fingers of his right hand into
the shoulder of **Hephaestion**.

Alexander

No? He was shamming dead.

Hephaestion

Was he? Well, I don't blame him.
He probably hoped they would be
frightened at what they'd tried to do,
and go away.

Alexander

When I opened his eye, he knew that it was
all over. He saw me; but gave no sign.

Hephaestion

Probably his head was spinning. I
expect he passed out again.

Alexander

He was awake. I was watching him.
He won't admit that he remembers.

Alexander releases the shoulder of **Hephaestion**, and turns fully on to his back, staring up at the ceiling.

Hephaestion

Well, he is the king. You know how
people twist everything.

Alexander
He doesn't want to admit that he lay
there. Trapped. At the mercy of the
mob, knowing he owed his life to me.
Now, he doesn't want to remember.

Hephaestion
He has his pride.

Alexander
Of course, but in his place I would
have spoken out.

Hephaestion slides his hand up across **Alexander's** gleaming shoulder and works his fingers through his golden hair. **Alexander** pushes, sensually against the touch.

Hephaestion
Soothingly.
Does it matter? Everyone knows.
He does; you do. No one can take
it from you.

Alexander inhales deeply and sighs.

Alexander
I suppose you are right. You
always understand. He gave me
life, or so he claims!
Chuckling.
Even if the Queen prefers to blame
the god. Now we're quits.

Hephaestion
Yes. You've returned the compliment!

Alexander turns back to **Hephaestion**, and their arms cross, as he reaches out to stroke the fair hair of the other.

Alexander
No one can compete with a gift from
the gods; but it is good to be free of
a debt to man.

Cut to:

115. EXT/The Palace Gardens, Pella/Morning

We **track beside** a pathway flanked by small cypress trees and leading to the seclusion of the Queen's garden. In the gaps we see the **camera is keeping pace** with a running, fourteen-year-old Nubian girl, dressed in black with a red girdle and red arm rings. The barefoot **Melissa** is the slave-companion and close friend of **Alexander's** sister **Kleopatra**. In the background we hear the metallic jingle of a sistrum, accompanied by the thumping, hand-drum of Dionysian sacrifice.

Nearing the end of the pathway, **Melissa, outruns the camera**, which **dollys up** and through the gap between two cypresses. Above the pathway, we see **Melissa** run on to the enclosed, split-level arena, where **Lanike** is teaching dance steps to **Kleopatra** and three of her fourteen-year-old friends. At the back, beside the altar and bust of Herakles where **Alexander** received the sword belt, two, female musicians, sit on stone seats. The girls dance barefooted, and wear highly coloured, thin, floating dresses; but no animal skin capes.

Without hesitating, **Melissa** runs across the mosaic floor, toward **Kleopatra**.

Lanike
Melissa no! Wait!

350

Melissa runs on and throws her arms around **Kleopatra**.

Cut to:

CU of the two girls with their arms around each other. In the background, the sistrum and then the drum, raggedly, fall silent.

Melissa

In an urgent whisper.

Your brother!

Kleopatra
Alexander? Where?

Melissa
Here. In the garden.
He's looking for you.

In the **CU** we see the anxiety in her eyes.

Cut to:

Overview of the Queen's garden arena and the approach pathway. **Alexander** comes on to the pathway at the top of the shot. As always his is moving quickly. A cool wind blows his hair and billows out the shoulder cloak from his throat. **Kleopatra** walks slowly from the arena to meet him on the pathway.

Cut to:

Kleopatra standing alone on the pathway. We hear the sound of the wind. She shivers and folds her arms around herself. She is very much **Philip's** daughter, dark curly hair, swarthy, square-featured and chunky. **Off camera**, **Lanike** claps her hands and the jingling, thumping music restarts.

Alexander reaching the solitary little figure of his sister. He takes her hand; but neither smile.

Alexander
You're cold, Kleo.

Kleopatra nods and gives a slight shiver. **Alexander** unclips the gold brooch at his throat and wraps **Kleopatra** in his cloak.

Alexander
We'll walk. I must speak
with you.

Kleopatra holds the cloak close up under her chin and keeps her eyes on the ground. They walk through the garden beyond the pathway.

Alexander
You heard what happened to
father at Byzantion?

Kleopatra
He got a spear in his leg.

Alexander
Yes. Dogs betrayed his attack.
Dogs, and the sickle moon.

Kleopatra
Mother says ...

Alexander stops abruptly and looks at her fiercely.

Alexander

Yes?!

Kleopatra shakes her head and remains silent. They stand together beside a stone bench, and a circular stone fish tank sunk in the ground. The palace looms behind them. **Alexander** relaxes and holds her hands inside the cloak.

Alexander

Did she do anything? You know,
the rites I mean. Did you see
anything? …

Kleopatra shakes her head.

… I won't say you told me. I swear.
By Herakles. I can never
break that oath …

They look at each other in silence.

Kleo, tell me. You must. I have
to know.

Kleopatra

It's always the same. If she did
anything different I didn't see it.
Truly Alexander.

Alexander

Impatient.

Yes, yes, I believe you …

Softening, he puts an arm around her.

… Don't let her do anything. She
has no right to now. I saved him at
Perinthos, but for me he'd be dead.

Kleopatra leans her head against her brother, and puts her left
hand on his breast.

Kleopatra
Why did you?

Alexander
It would have been dishonourable
not to.

Still with his arm around her, **Alexander** points towards the palace.

Kleopatra
Shaking her head.
      No. I'll go back to my class.

Alexander puts his hands on her shoulders, turning so that they
face one another as he does so.

Alexander
If she wants to send him medicines,
sweets, a doctor – anything – you must
let me know. I charge you.

Kleopatra
Shocked.

      Alexander! No! What she does may
seem terrible; but she must know it
doesn't work.

Alexander

She means them. I remember
only too well.

Kleopatra

When life is too hard, they help her
purge her soul. That is all they are.

Alexander

After a brief pause.

I expect you're right.
It was a long time ago …

He pulls **Kleopatra** into an embrace, and kisses her head, before taking back his cloak.

… You're a good girl.

Kleopatra stands for a moment watching, as he strides off, swinging the cloak around his shoulders, before vaulting a low wall on his way towards a palace entrance.

Cut to:

116. INT/An Entrance Hall of the Palace/Moments Later

Steadicam shot across the hall, looking towards the open doorway. **Alexander's** head and body rise up into shot, as he bounds up the steps from the garden, and in through the door. **Hephaestion** and **Antipatros** immediately converge on him, one from either side. **Antipatros** hands him a bound and sealed letter.

Antipatros

A second courier brought this.
The king says you may tell me
the contents.

Alexander
Smiling.

I will decide when I've read it.

Antipatros
The king says …

Alexander
When I've read it, Antipatros.

Antipatros walks away. As he starts along one of three corridors leading off the hall, he looks back, he is not pleased at seeing **Hephaestion** reading the letter over Alexander's shoulder.

Cut to:

Alexander and **Hephaestion** in **CU**.

Hephaestion
He commends your work as Regent.

Alexander
Mmm.

Hephaestion
Oh, good. He hopes to be fit enough
to come home soon.

Alexander looks sidelong at the face, just a few inches from his own.

Alexander
You like the king, don't you?

Hephaestion
He always makes me feel welcome.

Alexander

He's not jealous of you like my mother.

Hephaestion

Look! He wants you to mobilise
all the reserves.

Alexander

Mmm.

Hephaestion

But only Antipatros must know that the
plan is to invade the south.

Alexander

Mmm.

Hephaestion

You will have to invent a diversion.

Alexander

Mmm.

Cut to:

117. INT/The Queen's Sitting Room/Moments Later

Olympias sits very upright in a gilded, high-backed chair, from
which she can see through the window to the palace garden below. **Alexander** stands facing her, on the other side of the window. He leans against the stone window surround, looking down
on **Kleopatra's** dancing class, and the spot in the garden where
they talked.

Olympias

You look a picture of health
and vigour, considering you so rarely
come near me. Have you won the girl
of your dreams?

Alexander

I don't have time to be playing
about with girls.

Olympias

You should find time. People will
say you do not care for them.

Alexander

I will give them something else
to talk about.

Olympias

You always have time for Hephaestion.

Alexander

He helps my work.

Olympias

What work? You tell me nothing.
I hear that Philip has sent you a secret
letter. What did he say?

Alexander

That when he returns, he intends
to invade the Illyrians on our
north west frontier.
He wants me to mobilise the reserve
phalanx, and give the Pella garrison
some real exercise.

Olympias

You are lying to me.

Alexander

It you think so, why ask?

Olympias

I am sure that you told Hephaestion.

Alexander

No.

Olympias

People talk. Hear it from me,
they talk. Of your shaving.
Why shave, like a Greek?

Alexander

With a laugh.

Am I not a Greek then?
You should have told me sooner!

Olympias

Becoming ruffled.

You and your friends are known
for your shaving. Women point.
Ptolemy, Harpalos …

Alexander

Ask Harpalos why women point!

Olympias

You should consider a girl to marry …

Alexander

Marry?!!

Olympias

Before Philip makes you a marriage.
It is time you showed him it is a
husband he has to offer, not a wife.

Alexander turns slowly towards **Olympias**. His look becomes
a glare. Totally without humour, he stalks towards her, deliberately, cat-like. She presses back into the chair, as he stops, looking down at her.

Alexander

Almost hissing.

Never … say that to me again.

For an appreciable moment neither move, then **Alexander** turns
abruptly. He strides **towards the camera and out of the frame.**
We hear his receding footsteps. **Olympias** is **alone in the frame,**
unmoving. A door slams. She blinks and quivers. Slowly she
stands up and walks limply from the room.

Cut to:

Olympias walking, almost dreamlike, through her hallway, and
into another room off it, where **Hyrminia** and **Lanike** stand
at a table, unpacking and re-folding material, from a big, sack-
ing parcel. They stop in mid-movement, and in silence, watch
her approach.

Olympias

In a dull voice.

When my son comes to my door,
you will turn him away.

They nod. She walks away. They look at each other with concern and stand up to follow her.

118. EXT/Pella Stadium/Day

Fade up on the rippling, black hide of **Bucephalus**. **Alexander** and **Antipatros** talk, as they ride beside the stadium, where the Reserve Phalanx is drilling to commands given by blasts from a trumpet.

We track into the oncoming path of four lines of sarrissa carriers, twelve men wide and advancing with spear points lowered to **throat/camera height**. The **track stops** at the middle of the line, and the men and spear points begin to **pass out of shot**, six on either side of the camera.

A trumpet blasts twice, and the lines halt, with two men of the rear line **in shot, on either side of the camera**. Some fifty yards away, six lines, twelve men wide, advance towards us, with their sarissas all held point up, at an angle of forty-five degrees to the horizontal.

Throughout these manoeuvres we hear **Alexander** and **Antipatros** talking in **VO**.

Antipatros
These reserves are all farmers and
foresters from the western hills.
Another day of drilling and they'll be
ready for the field.

Alexander
They will need to be.
The tribes are concentrating all
along our northern border.

Antipatros

I'm not surprised. The price of a good
lie is that it gets believed.

Alexander

We must make certain it is. If
the King has not returned, I
will leave for the northern borders
the day after tomorrow.

Antipatros

How many men will you take?

Alexander

When I've finalised my plans, I'll let
you know, but back or not,
and if we have the word from Delphi or not,
the King will need to be represented
at Thermopylae when the League
meets there at the end of the month.
I'm sure that he would want you to represent him.
Will you?

Antipatros

Gladly …

One long blast on the trumpet brings the advancing lines to a
halt, behind the men in shot who are already halted. Two short
blasts, and the first two lines of the second group lower their
spear points in line with the first four lines.

Cut to:

The **camera swivels up and out**, to a **high angle shot** looking
across from the side of the phalanx, with **Alexander** and **Antipatros** in shot beyond. One long, one short, and one long blast,
on the trumpet, and the rear four lines turnabout. A pair of two

short blasts, and they lower their sarissas to the horizontal. The phalanx is formed for attack to front or rear.

Antipatros (continues)
... I will influence those I can;
but wherever possible, I'll have
decisions postponed for Philip.

We **dolly in** towards the side of the phalanx. One long and two short trumpet blasts are repeated once more. Immediately, on the left of the phalanx, two lines raise their spear points, turn left and right respectively, and lower their sarissas back to the horizontal. A total of twenty-four men are now facing the camera with their spear points lowered to the horizontal.

As we **continue to dolly** through the phalanx, along the central axis, a once repeated sequence of one long and three short trumpet blasts, has the two outside lines on the other side, turning to face outwards.

Cut to:

The phalanx, **from the POV** of **Alexander** and **Antipatros**, stands now with spears facing outwards on all sides. A continuous ripple of trumpet blasts, and the lines quickly space out, to leave corridors in the ranks wide enough for chariots to pass through.

Cut to:

119. EXT/The Palace Stables/Dusk

A pretty flirtatious girl in her early twenties, walks along the colonnade of the stables, carefully avoiding the grooms hurrying between loose boxes and the drinking fountain – either leading horses, or carrying feed. In gathering twilight, slaves place flaring torches in the wall sconces. Amongst the clumping of unshod hooves, we hear the many cavalry horses moving about their boxes, whinnying and snorting. The girl stops behind a Doric column and looks about her.

Alexander rides up to the colonnaded area. As he dismounts, a groom runs up to take the reins of **Bucephalus**. He walks quickly away towards the drinking fountain. The girl runs after him. We cannot hear their brief exchange; but we see **Alexander** laugh and shake his head. He continues on without breaking his stride. She walks out of shot, and **Hephaestion** walks up from beyond the fountain. He falls into step with **Alexander** and briefly puts an arm around his shoulders.

Hephaestion
No luck for Doris then?

Alexander
She wants me to marry.

Hephaestion
Marry!
How could you marry Doris?

Alexander
Don't be a fool. She's married.
– she's a whore –
she had her last child
by Harpalos.

An irritated **Alexander** walks on in silence. They approach a gate in the palace wall.

Alexander
Mother wants to see me going
with women, to know I'm ready.

Hephaestion
Only girls marry at our age.

Alexander
She has her mind set on it,
and wishes I had too.

Hephaestion
But why?

As they pass the sentry and the gate, **Alexander** looks sharply at his friend. Then, his look softens, and he reaches out a hand to hold the back of **Hephaestion's** neck.

Alexander
Dearest innocent!
I might die in battle before giving her
an heir to dominate.

Hephaestion looks thoughtfully down at **Alexander**.

Cut to:

Alexander and **Hephaestion** nearing a palace doorway.

Hephaestion
Will you do it?

Alexander
Marry? When I'm ready.
I'll suit myself.

Hephaestion
It's a great deal of business
running a household.
Girls you can take or leave.

Alexander
That's what I think …

Alexander moves ahead of **Hephaestion**, onto the top step before the doorway. Looking intently back, **Alexander** holds him by the shoulders.

Alexander
You are not to worry about this.
She would never dare do anything
to take you from me.
Believe me, she knows me too well.

Hephaestion nods. **Alexander** lets go of his shoulders and he becomes brisk as he turns to go inside.

… Now! We'll meet at early dawn.
I have a great deal of planning to do.

Cut to:

120. INT/King Archelaus Study/Night

The great desk is bathed in light from a single flickering lamp. The rest of the study is in darkness, apart from a shaft of light from the partly open door, and the dying embers of the fire. Two scribes droop on stools, at the edge of the circle of desk light, and on the opposite side of the desk to **Alexander**, who scans a model of Macedon's northern border. Deep in thought, he looks up at the scribes, his mind elsewhere, a pause, and he speaks slowly.

Alexander
Be off both of you.
We'll continue this
in the morning.

The two start at his words, then slide off the stools, before returning their writing tablets to the reading alcove, and hurrying from the room.

Alexander

Under his breath

> There! We will fight the
> Illyrians there.

He puts a stylos in the model and moves the top as he looks around it at the ground between the lake and the gorge.

He lets the stylos fall across the model and sits back in **Philip's** great chair. Still looking at the model, he puts his hands together behind his head and ruffles his hair. Slowly he stands up, and reaches for the dagger hanging from the back of the chair. Letting it dangle from one hand by the telamon, he takes a last look at the model, and then walks out of the study.

Cut to:

121. INT/The Approach to the Prince's Quarters/Moments later

Still swinging the dagger in one hand, by the soft leather of the telamon, **Alexander** walks along the dimly lit corridor leading to his quarters. He turns into the small, internal hallway. **Two Sentries** move apart at his arrival, and the younger runs across to the bathroom area, and reappears carrying a burning taper, which he hands to **Alexander** as he puts his right foot on the bottom step leading up to his bedroom door.

Alexander
All quiet?

Sentry
The last of the companions
went to bed over one hour
ago, Lord.

Carrying the taper and the dagger in the same hand, **Alexander** takes the remaining four steps in two strides, and reaches to open the bedroom door.

Cut to black

122. INT/Inside Alexander's Bedroom/Moments Later

For a fleeting moment the room is in complete darkness, before **Alexander** opens the door, enters, and closes it behind him. The taper provides the only light in the room. Walking across the room to his left, **Alexander** drops the dagger on one of his two clothes chests, and lights a small wrought iron oil lamp, standing on a delicate, cornel-wood table, amongst a pile of scrolls, writing tablets, brooches and a comb. He extinguishes the taper and drops it on the table. As he slips off his sandals, he unbuckles the shining, red-leather sword belt, and throws it across the curved back of a leather chair with flat, rectangular, decorated legs. Unpinning a gold brooch, he puts that on the table, and slips off his chiton, throwing it across the sword belt.

As he does so, there is a slight gasp from the darkness behind him. The naked **Alexander** turns to see a beautiful, watery blonde **Girl**, aged about sixteen, barefoot, and wearing a diaphanous white dress, with two gold shoulder brooches and a gold girdle, sitting on the edge of his bed. He steps across to her. She leans away, clearly frightened, and then she slides along the bed and stands up. With her hands at her face, she looks at the floor. **Alexander** looks straight at her without speaking. Dropping her hands to her sides, she raises her eyes to his face, and says haltingly, as if repeating a lesson.

Girl

I am here, because I have fallen
in love with you.
Please do not send me away.

Alexander

Gently

How did you get in?
There are guards.

Girl

I have been trying for a long
time to come to you. Tonight
I saw a chance and took it.

Shaking, she clasps her hands and puts them back up to her face.
Alexander reaches out, and gently touches the long hair framing
her unpainted face. He puts both hands on her shoulders, holding her carefully. She shakes less. He draws her towards him and
kisses her lightly on the lips.

Alexander

The guards must have gone to sleep,
or were they bought?...

His voice takes on a stern edge.

... If they let you in, we must be sure
that there is no one else here.

She grasps him out of fright. He kisses her again, and then gives
her a smile, as he disengages himself, and strides over to the window to give the curtains a brisk shaking on their jangling rings.
He flings back the lid of one great chest and, leaving it up, strides
to the main door, and rams home the bronze bolt. The dagger
slides to the floor as he lifts and peers into the second chest, before

slamming down the lid. He goes to the postern door, wrenches back the curtain, checks that the bolt is in place and swishes the curtain closed.

Frowning slightly, he goes back to the **Girl**. He unties her girdle and unclips the shoulder brooches. He slides the thin dress down her arms, and lets it slip to the floor. Gathering the **Girl** in his arms, he reaches down and throws back the bed cover. Laying her on the bed, **Alexander** lies down beside her. His arm across her breasts. She buries her face in his shoulder and, slowly, moves her trembling fingertips down over his torso, stopping just below the waist. He takes her chin in his left hand and turns her face towards him.

Alexander
Why you have been brought to this,
I do not know. Perhaps the gods…
Don't be frightened. We are both being
challenged. Together we shall triumph.

Smiling, he leans forward and kisses her forehead, her eyes, then her cheeks, her lips and her chin. As his lips seek her throat, his hand reaches for her breast.

Fade to:

The great gate of a city under siege, in **CU**, from inside, the besieged and burning town. Battered from outside, the gate quivers, splinters, and wreathed in smoke, collapses in **towards the camera**. Armed men rush in through the smoke, passing around and **over the camera**, and **out of shot**.

Cut to:

Reverse shot from the gate: The narrow town street runs uphill, quickly disappearing in the smoke. On either side, women and children run from blazing houses. The attackers spear or cut down the children, and, seizing the women, run on to vanish in the smoke.

Fade to:

Alexander and the **Girl** in the act of making love. We see her face and his back in **CU**. He is sitting on the edge of the bed, and he supports her strongly beneath the armpits, as she eases down on to his thighs, with her arms and her legs around him. Her head goes back in a silent gasp. They clasp each other.

Fade to:

The deserted street of the besieged town still wreathed in smoke. Blood flows in the shallow drains that run the full length, and on both sides, of the street.

Cut to:

Alexander and the **Girl** lying together beneath the coverlet, apparently asleep. She rolls away from him and tries to get up without waking him. As her feet reach for the floor, he puts out an arm, and gently restrains her with a hand on her shoulder.

Alexander

Quietly.
> Don't go. Let them wait.
> Stay with me until morning.

She looks back over her shoulder and lies back next to him. Twisting around, and still under the coverlet, they embrace, with her face in his neck, and his face buried in her hair.

Fade to the bed and the couple in silhouette:

Fade up to dawn overcoming the lamplight:

Alexander gets up and going around the foot of the bed, snuffs out the lamp. He looks down at the sleeping girl and draws back the curtain. She wakes and looks up at him. They exchange smiles.

Alexander
I wish we could stay longer; but I
have work to do.

Alexander reaches for his chiton. The **Girl** stretches. As she swings her legs to the floor, we glimpse blood on the sheet. **Alexander** goes to the chest with the open lid, and rummages inside, finally finding a worn, soft-leather pouch. Straightening up, he empties the contents into the palm of one hand.

In **CU** we see a solid, gold and enamel brooch depicting two crowned ibis, their necks caressing. He grimaces, drops the pouch on the floor, and turns to the **Girl**. She is looking down, fastening one of the gold shoulder brooches to her dress.

Alexander
When you are old, and I'm long gone,
you will boast to your fellows –
silently rocking, and sucking soup
through toothless gums –
that one night, in a summer long ago,
you had the maidenhead of Alexander.

Girl
Don't say that.

Alexander
This will remind you.

He hands her the brooch.

Girl

Oh, how beautiful!

Alexander

They have been passed down
from queen to queen
for two hundred years, and
were given to me as an heirloom
for my bride.

Alexander strides to the door, and the girl stands up, half-handing back the brooch.

Girl

Shouldn't you …

Alexander opens the door and looks back.

Alexander

Tell the Queen how much you
pleased me.
Then show her the brooch –
and be sure to say I told you to.

From the **Girl's POV** we see him step out of sight. The door closes firmly behind him.

Cut to:

123. EXT/The Palace Stadium/Late Afternoon

A **slow zoom** through swirling dust, rolling past the camera in great clots, tinged crimson by the late afternoon sun. The thin black lash of a driving whip curls through the dust. **Crack!** And again, **Crack!**

Still in the zoom, the **camera cranks up** to show us the heads of **Alexander**, beside that of a driver, and the outline of the synoris, amidst the dust thrown up by a pair of galloping ponies. The stadium floor is largely obscured by a languid pall of dust from previous circuits, which hangs, without rising, on the still air.

Alexander
Faster!

Alexander seizes two spears from a case fixed centrally on the front grab-rail of the synoris. The driver cracks his whip. **Alexander** vaults over the side. He runs beside the chariot for a few paces, his right hand holding the rail, and then sprints away towards a row of eight effigies of Persian 'Apple bearer' spearmen, in the centre of the stadium. Still running fast, he hurls the spears in rapid succession at the two nearest, hitting both. Beyond him, as he recovers the spears from the effigies, we see the synoris come around the corner, into the back straight, and slow to a brisk trot. **Alexander** lopes across, running beside the car for twenty yards or so, before vaulting aboard.

Alexander
Go!

The driver shakes the reins, and the ponies break into a canter. As the synoris swings around the 'bottom bend', we see, beyond them, **Harpalos** arriving at a limping run, where **Hephaestion**, also caked in dust, lies stretched out beside the track. Nearby, the ponies harnessed to the second synoris, crop the rough turf between the stadium and the track from Pella and the palace. The driver walks back to his team, carrying a ceramic bowl of water from a nearby Hermae – a wayside bust of Hermes incorporating a drinking fountain. **Harpalos** waves frantically to **Alexander**, who acknowledges the sign. The ponies swing into the home straight. Their pace increases to a full gallop. **Alexander** vaults over the side, runs alongside for a few strides, and then peels away, to run behind the synoris and over towards **Harpalos**.

Cut to:

Harpalos, with **Hephaistion** now standing beside him, as **Alexander** runs in to join them.

Harpalos

Excited.

The word has arrived from Delphi!
I passed the king's messenger
on his way to the palace.

Alexander
When?

Harpalos
Not five minutes ago.

Alexander beckons urgently to the drivers of both the synoris, and as they run over, he turns, putting a hand on **Hephaestion's** shoulder.

Alexander
See to the ponies. Tell the groom master
to clean the cars thoroughly. If the news
is good it will be sometime before we can
use them again ...

Alexander moves his hand from **Hephaestion,** and points at his driver.

... Send one of the Royal Household
to the wicket gate guardhouse
with a clean chiton for me.

Immediately! ...

The driver runs off. **Alexander** looks at **Hephaistion** and **Harpalos** in turn

> ... As soon as I know what the oracle
> has said, and what the King
> has in mind, I'll come and find you.
> Golden intelligence Harpalos,
> my friend, thank you.

Alexander runs towards the fountain.

Cut to:

Hephaistion summoning **Alexander's** synoris, and in **CU** with **Harpalos**.

Hephaistion
Over here.

Harpalos
(giggling)
Have you noticed he never stinks? No
matter how hard the exercise. When
everyone else,...

He wrinkles his nose and steps away

> ... including you right now, is as
> rank as an old badger.

Hephaistion looks at him impatiently, and as if he is quite mad.

Hephaestion
Perhaps he burns it up.
I don't know. Ask Aristotle.

Alexander stands with his head under the jetting fountain, working the dust from, his face, neck, and heavy mop of hair, with his fingers. He picks up a strigil, and begins to scrape the dust from his left forearm.

Cut to:

124 INT/Philip's Bathroom/ Early Evening

Philip sits on a stool, naked, apart from a towel thrown across his lap. His **Doctor**, and the **First Royal Lad** look at the newly healed spear thrust to his thigh and side. In the background, slaves, supervised by the **Second Royal Lad** are filling the sunken bath.

Doctor
Both thigh and side have
healed well, King.

Philip

Laughing.

So, they should. My flesh has
had enough practice, doctor.

He glances at his body, and we see, in **CU**, that almost every exposed part has a wound scar of some sort. The **Second Royal Lad** approaches.

Second Royal Lad
Shall I warm the water, Lord?

Philip

Abruptly.

No! In Macedon,
kings, like our pregnant mothers,
bathe in cold water.

There is a rap at the door, and **Philip** jerks his head to the **First Royal Lad** to go and answer it.

Philip
Certainly, they've healed enough
to play the soldier.
I shall spend tomorrow exercising cavalry.
Philip stands up, holding the towel against him with his right hand. The **First Royal Lad** reports back.

Philip
What do they want?

First Royal Lad
The messenger from Delphi, Lord.

Philip
Ah! Bring him to me …

Looking at the **Doctor**, he steps over to the bath.

… Well, doctor, is it the word we want?

Doctor
The families of Delphi are friends
of Macedon.

Philip gives a cynical laugh as he steps down into the bath.

Philip
You mean the gold poured
into the navel of mother earth
has been well spent!

Cut to:

The travel-stained Delphic messenger entering the bathroom, is accompanied by a clean, if still damp, **Alexander**, wearing a clean chiton. He looks at his father standing, nude, in the bath, and he stops, his face clouding over.

Flashback to:

A scene from the prologue, only half-remembered in detail by **Alexander**, with a naked **Philip** beginning to confront mother and child in bed. The flashback itself is silent; but **Philip's** voice intrudes from the bath.

Philip (VO)
Finally, a parade ground bellow.

> Alexander ... Alexander! ... Alexander!

Cut to:

Philip now seated in the bath. The **Doctor,** The **Royal Lads,** the slaves and the messenger are all looking at **Alexander**, who is still looking puzzled.

Philip
Impatient.
> Read the verses.
> My hands are all wet.

Alexander
Hesitant.
> Yes ... yes, all right father, I will ...

In **CU**, he takes the scroll from the messenger, unrolls it, and reads:

> ... Here to my temple, enriched
> from Mount Pangaion. You have come.

Is your Messenger a man of Hermes,
favoured as you are by the gods?
To direct, and be directed, as in all else,
would now be the Archer's aim, Just as …

Philip
Enough!

Cut to:

Philip stretches down in his bath. There is a long silence. **Alexander** walks to the edge of the bath.

Alexander
Well, father?

Philip

Quietly.

We go south, it is time all Hellas
acknowledged Macedon.

Alexander
And the northern border?

Philip
If, the Illyrians do more than
run about like headless goats,
which I doubt, then Antipatros
can deal with them.

Alexander
As Regent?

Philip
As Regent, yes. You my son,
will command my cavalry.

Alexander
Thank you, father.

Philip
Come to the study when
I've finished here, and
we'll discuss what will happen.

Cut to:

125. INT/The Approach to the King Archelaus Study/ Late that Night

The area is crowded still, with those summoned by **Philip,** as well as the usual guards. The study doors open and the murmur of conversation ceases. Watched by everyone, **Alexander** walks out. He is enveloped from neck to ankle in a black cloak. Without either looking at, or acknowledging anyone, he walks through the throng and starts down the steps.

Dissolve to:

Alexander walking the full length of the corridor towards the half-life size statue of Herakles at the foot of the steps leading up to the Queen's Apartments. Thoughtfully, he stops and rubs the toe of the statue. Looking up he sees the duty sentry, standing at the top of the steps, shield up and spear pointed. He is bent and old, with a white beard. Hesitant about **Alexander's** identity, he half lowers the spear. **Alexander** strides up the steps. The sentry only just steps aside in time to avoid being brushed aside. **Alexander** draws his dagger, and raps with the hilt on his mother's door.

Female Voice
It is late. The Queen is asleep.

Alexander

It is Alexander. Open the door.

Olympias (VO)

More distant.

Let him in.

Cut to:

126. INT/Olympias Bedroom

With just one of the triple-snake oil lamps alight, the extremities of the room are in deep shadow. **Olympias** sits at her dressing table. Her only make-up is the antimony highlighting her eyes, and the shining of her lips. She is wearing an ankle-length cream robe, trimmed with gold, tied with a twisted gold girdle, and with a rich, dark fur collar, which mingles with her gleaming, henna-dyed hair.

She stands up as **Alexander** enters, and immediately dismisses the bleary-eyed slave who has followed him into the room.

Olympias

Leave us. Go back to bed.

As they approach each other, **Alexander** looks across at the mural of the sack of Troy, now above a fireless grate. They come together, kiss, a trifle superficially; but do not fully disengage. **Olympias** lightly straightens his hair with her fingertips.

Olympias

You should be in bed. There will be
a lot to do before you can march.

Alexander

You know?

Olympias

Looking at him closely.

>Of course. What is it? You look
>strange. Have you been dreaming?

Alexander

>Knowing, I though you would
>have sent for me.
>You must know what brings me
>at this time.

Olympias

>Do you want me to make
>a divination for you?

Alexander backs away and begins to pace between **Olympias** and the fireplace.

Alexander

>I want no divinations, Mother.
>I need the truth ...

Olympias looks away, smoothing her hair with one hand.

>... This will be no little war. It is the
>beginning of everything ...

He stops in front of her.
>... Tell me who I am!

In **CU**, **Olympias** starts, and looks at him, clearly surprised and relieved.

>Never mind what you have
>been up to. I want nothing of that.
>Just tell me what I ask.

Olympias

Quietly.

> Sometimes it is I who need
> to ask who you are.

Cut to:

Alexander moves away a few paces, and then comes back to stand directly in front of his mother.

Alexander

> I am Philip's son, am I not?

Olympias

Firmly.

> Do not pretend you can believe that.

Olympias reaches out, and taking both his hands draws him towards her.

Alexander

> Well what then? I have come to hear.

Olympias

> This is too solemn a matter for
> a midnight whim.
> The gods must be placated.

In **CU**, **Alexander** looks deeply into her eyes.

Alexander

> Mother, what sign did my
> daimon give you?

She embraces him closely. We cannot hear what she whispers in his ears. **Alexander** leans back to look at her.

Alexander
And that is everything?

Olympias
Even now you are not satisfied.

Alexander embraces her passionately, and then holds her at arm's length.

Alexander
All things are known to the gods.
The trick lies in knowing how to
question them.

Releasing her, he turns and walks **towards the camera** and **out of the frame, leaving her alone**. **Olympias** goes to her dressing table, and picking up a spill, lights the other two snake-lamps. The room brightens. We hear the outer door closing, as she goes to a chair in a corner of the room. We move slowly in on her as she sits down, drawing her legs under her. Tears run down her cheeks. She pulls her robe tightly about her.

Olympias
My son.

Dissolve to:

The black-swathed figure of **Alexander** walking through the deserted, silent corridors of the palace. Finally, he reaches the foyer of the Prince's Quarters. With the doors to his own bedroom facing him, he moves to his left, and opens quietly, the first of two other doors.

Cut to:

127. INT/Bedroom of Hephaestion/Midnight

Moonlight floods the room, shining directly on to **Hephaestion**, who lies asleep, his naked upper body clear of the bed cover. **Alexander** approaches and stands looking down at his friend. He reaches out to wake him, then changes his mind.

Alexander
Nothing should disturb the
last sleep of childhood …

He walks to the window and draws the curtain, so that the moonlight does not strike **Hephaestion.**

… Certainly not the powers of the night.

He looks towards the camera.

Cut to:

Alexander's unblinking and smiling face filling the frame.

Alexander
Future ages will wonder at us,
as the modern age wonders
at us now.

Freeze frame

Cut to black

THE END

Credits

CHARACTER NOTES

CHARACTER NOTE ONE:

By any yardstick, King Philip and Queen Olympias were remarkable characters in their own right. Alexander was very much a son of them both, inheriting in spades his mother's beauty and her passion, and his father's brilliance – and more – as a statesman and a general. His amazing vigour, endurance, strength, bravery and brilliance stemmed from them both, and was honed by his own genius and implacable nature, together with the circumstances of his upbringing.

At the time of the Prologue, Philip is aged thirty, one-eyed, swarthy, grizzle-bearded, and heavily battle-scarred. Olympias is just twenty-two, a ruthless, imperious and streetwise mystic. Despite her smouldering beauty, Philip's lust is for the youth of either sex. He fell in love with the compelling Epirote child-princess on the cult island of Samothrace, and probably came to regret his obsession early on in their marriage, when Queen Olympias claimed the beautiful, fair-haired child – so unlike Philip's curly, dark-haired looks – as her son by the god Zeus-Ammon.

For Queen Olympias, the problem with Philip's philandering was, as much as anything, the fact that any resulting children posed a threat to the kingly inheritance of her beloved Alexander. As he showed, however, Philip was far too shrewd not to have appreciated Alexander's worth early on in life, even if the realisation came to be tinged with a certain old bull jealousy at some of his youthful achievements.

In the Prologue scenes Alexander is around five years old.

CHARACTER NOTE TWO:

Alexander was sensitive and secretive about his ancestry. Probably, in the first instance, because his mother claimed a god for his father. As an adult and king, he was far too shrewd a realist not to use the claim to his advantage. He probably always considered Zeus-Ammon as his spiritual father, and recognised Philip as his actual father. Such a consideration was in line with ancient thinking. Nonetheless, as a child, he may have been prickly on the subject, hence the angry reaction to the slur on his dog's pedigree, and the half-brother-blood-brother bonding with Ptolemy.

Although twice his age, Ptolemy was one of the constant friends (companions) of Alexander's youth. He served him loyally as a general and went on to found the celebrated dynasty of Egypt known to history by his name. Ptolemy hijacked Alexander's funeral cortege and established the Imperial cadaver in a golden mausoleum in the centre of Alexandria. Philip's two leading general-ministers, Parmenion and Antipatros would both go on to serve the son. While far out on the road to India, Alexander would have the former assassinated in the interests of strategic security. Throughout his absence, Antipatros would rule Macedon as Alexander's regent, and would spend the time wrangling, and being complained about, by the Queen Mother. For Alexander, friendships were everything and forever. The brother of his much-loved nurse Helanike (Lanike), 'Black' Kleitos, was an older brother type friend of his youth, who also would serve him with military distinction as a companion. He saved Alexander's life at the battle of the Granicus. Deep in the deserts of central Asia Alexander murdered Kleitos in an alcohol-fuelled brawl. History records that the celebrated orator Demosthenes had an intense dislike for the child Alexander. It is entirely possible that this seemingly irrational feeling against someone so young had its origin in the humiliation of Demosthenes during the visit of the Athenian peace delegation to Pella.

Subsequent to the Prologue Alexander was around eight years old.

CHARACTER NOTE THREE:

We know that Alexander was a musician with a beautiful singing voice; but that at some point during childhood, he decided never to sing again, and thereafter, to listen only to martial music. The club footed Harpalos was a Companion from childhood with whom Alexander, typically, would never lose faith. Harpalos repaid his friend by stealing vast sums of public money, when put in charge of the hugely wealthy treasury of Alexander's Persian Empire, at Babylon. Hephaestion was also fair haired; but, when fully grown, a good six inches taller than Alexander. As has been said before, he must be one of the great unknowns of history. Little is known about him, and yet Alexander, nothing if not the consummate professional, came to entrust his friend with extremely important tasks, both military and diplomatic. All of these he seems to have carried out successfully. The response to the rebuke of Leonidas for wasting resin is famous. Some ten years later, on becoming master of the lands of supply, Alexander sent his old tutor a sack of the stuff. Doubtless accompanied by a hand-written note.

From the scene in the marketplace Alexander is around twelve years old.

CHARACTER NOTE FOUR:

Alexander's mastery of his celebrated charger Bucephalus was well documented in antiquity and is an incident which he himself was fond of recounting. Perhaps, as has been suggested, as an after-dinner story. At the siege of Doriskos, it is from Kassandros, the son of Antipatros, that Alexander saves the young mother. Although Kassandros was a Companion, it was only by virtue of his father's relationship with Philip. He would serve Alexander as a general; but admitted, after Alexander's death, that he could never pass his statue or likeness without a shiver of fear. Alexander's appointment by Philip as Regent of Macedon is an historical fact. Philip was a good judge of character and it is virtually certain that he made the appointment because he recognised the ability of his son, rather than for reasons of nepotism. The incidents illustrating Alexander's campaign against the northern tribes in revolt, depict the future characteristics of his generalship. Most notably the lightning speed of movement, his ingenuity and thoroughness. Equally typically, he leads from the front, and is considerate of both the defeated and the wounded enemy.

From the scene where Alexander and Hephaestion find the Senoris, both boys are around sixteen years old.

ACKNOWLEDGEMENTS

This virtual film text has been created using additional material from works by the following writers:

Ancients
Euripedes, Plutarch, Arrian, Theognis of Megara, Isocrates, Curtius, Diodorus.

Moderns
Andre Bonnard, Mary Renault, Arthur Weigall, Ulrich Wilcken, J.F.C. "Boney" Fuller, George Finlay.
Of the modern writers – that is, those writing in the Nineteenth and Twentieth Centuries, Mary Renault would seem to me to have understood the man more completely and more precisely, than any of her contemporaries. See her biography:
"The Nature of Alexander"

The cover design was created by Andrew Cachia, in Malta. My grateful thanks also, to all at Novum Publishing, and especially to Bianca Bendra

By the same Author:

"O Laughing River":
Stonewall Jackson: The Reality of Military Genius

E-Mail: mwnestor1@gmail.com

The author

M W Banks hails from Devon, England. He attended the Prebendal School in Chichester, followed by Pangbourne Nautical College. He was commissioned into the Royal Marines directly from school and thereafter served with the Fleet Air Arm.
He received commando training, as well as training as a shallow water diver, and qualified as a Royal Navy helicopter pilot and flying instructor. He served actively in the military in Cyprus, Malaya and Borneo and thereafter, joined the Scotch Whisky industry, followed by NGO management and fundraising. He is a widower with one stepson. Favourite activities include aviation, writing and reading, and sporting activities: cricket, skiing, golf, swimming and horse riding. His previous publication was O Laughing River, a biography of Stonewall Jackson.

The publisher

> ,,
> *He who stops*
> *getting better*
> *stops being good.*

This is the motto of novum publishing, and our focus
is on finding new manuscripts, publishing them and
offering long-term support to the authors.
Our publishing house was founded in 1997, and since
then it has become THE expert for new authors and
has won numerous awards.

Our editorial team will peruse each manuscript
within a few weeks free of charge and without
obligation.

You will find more information about
novum publishing and our books on the internet:

w w w . n o v u m - p u b l i s h i n g . c o . u k

M W Banks

O Laughing River

ISBN 978-3-99064-554-3
476 pages

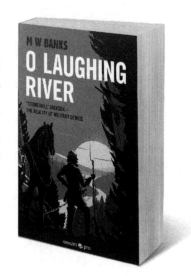

O Laughing River is a must for everyone interested in the art of war, as well as being an inspiring account of the life of a great man and and military genius; "Stonewall" Jackson. Forget "dry as dust" history, this is a story which will endure for all time.